D1505438

Steps Going Down

Other books by Joseph Hansen

Brandstetter & Others
Nightwork
Job's Year
Backtrack
Gravedigger
A Smile in His Lifetime
Skinflick
The Dog & Other Stories
The Man Everybody Was Afraid Of
One Foot in the Boat (verse)
Troublemaker
Death Claims
Fadeout

Steps Going Down

JOSEPH HANSEN

A Foul Play Press Book

The Countryman Press
Woodstock, Vermont

Library of Congress Cataloging-in-Publication Data

Hansen, Joseph, 1923–
    Steps going down.

    "A Foul Play Press book."
    I. Title.
PS3558.A513S7   1985   813'.54   85-17134
ISBN 0-88150-054-2

For Charles Osborne of London

Whoever loves, if he do not propose
The right, true end of love, he's one that goes
To sea for nothing but to make him sick.
                              —John Donne

Steps Going Down

1

Cutler carries supper on a tray along the hall to Moody. A thin tube of opaque yellow plastic leads from an oxygen tank beside the bed to Moody's head. Elastic around Moody's head keeps the tube in place, so that the short ducts at the end of the tube poke up the nostrils of Moody's thin, aristocratic nose. He wears the tube much of the time—he has emphysema. Sixty-five, thin, gray, he sits propped by pillows, gazing at a television newscast. He looks neat, in a green turtleneck jersey, tan widewale corduroys, green wool socks. He thinks, sick as he is, that he is going for an outing, tonight. But then, he always prefers being dressed during business hours. Every morning, as Cutler helps him totter into the shower, he says, "I may be needed."

In this delusion, he sometimes takes off the oxygen tube, sits on the edge of the bed and, breathing hard from the exertion, puts on his shoes. He makes his way downstairs to the office to see that everything is running smoothly. Even the descent is heavy going for him. When he appears in the doorway, Cutler, Fargo, or one of the others hurries to help him into a chair. Everything is running smoothly. Fargo sees to that, although Moody prefers to give the credit to Cutler, and Cutler accepts it—why not? After all, Fargo is one of those office females who thrive on being overworked and underpaid. What reason has Cutler for ruining her life?

Moody can't stay long. Oxygen would be unsafe down here. A machine might spark. A customer might light a cigarette. NO SMOKING signs are posted, but not everyone notices. Anyway, Moody can find no fault with the way his business is being operated. And if he could, it still wouldn't be long before he had to be carried upstairs to his bed again. Fargo would jump at the chance to carry him, but she is no longer young, is scarcely five feet tall, and weighs less than a hundred pounds, while Cutler is six foot two, weighs a hundred eighty, and is young, though not as young as he pretends. He has never been athletic, except in bed. But he is strong, and Moody is, these days, not much more than skin and bone.

So go the times when he is not needed, but simply wants to feel still a part of things. The times when he regards himself as indispensable are when old customers ask for him. Men like Irv Liebowitz, Tony Baron, Phil Quinn, writers whose scripts Moody began typing and duplicating back in the mid-1950s, when television started dismantling the old, self-contained motion picture studios, and writers, actors, and a good many others found themselves on their own, scrambling to survive. Moody had struck a golden moment to found this business in the living room of his dead mother's frame house on a side street in the middle of Hollywood, with one used typewriter, one used mimeograph cranked by hand, and himself as the only worker.

Now the business occupies the entire downstairs of the house. The typewriters are electronic, there are big, glossy Xerox machines of the latest model, computerized typesetting machines, glittering, frisky offset printing presses. Monday through Friday, from nine to five, everything hums, clicks, beeps, bustles. The paint on the old woodwork shines, the carpet is deep underfoot, the new wallpaper is cheerful. Everything says prosperity. And Moody insists that he owes it all to the screenwriters who have kept coming back to him down the long years. The least he can do, he says, is struggle downstairs, give them a smile, a handshake, a few cordial words.

"They're healthy," Cutler says. "Let them come up here if they want to see you. Stewart, it's only a formality with them, a reflex. If they knew what it costs you, they wouldn't ask for you."

Only this morning, Cutler said this. For the hundredth time. Fargo had barely got the office door open when Cutler, upstairs, rubbing down Moody's wasted limbs with a big, thick bath towel, lathering the beard stubble on Moody's sunken cheeks, unwrapping a yellow plastic throw-away razor, heard Phil Quinn's booming voice below, his bellow of laughter. He couldn't make out the words, but he knew Quinn's line with withered, painted Fargo—how pretty she looked today, how young and fresh, and how attractive were the mismatched rags she had thrown on before she'd rushed eagerly off to another day's slavery.

"That 's Phil Quinn." Moody began to tremble. "He hasn't been in for ages."

"Take it easy," Cutler said. "You'll make me cut you."

Moody pushed him away, struggled to his feet. The bathroom door was open. "Phil!" Moody tried to shout the name, but he is past shouting. It only made him cough and wheeze, gaunt belly pumping, ribs moving like the gills of a stranded fish. He clutched feebly at Cutler. He gasped, "Tell him to — wait. I'll be — down — as soon as I — can get — dressed."

"Sit down, Stewart. You're getting all sweaty."

"Please!" Moody sat again on the closed toilet, huddling the towel around him. He looked up at Cutler, hollow eyes begging. "I mustn't lose Phil Quinn. Not for a customer, not for a friend. Not after — all these — years."

"Ridiculous." But Cutler rattled the razor into the washbasin, dried his hands, called out, "Mr. Quinn?" and ran, two at a time, down the stairs, snarling under his breath. The screenwriters didn't represent a meaningful fraction of Moody's business anymore, hadn't for years. But, luckily for Cutler, Moody has a soft spot in his head for writers. Also, he adores tinsel success, and Quinn has a box office smash going for him right now. Cutler put on his best hale-fellow grin, jogged into the office, held out his hand. "Good to see you," he said. "Stewart's just getting dressed. He'll be down in a few minutes. Will you wait? He's anxious not to miss you."

"Of course." Quinn is a brown-skinned, muscular man in his fifties, big head, big chest. Cutler suspects him of possessing too many Y chromosomes. He's had four wives, and probably beat them all, regularly. He's always polite to Cutler, but Cutler senses contempt in Quinn's eyes, and imagines that as a high school kid, Quinn stomped queers in alleys. His smile was brief this morning. Letting go Cutler's hand, he looked concerned. "Tony Baron tells me Stewart's health is failing. Is that true?"

"He has his good days," Cutler said. "He still takes a lot of interest." Cutler started for the stairs. "I'd better go see how he's doing."

"You looking after him yourself?" Quinn said.

"It's no trouble," Cutler said. "Excuse me." He ran back up the stairs, two at a time, to finish shaving Moody and to get him dressed. But Moody was not in the bathroom. He lay on his bed, wrapped in the towel, patches of lather drying on his face. He had fumbled the oxygen tube into place. He turned pitiful damp eyes to Cutler and rolled his head against the pillows.

"I can't do it," he said. "What will he think?"

"Relax." Cutler gave Moody an encouraging smile. "We'll get you into fresh pajamas and your new robe, and he can come up here."

Cutler didn't know why, but making a good impression on Quinn seemed important to him. Maybe only because the man was so thunderously masculine. Cutler was pleased that he had redecorated the apartment before Moody's illness began to take up all his time. Cutler had a knack for pattern, balance, line. Moody liked green, so this room was a medley of understated greens.

In high school, Cutler's art teacher, Warren Fisher, had praised the boy's color sense—before he took him to bed. At sixteen. He kept whispering in the dark, his voice trembling, *So lovely, so lovely. And I'm the first to have you. I'm the first.* It wasn't so. Far from it. He had picked up timorous, skinny Harvey in a springtime Portland park two years before. And there had been other men. But he didn't tell Warren Fisher so.

Cutler motioned Quinn to the bedside chair. Quinn sat.

"Pleasant room," he said, "if you have to be sick."

5

"Darryl did it," Moody said. "Like a professional."

"They often are," Quinn said without expression. The oxygen tank stood near him. He eyed it thoughtfully. The tanks are rented, their red paint scratched and chipped from rough handling by truckers. Quinn said, "Good nurses, too, I understand." He looked at Cutler, who stood at the foot of the bed, but it wasn't Cutler he spoke to. It was Moody. "You see a doctor regularly, I suppose?"

Moody nodded. "Darryl drives me to the hospital."

"Chauffeur too," Quinn said, as if adding something up. "Cooks the meals, does he?"

"Like Julia Child in drag," Cutler said.

Moody frowned at him with a quick cautionary shake of the head. He told Quinn, "And cleans the house and manages the business. I'd be lost without Darryl." His eyes were moist again. Odd. Weepiness, in anyone's presence but Cutler's, was not Moody's style. He must be feeling really sick. Moody said, with a tremulous try at a smile, and one of those awful, old-auntyish dissimulations that fool no one, "He's like a son to me."

"Or a daughter," Quinn said.

"I understand," Moody said hastily, "that *Touch and Go* is being a terrific success. I'm so pleased for you. It's absurd"—Moody simpered like a girl, and would have blushed if he could—"but I feel a little proprietory, a little proud, even though all we did was type the scripts and run them off for you."

"I'll mention you when they hand me my Oscar." Quinn smiled and took Moody's hand. "You get better now, you hear? I want to find you running things, next time I come by."

"It was kind of you to visit me." Moody patted Quinn's hand. "Old friends mean so much." A shadow crossed his face. "It's been a year, now, but I still can't get over poor Irv Liebowitz."

"I miss him." Quinn looked grim. "He fell apart fast after the divorce. That bitch. Her lawyers destroyed him."

"And drink." Moody sighed. "He was drinking heavily."

"He was going on the wagon," Quinn said. "He had a script to write."

"What a ghastly way to die, lost in the desert. That ravine where they found his body"—Moody shuddered—"swarmed with rattlesnakes. Miles from anywhere. No water. Coyotes had eaten him, buzzards. I dream about it sometimes. It seems impossible. Could it really have been him?"

"His clothes, his wallet, his car." Quinn rose. "The Sheriff doesn't have any doubt. That dump where he holed up in Perez—the Golden Poppy motel? They said he'd wandered off drunk before." Quinn looked at Cutler. "Darryl? Suzie says she'll have those pages ready for me by five. Can you run them down to me at the beach?" He glanced at Moody. "I'll pay the extra cost, of course."

Cutler raised his eyebrows at Moody. He hoped he was showing no eagerness, but he was eager. It seemed to him that he'd been cooped up here forever. Oh, he got out to the supermarket and drugstore every few days, the laundromat once a week. But that was the extent of it. Life was going on out there, and all he could do was press his nose to the windowpane. He knew what was good for him, so he never complained to Moody, nor to Fargo, nor to anyone in the shop. But, God, how he longed to touch life once again, to be part of it, if only for a few hours. At the unlikely thought, right now, his heart pounded.

"There'll be no extra cost." Moody waved the idea away. He studied Cutler. "It will do Darryl good to get out for a little while." Moody smiled wanly. "Maybe I'll go along for the ride. We always spent vacations at the beach. I'd love to see the ocean again. It seems ages."

Cutler swore to himself. But he smiled, and smacked his palms together in a show of pleased anticipation. "Hey, that would be great," he said, and showed Quinn out and down the stairs, telling himself Moody was too sick. He hoped to God that Moody was too sick. His heart sank when he came up to fix Moody's lunch at noon and Moody had, somehow, got himself dressed. Cutler, bringing potato and leek soup and rye toast into the sunbright room said, "You should have called me to help you dress. That drive's going to be tiring, you know. You should have saved your strength."

"I'll be fine." Moody unfolded the napkin and tucked a corner of it in at the high neck of his sweater. "I'm feeling better than I have for days." He reached for the tray, eager as a hungry teenager. He almost laughed. "Won't it be a treat? Just like old times? Driving to the beach. Just the two of us. Lovely."

"Just the two of us," Cutler said.

And now he fetches Moody supper, bits of veal in a white wine sauce, with pureed carrots and fresh steamed green beans, and a glass of chilled pinot blanc. Moody, his gaze on the television screen, doesn't even notice when Cutler arrives. Cutler pauses in the doorway, looking at the old man for signs that he is fading. He sees no such signs, and swears to himself again. Only to himself. He works up a smile and a cheerful tone of voice, and carries the tray to the bed. "Here we go—one of your favorites."

Moody's head, circled by the elastic and the tube, jerks up. "Don't do that," he snaps. "You frightened me." Grumpily he accepts the tray.

"The sun's in your eyes." Cutler starts for the window.

"Don't walk in front of the television," Moody says. "Have you no consideration?"

"Sorry," Cutler goes behind the television set and draws the curtains. "There's chocolate mousse for dessert."

Moody snorts. "Chocolate mousse!" He pokes with a fork at his food. "Instant pudding from a box."

"Come on Stewart," Cutler says gently. "What's the matter? That's a lovely supper. And I never made pudding from a box in my life."

"I can't go." Moody's voice is small and quavery. Tears are in his eyes. "I wanted so much to go." He shakes his head mournfully. "I can't. I'm utterly exhausted."

"Never mind." Cutler bends, gives his skeletal shoulders a hug, kisses him lightly on top of the head. "The beach is always there. We'll go some morning, when you're fresh."

Moody sulks, pushes at his food again. "I wasn't

very fresh this morning, was I?" He darts a sharp glance up at Cutler. "You come straight back, do you hear me? I don't like being alone here. You know what this neighborhood's turned into. It's very dangerous."

"That will be on my mind," Cutler says.

2

He drives out the Santa Monica freeway, the envelope of Quinn's pages lying on the empty passenger seat. The sun is still well up. The sky is a rich blue. Through the window, the breeze brings the tang of sea air with it, and Cutler breathes it in gratefully. He almost laughs aloud, he feels so free. The car is nothing, a Japanese compact, five years old. He keeps it washed and waxed, so it looks nice, keeps it serviced so it runs well. But with Moody's kind of money, Cutler would have bought a Porsche.

And that, Cutler's mother says inside his head, *is why he has money, and you don't, and never will. Like your father. You think your looks will get you anything. Well, life doesn't work that way.*

Cutler hopes that at this very moment, a pyromaniac is setting a fire in her basement. He leans for a second to see himself in the mirror, and smiles a tight little smile. He's going to be all right. Moody likes his looks. Moody is in love with him. Moody has made him his sole legatee. And Moody is a sick man who can't last forever. Then Cutler will buy a Porsche, a Rolex watch, and a Brooks Brothers suit, and drive up the coast and show her whether looks will get you anything you want, or not.

Traffic on the coast highway moves slowly. Only two days ago, a storm up from the Gulf of Mexico battered it with fifteen-foot-high breakers. Lanes are closed. That's fine with Cutler. It will give him an excuse for getting home late. Moody saw the storm damage on television, million dollar beach homes smashed, their movie-star owners out stacking sandbags against the next high tide. Moody will accept the excuse—he'll have to. Cutler grins. Quinn's timing couldn't have been better.

An out-thrust of sea cliff protects the houses on the beach at Cormorant Cove from storm damage. The tide is still high today, and the big waves crash over the stands of ragged black rock off shore. No cormorants perch out there now, in the coppery light of the downing sun. The streets of the little community of low-roofed, sprawling, expensive houses twist back on themselves, like a climber making a difficult descent. As he threads his way among them, he begins to wonder if he will find Quinn's place, when suddenly he is there. A red Alfa Romeo two-seater, and a new four-door BMW are parked beside the mailbox.

Carrying the envelope, Cutler takes a flight of wooden steps down to a deck where plantings flourish in raw cedar boxes. The raw cedar house has many French doors. He can see straight through rooms that seem shadowy because the far French doors show him the wide ocean, sheened with sunset gold. He can't locate a bell-push, so he unlatches a door and walks on deep carpet through long rooms, sun and sea-dazzle half blinding him, so that he knocks into furniture. He makes out human shapes beyond the far doors, which stand open.

He pauses in the doors and sees Quinn plain, seated in a chair on a slatted plank deck, smoking a cigarette, a drink in his hand. He wears a Hawaiian shirt, unbuttoned, showing a brown chest and belly. He wears shorts, sandals, dark glasses, and looks at if watching the tide break out there on the rocks relaxes him. A slim blond in a bikini sits in another chair, a big portable cassette machine on the deck beside her, playing gentle jazz. She, too, wears sunglasses. A crossword puzzle book lies in her lap. A pencil is stuck through her piled up hair. She notices Cutler in the doorway, leans across and speaks to Quinn, who turns.

Cutler smiles and holds up the envelope.

"Ah-ha!" Quinn gets out of the chair, moving younger than his years, brisk, athletic, probably to convince the young woman of something, certainly not to convince Cutler. "Thank you." Quinn sets his drink on the broad wooden arm of the chair and comes to Cutler, holding out a hand. Cutler doesn't know whether the writer is reaching for the envelope or wants his hand shaken. He shakes the hand, then puts the envelope into it. "Come on out." Quinn makes a broad, hostly gesture. "Join us. This is our favorite time of day, here. Tides the last few days have been spectacular. Great cloudscapes, too."

Cutler has followed Quinn. They pause beside the woman's chair. "My wife, Veronica." Cutler runs his eyes over her near-nakedness. She is flawless, living proof that money can buy anything. She smiles up at him with amazing teeth, speaks his name as if it were the least interesting thing she has ever heard, then studies her crossword puzzle again, frowns, pulls the pencil from her hair, and makes a mark on the page. Cutler knows what she is thinking—that he is too old for an errand boy. She is right.

Quinn drops the envelope onto the flowered cushion of his chair and steps to a wooden cart that holds bottles, glasses, an ice bucket. "Drink, Darryl? Martini?" Quinn's brown hand hovers, touches this bottle, that one. "Scotch? White wine?"

"I don't like to intrude," Cutler says. He doesn't recognize this friendly Phil Quinn, and he feels uneasy. The idea appeals to him, of sitting here, sharing for an hour the kind of life he has always craved, opulent, easy, never a worry in the world, achievements, honors, fame. Inside his head, his mother says, *You have to earn those things, you have to work for them. No one's going to hand them to you.* Someone has handed them to Veronica Quinn. Cutler turns away. "I'd better get back."

"Sit down. I appreciate your bringing me those pages. That's a long drive. You deserve at least a drink." He nods at a third chair in the group. Cutler murmurs thanks, sits down, and gazes at the crashing waves while behind him ice jingles in a martini pitcher. Quinn puts a big, chilly glass into his hand. "There you go." He sits, picks up his own glass again, lifts it to Cutler. They both drink, then Quinn settles back in the chair, tilts his head, and cranks up the friendliness. "Tell me about yourself. You've been with Stewart quite a while, now, haven't you?"

"Six years," Cutler says. It seems impossible.

"A writer has to know something about people," Quinn says, "and I wouldn't type you as an office manager." He frowns. "Didn't Stewart tell me you're a writer, too?"

Cutler's laugh is short. He shrugs. "In the sixties, there were a lot of sleazy little publishers around L.A., putting out sex paperbacks. It was easy money. It was writing. Of a sort." He doesn't add

that the sex in his books was gay, or that Ralph
Pullen, an editor he lived and slept with, outlined
the stories, and all young Darryl had to do was fill
in the blanks. "But after ten books or so, the market
dried up. Graphic sex got into mainstream fiction.
Most of the hacks switched to writing gothics."

"But not you?" Quinn is listening carefully, frown
lines between his brows. Cutler wishes he could see
the man's eyes. Why is he suddenly so interested?
"Why not?" Quinn takes a cigarette pack from his
Hawaiian shirt, leans across, holds it out.

Cutler shakes his head. "I gave up smoking when
Stewart had to have oxygen around. It's explosive."

Quinn lights a cigarette. The blond young woman
shuts the crossword puzzle book, tucks it down between the arm of the chair and the cushion, gets up,
and goes into the house. She moves like a figure in
a wet dream. Quinn asks, "Was that when you went
to work for Stewart?"

"No—I thought I could write the Great American Novel, didn't I?" Cutler sips at the icy drink.
It is very good. He peers at the bar cart to read the
gin label. "I didn't try to get a job until I found out
that none of the publishers wanted the Great American Novel—at least, not my version of it."

Cutler has told two lies here. He never finished
the book he meant to be the fictionalized story of
his life. Facing his mother, even as words on paper,
day after day, re-living her slaps and sneers as a little kid, a gangly adolescent—guilty all the time, but
never sure of what—was more than he could bear.
And he never applied for jobs. He lived off older
men—Clark Calhoun, until fat Clark decided Cutler
was having boys on the side; Dean Schuller, till

withered Dean hired an accountant to check out why his bank balance was always so feeble; Lawrence Askew, whose car Cutler had totalled. He didn't go to Stewart Moody Script Service for a job—a nervous Moody picked him up on sunny Hollywood Boulevard when Cutler was broke and, after ten years of it, fed up with hustling. 1976. And they lived happily ever after.

"Not to worry," Quinn says. "You'll write again. If you're a writer, writing is what you do."

Cutler gives him a sad smile. "I think about it. But Stewart keeps me pretty busy right now. Anyway"—he lifts his glass to Quinn—"thanks for the encouragement."

Quinn says, "Where do you come from?"

"Oregon." Cutler laughs wanly. "Sleepy old Portland."

"Pretty country, though. How did you come to leave?"

"It's always raining." Cutler likes attention, but Quinn's bothers him. He is too bloody inquisitive. What business of Quinn's is Cutler's history? Until this afternoon, Cutler would have said that Quinn despised him. He takes another swallow of martini and sits for a moment, frowning into the glass, answering his own question. *A writer has to know something about people.* Maybe this is how Quinn learns. Maybe this is how he gets the stories he turns into film scripts. They have to come from somewhere. Well, this is one story Quinn isn't going to get. No one is ever going to get this story.

How did you come to leave? Cutler gets quickly out of the chair, walks to the deck rail, stands there clutching the glass and staring out at the horizon

16

where the sun hangs red over the ocean. But that is not what he sees. He sees a kid on a bicycle charge out of a dark side street right into his headlights — a small boy, not ten years old, riding a racing bike. At midnight, almost midnight. A big blue crash helmet makes the boy look like some creature from a space ship.

Cutler is driving the Sunbeam his mother has just given him as a graduation present — not knowing how bad his grades are, that he will never graduate. Cutler shouts and steps on the brakes and the new tires scream. He has been driving fast through a neighborhood asleep, not a car on the streets. Only this young boy on a bicycle, who ought to have been in bed hours ago. Cutler jerks the steering wheel, but it is too late. There is a thud, and he sees the boy looping through the air, away, high, the crash helmet flying.

"I was eighteen," Cutler says. "It was time to leave the nest."

Quinn stands beside him. "You're shivering." He takes the empty glass from Cutler's hand. "Can I get you a jacket?"

"It's a warm wind." Cutler tries for a smile. "I feel a little shaky, that's all." He reads his watch, looks toward the French doors. Is the dream creature cooking Quinn's supper? Would she do that, could she? No. There must be a fat cook. He hates remembering that night. It always makes him sick. "Look, I don't want to keep you from your supper, but can I beg another drink?"

"I was about to suggest it." Quinn takes off the sunglasses and peers at Cutler. "You look pale. Sit down." He walks to the cart. "This will only take a minute. No rush about supper. Will you eat with us?"

Cutler drops onto his chair, swallows hard, shakes his head. "I have to get back to Stewart. He shouldn't be alone." Cutler leans his head back, shuts his eyes against the flame colors of the sky.

It wasn't his fault. What was the kid doing there? Yes, there was a boulevard stopsign, but the neighborhood was deserted. It was midnight. He was speeding. He had a brand new car, his very own. He was young. Of course he wanted to test how fast it would go. Who could blame him for that? He laughs bitterly to himself. He knew who could blame him for that—his mother.

He sat in the little car, unable to move, silence all around. He must get out and find the boy. Maybe he wasn't dead. That was a lie. He knew the boy was dead. He couldn't make himself touch the door handle. All he could think of was what his mother was going to say. He had to call the police. Go to that house right there, climb the porch steps, ring the bell, ask to use the phone. There'd been an accident. Suddenly a light went on in that house, at an upstairs window. The window went up, someone leaned out, a woman in a nightgown, hair in curlers. Cutler started the car, stalled it, started it again, and drove off, clattering over the bicycle in his panic.

"Here you go." Coldness touches Cutler's hand. He flinches and opens his eyes. Quinn bends over him, offering another big martini. Cutler laughs weakly, extends a shaky hand, and takes the drink. "Thank you." He puts the glass hastily to his mouth, dribbling some of the gin and vermouth down his chin. The rim of the glass rattles against his teeth. Quinn says, "You're ill. What do you think it is. Flu? Flu can be vicious in hot weather." He tilts his big head. "Why don't I call my doctor?"

"It's not flu." Cutler sits up straight. "It's nerves, stupid nerves." He takes another drink. "You see, I don't get out much." He tries for a laugh again, and this time almost manages it. "Driving freeways when you're not used to it can shake you up." He drinks again. "Forgive me? I feel like a fool. I damn near came completely unglued on the coast highway, almost got out of the car and walked off and left it."

Quinn rumbles a laugh. "I can identify with that."

"The traffic will be lighter going home," Cutler says.

"You feel free to wait here till you're steady again." Quinn sits down, picks up the envelope of his pages, opens it, slides the pages out, and looks them over quickly. "Good," he says to himself, "good." He looks at Cutler. "You know, I've tried other typing services. After all, Stewart's not exactly in the neighborhood. But none of the rest of them is any damn good. At Stewart's someone can always read my scratchings-out and scrawlings-in."

"Stewart's a perfectionist," Cutler says. "He demands the best of everybody and won't settle for less."

"I suppose I'll have to get a damned word processor." Quinn slides the pages back into the envelope. "Start doing it all myself." He looks gravely at Cutler. "I mean, Stewart's dying—that's the truth, isn't it?"

Cutler wonders who Quinn is to demand the

truth. Cutler feels steady now, in control. He says in light disparagement, "Emphysema doesn't strike you down like that. I look after him. He gets the best treatment. He'll live for years yet."

Quinn says, "I certainly hope you're right."

3

The setting sun casts dark shadows in the notches of the brown hills across the highway from the beach. In one of those notches, someplace along here, crouches a rickety wooden bar and restaurant called the Sea Shanty. It half hides behind eucalyptus trees purposely untrimmed. It isn't eager to draw travelers off the highway. It has all the customers it wants. Cutler used to be one of them, seven, eight years ago. Then he could find it in his sleep. Now he has twice passed the place where he would have sworn its access road crept off the highway.

No access road. He doesn't understand, and it is making him frantic. He begins to quiver inside. His hands sweat on the steering wheel. He is losing precious time. He has been shut up too long. Everything has changed. Damn. There's the abandoned gas works again. He looks in the side mirror, glances through the windshield, makes a fast U turn, tires squealing, and heads into the sun and sea glare one more time. He didn't drive far enough before.

Or did he? The way storms have been punishing this coast, shattering piers, toppling houses into the surf, bringing cliffs down onto the highway, eating up miles of beach, maybe the Sea Shanty is gone — buried by a mud slide, or caught in a flash flood from the hills and washed out to sea and sunk with all faggots on board. How the hell would he know? He never sees anyone from those days. Moody wouldn't like it, and he doesn't want to make any mistakes with Moody. But he has dreamed of the place a thousand times. And tonight he wants to be there again. God knows how soon he'll have another chance. He squints into the harsh red light. Where the hell is it?

It is where it always was — miles farther north than his tricky memory put it. He swings the compact off the highway, and follows the patchy asphalt access road to a gravel area under trees thicker and taller than they used to be, and scruffier. Pods and leaves and peeled brown bark from the trees litter the gravelled patch. Few cars stand here. That's as it used to be. Not many came to the Sea Shanty to eat. They didn't come to drink either. To be accurate about it, they came for each other. He hopes that hasn't changed. Crossing the gravel, his heartbeat quickens. He is excited and a little scared. It's been so long — will he remember how to act?

The black door must have been painted more than once since he last saw it, but its paint is cracked and peeling now as it was then. The door handle is pitted with corrosion from the salt in the sea winds. He pulls the door open and steps into darkness, cold air conditioning, and the blare of Judy Garland singing "The Man that Got Away." A television set hangs over the back bar. It is playing a video tape of *A Star is Born*. She sings in a bistro closed for the night, the chairs upended on the tables. The faces of men seated at the bar are turned up to watch her. They are like all the faces he has ever looked at in this place, yet he knows none of them. The most beautiful of the faces turns toward him for a moment, blue eyes size him up, the face turns back to Judy Garland.

The bar is a low bar, now, each seat an armchair on a swivel. He settles into one. The bartender is tall, with a receding hairline, the usual mustache. Four out of the five men at the bar have the usual mustache. Only the most beautiful is clean shaven, but he is hardly more than a boy, and he is extremely blond, so blond his hair is almost white. The bar curves, and Cutler can see that the boy's glass is empty except for half-melted ice cubes.

The bartender says, "How are you tonight?"

Cutler says, "I'll be better when I've had a martini on the rocks. And give that one whatever he's been drinking, will you please?"

The bartender arches an eyebrow. "Fast worker."

"Foreplay bores me," Cutler says. The bartender twitches a smile and turns away, and Cutler looks at his watch. He hasn't much time. This is a bad hour of the day to try to make a pickup, but there's no choice, is there? Moody, propped by pillows on the green counterpane, will be watching television, but only half of his attention will be on it. The other half will be on the clock. Cutler dares not be too late. It's unfair, after years of self-denial, but he has to get what he wants tonight quickly or not at all.

With a small, amused flourish, the bartender sets the martini in front of Cutler on a cocktail napkin. The glass is small, the olive is large, and there is much ice. The bartender carries what appears to be Scotch to the blond boy, says something to him, nods in Cutler's direction. The boy doesn't seem surprised. He looks toward Cutler, however. Cutler gives him a smile. The boy blinks, lifts his glass to Cutler, drinks. Cutler tries his martini. It is a poor thing next to Quinn's. Absentmindedly, he touches his shirt pocket. He wants a cigarette. Oh, this is going to be a wild night. With a wry shake of his head, he goes to the cigarette machine. When he returns, the boy is in the chair next to his.

"Thank you for the drink," he says.

"My pleasure." Cutler drops into his chair, takes the cellophane off the cigarette pack, opens the flip top, removes the gold paper, holds the pack out to the boy, who shakes his head. Cutler lights a cigarette, drinks, says to the boy, "Have dinner with me."

The boy makes a wry face. "I'm meeting someone."

Cutler looks at the far tables laid with silver, napkins, glasses, where candles flicker inside amber glass chimneys. "You're not going to eat here, surely."

"I don't know where. He's picking me up here."

"I'm Darryl Cutler." Cutler holds out his hand.

"Chick Pelletier." The boy shakes hands limply, awkwardly, like a little kid who hasn't learned the knack. Or like a girl. Cutler's handshake is strong, manly. His mother made him practice. *A good, firm handshake makes people respect you.* The boy is looking intently at Cutler, and when Cutler lets his hand go, the hand reaches out and a finger makes a cool line down the side of Cutler's face. "Rugged. I love those deep creases. Mmm."

"You're a study in contrasts," Cutler says. "Fair hair, tan skin. Are you a surfer?"

"Will it be kickier for you if I say yes?" Chick Pelletier's blue eyes mock him. "Or have you got a thing for the absolute truth?"

Cutler laughs briefly and turns away to get the

24

last of the very little gin and vermouth from his glass. "Nobody tells the absolute truth."

"I do. It makes people furious." He reaches out again, undoes two buttons on Cutler's shirt, parts the shirt, smiles, hums, strokes Cutler's chest. "Lovely fur," he says. "Are you Greek or something?"

"Black Irish—or something." Cutler coughs on cigarette smoke. He isn't used to it anymore. "You're not drinking," he says. "Something wrong with the Scotch?"

"It's rum," Pelletier says. "What's the hurry?"

"I want us to be gone when your date gets here."

The boy wears a skin-diver's watch. He reads it. "I live with him. He's older." He looks into Cutler's eyes and the corners of his pretty mouth twitch. "I have this thing for older men."

"Jesus," Cutler says. "What do I do now?"

"I can make an exception in your case," Pelletier says. "But if I stand Wrigley up, he'll kick me out."

Cutler touches the thick black watch. "Is there time for another drink, or not?"

"There's time. He said seven fifteen. But he has a sadistic streak. He likes to keep me waiting."

Cutler signals the barman, who nods and gets to work.

Pelletier goes on, "To scare me, make me wonder if he's grown tired of me."

"Are you saying you want to move in with me instead? How do you know you won't be disappointed in the sex?"

"With a body like that? A face like that? A girl would be crazy." Pelletier suddenly drinks off his rum, reaches for the Marlboros and matches on the bar, lights a cigarette. He handles it like Bette Davis, and

blows smoke into Cutler's face. "Do you believe anything I'm telling you? Why would you trust someone who'd have sex with you for a lousy glass of rum?"

"Because you have a snub nose and baby blue
eyes," Cutler says, "and all the world knows those
are sure signs of total innocence." He crushes out
his cigarette in a little glass ashtray. The bartender
brings fresh drinks. Cutler pays for them, tries his
martini, finds it stronger than the first, and lights
another cigarette. "Why would you trust me? I look
like Mephistopheles."

Pelletier broods over his rum. "That would be a
better reason. Don't you know looks can be deceiv-
ing? I could be evil as a snake. Wouldn't it be easy,
looking like I do." He watches Cutler sidelong. "What
if you take me someplace for sex, and I kill you, steal
your money and your credit cards, and drive off in
your car? Why wouldn't I do that?"

"Because that's not why you're here." Grinning,
Cutler touches the boy's crotch. "Some motives can't
be hidden. Yours is making a bulge, didn't you
know?"

"Thinking about murder does that to some of us."
Pelletier stares menacingly into Cutler's eyes, but he
can't keep the pretense up. His mouth twitches, he
laughs and turns away, shaking his head. "God—
and I'm supposed to be an actor. You're right." He
swivels the chair and stands up in his blue tanktop,
yellow running shorts, bare feet. "Let's go do it." He
starts for the door, drink in his hand. Over his shoulder, he says, "Then you can drop me back here, and
Wrigley will never know." He edges out the door,
sucking at his drink. Cutler gathers up the Marl-

boros, matches, keys, glances at the mustached men at the bar, who watch him with what he takes to be envy, and goes after Pelletier.

Under the tall, rustling trees that are brushy silhouettes against a fiery sky, the boy perches on the trunk of a Mercedes sports coupe and sips his rum. The sea wind blows his pale hair. Cutler crunches across gravel, dry leaves, pods, to smile at him.

"Wrong car," he says.

"Oh yeah?" Pelletier's face falls. He lets himself down off the trunk, glances around. "Which one, then?"

Cutler points at the compact. "Boring, right?"

Pelletier squints, pushes hair out of his eyes, and shakes his head. "You're putting me on. You wouldn't be caught dead in a car like that."

Cutler shrugs. "It's a company car—all right?"

"What kind of company?"

"Secretarial service, instant printing, all that. My lover owns it. He's an old man, sick. I run it for him. Actually, I'm a writer." Cutler starts toward the car, Pelletier hobbling beside him, wincing. Cutler says, "Gravel hurt your feet?"

"Yeah. Why don't you carry me?"

"Give me your glass." Cutler takes it, bends his knees, bends his back. "Climb on," he says.

Pelletier paws at his hair, giggles. "You're kidding."

"I won't drop you," Cutler says.

"I'm not a little kid," Pelletier says.

"You're not a big kid, either, or you wouldn't go around barefoot. Why do you do that?"

Pelletier grins. "Because it drives Wrigley crazy." Pelletier frowns. "You like carrying people?"

"Not people," Cutler says. "You."

Pelletier snorts, wags his head, holds out his hand. "Give me back my drink." He takes it, swallows from it, brushes gravel off the sole of one foot, then the other, and limps off. Cutler follows. In the car, poised at the edge of the highway, Pelletier directs him northward.

"I know a place," he says, "where we can get it on. Nobody goes there. I'll show you the road." He takes the cigarettes from Cutler's pocket and lights one, lays pack and matches on the dash, leans back smoking, drinking. "What kind of writer?"

"Novels, but there's no money in that. The big money is in movies and TV. I'm working on a screenplay. I've got friends in the industry. Bigtime screenwriters. It's the only way into pictures. You have to know people."

"You don't have to bullshit me," Pelletier says. "I like you. You're gorgeous. How tall are you?"

"Six three," Cutler lies, "and I'm not bullshitting you. I was down in Cormorant Cove only this afternoon. At a meet with Phil Quinn. At his house. You know who Phil Quinn is? He wrote *Touch and Go*."

"It just opened," Pelletier says. "Big boxoffice."

"You got it." Cutler nods. "Who is Wrigley? Is that the chewing gum Wrigley? Wrigley field?"

"Please." Pelletier scoffs. "Gourmet cookware."

"Someday I'm going to own a house in Cormorant Cove," Cutler says. "You want to live with me in Cormorant Cove?"

"When you sell your screenplay?" Pelletier's bored tone says he does not believe in the screenplay.

28

"There's a part in it for you," Cutler says. "The lead. You'll be a star."

Pelletier shrugs. "Sure, why not?" His rum is gone. He tosses the empty glass out the window. "Here comes our road," he says.

They drive back into the hills.

4

The air conditioner in the night window blows cool-ness across him in his bed but it doesn't help. He sweats, turns from side to side, checks and rechecks the red numbers on the clock radio beside the bed. Two forty eight. Two fifty two. Two fifty nine. He groans and sits on the edge of the bed and lights a cigarette. It is the last in the box he brought back here from the Sea Shanty. It has been days, but he only smokes in here, alone.

It has been days, but he can't get Pelletier out of his mind. It isn't so bad during business hours, and when he has Moody to look after. But at night it is torment. Pelletier's voice speaks inside his head, Pelletier laughs, mocks, flatters. When Cutler shuts his eyes, he sees Pelletier. Naked in the car up there in the empty sundown hills, or hopping on the gravel of the Sea Shanty's parking space, or looking sober while he touches Cutler's face at the bar.

This has never happened to Cutler before. He wants Pelletier so badly he is ready to cry about it. It makes no sense. He has had sex with scores of strangers in his time and walked away without regrets or feelings of any sort except satisfaction that didn't last. The faces and voices never stayed with him. He never wanted to go back and find any of them. Yet now he is half out of his mind worrying that he has lost Pelletier forever. If this is love, what the hell is there to like about it? He has never felt so sick in his life.

It was the long wait, wasn't it — all those years stuck here with Moody, under Moody's watchful eye, never once breaking cover? Here in the dark, film clips of memory jitter past — faces, bodies seen in supermarket, drugstore, coin laundry, steady looks from knowing eyes. A hand seemed by accident to brush his fly. A leg pressed against his. He moved on, keeping his own eyes to himself, his own hands. Moody is going to leave him well-fixed for life. He is not about to spoil that. The fan inside the air conditioner rattles. It is scarcely audible, but it makes him furious. He jumps to his feet, runs at the metal and plastic box, bangs it with an open hand. The rattle ceases for the moment.

He stares out the window at the pale moonlit side of the old frame house next door, almost identical to this one. And he wishes he could bang his head with his hand and rid it of Pelletier. *When will I see you again?* Pelletier says in there, like the rattle of the air conditioner. It didn't mean anything. It was a mechanical phrase, obligatory, it went with putting your pants back on. It was a sort of thanks for the nice five minutes. Everyone said it, no one meant it. This makes Cutler's chest ache. He turns from the window in disgust. He is pathetic.

He leaves his room, crosses the hallway dimly lit by the fluorescent fixture that burns all night in the shop below. Softly he turns the knob of Moody's door, opens the door, puts in his head. Moody lies quiet in the moonlight. Cutler holds his breath and listens. He hears the thin hiss of the oxygen, and

Moody's regular breathing. All okay. He softly shuts the door again, visits the bathroom, returns to his bed. He switches on the lamp, piles up pillows, gets into bed and picks up the file copy of Quinn's script in its red cover. He will never see the picture — not until it reaches TV, and that won't be for years. He is curious about it.

But more than curiosity led him to bring it up here. Pelletier was right — Cutler isn't writing any screenplay. To begin with, he doesn't know the technique. For years he has managed this business for Moody, but he has scarcely looked inside the covers of any film script. The slaves type and reproduce the scripts, as they run the rest of the machinery. Cutler sends out statements, keeps the books, banks the receipts. He pays the bills, doles out the weekly wages, checks inventory, orders supplies. He never touches a typewriter.

The novel with his mother in it soured him. When he first won Moody, he spun fantasies for the old man about writing again, and Moody rushed out to buy him a typewriter. Dim, tidy-minded Moody had a romantic streak. He was going to feed, shelter, and finance a genius, and not just any genius — a tall, dark, handsome, young genius. Cutler laughs to himself. Where is that typewriter now? He can't recall. Under the bed? In the closet? Why has he thought of it now, at three in the morning, head aching, mouth bitter, insides noisy because not only can he not sleep, he can't eat?

He won't see Pelletier again. He doesn't dare. Still, he keeps thinking about writing that screenplay for him to star in. Trying to write it. Pointless, yet the idea nags him, through the days, through the nights.

So does the vision of Quinn's handsome house over-looking the crashing surf. He badly wants a house like that, and the money and fame that go with it, and someone as unearthly beautiful as Veronica Quinn to share it with — Pelletier, of course. *You'll never do it,* his mother says. *You give up too easily.*

He won't give up. Didn't Quinn encourage him? *You'll write again. If you're a writer, writing is what you do.* Sure. Cutler will pick up the knack from reading this script. And Quinn will help him sell the one he writes. He just needs time. Fargo can cover for him in the shop — the more work you pile on Fargo, the happier she is. All those evenings wasted sitting silent beside Moody while the old man dozes through hour after hour of idiot television, Cutler can use for writing. Moody will excuse him. He'll be delighted that Cutler is writing at last. And when the script sells — goodbye Moody. He can leave his boring little business to someone else. Who needs it?

"Do you realize what time it is?" Moody stands over him in pajamas and robe, hair spiky from sleep, his breathing wheezy. Bright daylight is in the room. Moody bends and picks up Quinn's script from the floor. "Did you stay up till all hours reading?" He slaps the script down pettishly on the night stand and examines the clock. "You didn't even set your alarm. Have you given up all sense of responsibility?"

"I'm sorry." Cutler blinks, runs a hand down his face, pushes wearily away from the pillows, swings his feet to the floor. "It won't happen again."

"Perhaps you're ill." Moody studies him crossly. "You certainly haven't been yourself lately. Not since you drove to the beach that night." He narrows his eyes, suspicion edges his voice. "Something happened, didn't it? Something you haven't told me about. You met some man, didn't you?"

"I met Phil Quinn." Cutler coaxes him with a smile. "Come on Stewart. You know half the coast road was washed out. The traffic was very slow."

"That's what you told me. You were very late. There was gin on your breath. You stopped at some bar and picked up some trashy boy for sex. Don't lie to me." He is trembling, his eyes fill with tears, his voice breaks. "Oh, to think you'd do such a thing to me when I'm dying."

"Ho." Cutler gets to his feet and takes the shaky, skinny little form in his arms. "Now, now. You know that isn't so. You're getting along fine. You're just upset because I overslept." Cutler with gentle fingers wipes tears from Moody's face, as if Moody were a small boy who'd scraped his knee. He takes Moody's face in his hands and looks into his eyes. "I had gin on my breath," he explains, smiling patiently, "because Quinn made me a martini — a very large martini."

"You should have refused. You were driving."

"I couldn't. You wouldn't have wanted me to be rude to Quinn. I know how important he is to you."

"Yes. Well." Moody's mouth twitches. "I'm sorry if I accused you falsely." A smile trembles. "You've been very loving and kind. I don't know what gets into me." He separates himself from Cutler, takes a step toward the door, and begins to weep, his bony shoulders shaking. Cutler puts arms around him again and gently steers him, whimpering, shuffling along the hall to the bathroom. He begins to help him out of his robe, as he has morning after morning now for many long months. But Moody is inconsolable. He weeps. He clutches Cutler's arms. "I don't want to die," he cries, looking up pitifully into Cutler's face, begging. "I don't want to die."

"And you're not going to." Soothingly, Cutler unbuttons and removes Moody's pajama top. "What a way to start the day. You know the doctor says you're doing fine, keeping your weight up, holding your own."

Moody nods, sniffles, gulps. "I know."

"Of course you do. You stop brooding about dying, understand? There's lots of wonderful years ahead. Come on, let's get you into the shower now, and then we'll have a special breakfast. Eggs Benedict — how about that?"

"You are good to me," Moody hiccups. "Don't leave me, Darryl. I know I'm cranky sometimes, but I don't mean it." His nose runs. "It's just that I don't feel well."

"I understand." With tissues from a box on the back of the toilet fixture, Cutler wipes Moody's upper lip. He kneels on the bathroom tiles to help Moody out of his pajama pants. "You know I'll never leave you. Why would I?" He stands, hangs robe and pajamas on the door hook. "Where would I go?" He puts a light kiss on Moody's mouth. "You're my whole life — you know that." He edges past the old man's skeletal form to turn on the taps in the shower. The plumbing shudders and clatters. Cutler adjusts the water temperature, then steadies Moody as he steps under the spray and carefully places on a no-slip rubber mat feet white and fragile looking as fine china. Cutler says, "Why would I pick up some stranger in a bar, when I have you?"

"Speak louder," Moody says. "I can't hear you."

Cutler smiles, shakes his head, wags a hand to say it wasn't important, and clicks shut the chromium-framed ripple-glass door of the shower stall. On the glass, a muscular young merman with seaweed hair blows on a conch shell. Cutler painted it there years ago. He grimaces. If he'd known then what he knows now, he'd have painted himself as a staggering Sinbad with a naked Old Man of the Sea on his back. Behind the shower door, feebly but unmistakably, Moody begins to sing.

"What about one of these?" Cutler has looked carefully for the ad and finally found it. It is for a chair that travels on a rail up and down stairs. He lays the magazine open to the ad on the blankets that cover Moody's thin legs. "It would let you go down to the shop whenever you wanted, and come back up here anytime you liked."

Moody picks up the magazine. Half-lens reading glasses perch low on his thin nose. He peers through them at the ad and sneers. "Look at that ridiculous old woman." He eyes Cutler over the tops of the glasses. "Is that how I seem to you? An old woman who can't walk upstairs? Well I can. If I take my time. I was a good runner once." He hands the magazine back to Cutler. "Captain of my high school track team. Faster than you ever were. You're too big and clumsy for a runner."

Cutler closes the magazine, lets it drop to the floor beside his chair. "I just thought you'd like the independence it would give you."

"You're tired of being on call every minute of the day," Moody says. "That's it, isn't it?"

"That's not it. I know you enjoy being in the office. It makes you nervous when you can't." The television is on. An actor in a scuba diving outfit and big flippers steps through a living room doorway. A laugh track laughs. Cutler adds, "You sit up here brooding too much."

The man in the wetsuit makes a sudden turn, and behind him the spear under his arm impales a cake on a table. Someone screams. Startled, the man turns around again, swinging the cake into a middle-aged woman's face. More recorded laughter. Moody stares at the television set without a smile. He says, "It's provoking when those you love try to change you." He takes off the glasses and regards Cutler coldly. "Why do you want to change me, suddenly?"

"I was trying to think of ways to brighten up your days, that's all." He wants to broach leaving Moody in here alone with the TV in the evenings while he writes. He is afraid to try. "I don't want to change you, Stewart. What a thought. I'm very happy here with you—you know that. You've done a lot for me, and I'll always be grateful."

"Hmm." Moody is skeptical. "I should be flattered to think I'm so much on your mind, shouldn't I? Why do you suppose I'm not? Why do you suppose I get the feeling that you're after something—for yourself?"

Now is his chance, and Cutler laughs. "You know me so well. It's true. Maybe you've heard the typewriter going in my room at night when you're supposed to be asleep?"

Moody's head jerks back, startled. The oxygen tube makes a flicking sound against the wall. "What?

You mean your typewriter, the one I gave you?"

Cutler ducks his head with an aw-shucks grin.

"Why, no, I hadn't." Moody starts to smile, frowns, smiles again. "You mean you're writing? You're writing your novel, at last?" He reaches out and catches Cutler's hands in his, and tries to squeeze them, though he hasn't the strength. Tears of joy shine in his eyes. "But Darryl, that's wonderful news. How proud I am. How happy."

"I thought you would be. But I don't want you to feel neglected. I'll need time to myself."

"Of course you will. I understand." Moody claps his hands. "Let's have some champagne."

Laughing, Cutler gets out of his chair. "Okay, but it's not a novel, this time. It's a screenplay. I figured if Phil Quinn could do it, so could I. He encouraged me, the night I was down there."

"Of course, he did." Moody scrabbles around him for the television remote control and switches off the set. He seems happy as a little boy. "Then something good came of that trip, didn't it? It was the writing that was on your mind—that's what made you seem different. Of course. What an old silly I am."

"A lovable old silly," Cutler says, and goes off up the hall, whistling, to fetch the champagne.

5

It is late. His back aches. He has sat for hours at the typewriter, lamp glaring white off the blank page that wraps the platen. The motor of the typewriter pulses. The fan rattles lightly in the air conditioner. From across the hall come voices, sirens, tire-squeals from Moody's television set. The sounds irritate Cutler. He jumps up and switches on the clock radio by the bed. He wants to drown out the noises with music, but no matter what station he tunes to, someone is talking. He switches the radio off. He feels helpless. It makes him angry.

Back at his desk, he lights a cigarette and stands staring down at the neat ream of paper beside the typewriter, paper he is supposed to be turning into a screenplay. He has taken to buying cartons of cigarettes with the household supplies. He could never write without cigarettes before. Now he can't write even with them. Wearily, he sits down again and without thinking reaches for the tattered paperbacks stacked on the desk. Covers faded, pages turning brown, these eight he has dug out of the closet, the eight he managed to hang onto through the years since he wrote them, even those times he had to leave everything else behind.

He thumbs through them, unseeing, and lays them back one by one on the desk. There should be two more, shouldn't there? Or three? He can't remember. It was a long time ago, and really only the first one mattered to him. He sits holding it now, gazing down at it through the smoke that rises stinging from the cigarette hung in the corner of his mouth. On the scuffed cover, a lost-looking, too-pretty teenage boy in tight Levis and an open shirt, lounges against a lamp post on a sleazy night street. *Boy Hustler,* the title reads. Cutler's remembering smile is thin. He had called it *Lonely in the Night.*

How had he come to write it? Memories come in a rush. He drove down the coast from Portland almost without stop, sleepless, frantic, the dead boy on the broken bicycle following him. Cutler's eyes kept falling shut. He had money, but he was afraid to stop. The dead kid would come to his bedside, all bloody and broken. Locked motel room doors didn't stop ghosts. When dawn came, he slept in the car on some forsaken beach, dunes and tufts of tall grass. Rain. He bypassed San Francisco. It wasn't far enough away.

In Los Angeles, he drove around and around in the dry, hot sunshine, nowhere to go, nothing to do. He ate at greasy spoons, hamburger stands, pizza stands, burrito stands, never going back to any of them twice. He was terrified that his mother would find him. Lorraine. It made no sense, but he was too shaken to be sensible, too scared. Stopping anywhere for more than half an hour—he did have the car washed: it was his car; it seemed terribly important—meant she could catch him. She'd have called the police, maybe sent private detectives. A truant officer in Portland had given him trouble more than once. He kept seeing this man in his old gray suit with the drooping shoulders—imagining he saw him.

He thought the man came and sat next to him at the counter of a Mexican take-out place on Vermont. *You're a long way from home,* the man said. *We all know what you did.* Cutler pushed him, the stool toppling backward in a long, slow arc, the way things sometimes fall in dreams. Cutler ran, ran until he was exhausted, and fell down, sobbing, vomiting. On someone's lawn. A woman came out on a stingy little concrete front stoop, staring, her hand clutching a padded housecoat closed at the throat. She scowled at him. In a crow's voice, she told him to get up and go away. He sat on benches on the City College campus until dark, then went back, got the Sunbeam, checked into a scaly stucco motel out Venice boulevard, and slept for two days straight.

He showered. His clothes were filthy. He went out and bought new jeans, underwear, socks, razor and shaving cream. In the motel office, he waited for the beard-stubbly manager to check in a whore with her john, an early drunk, then paid his bill. It left him with a few ones and some loose change. He put gas in the Sunbeam and drove back to a cafe in Venice. Shirtless druggies with long, tangled hair and dirty feet tried to bum quarters from him. On the pot-holed gray blacktop of the street gulls stood around. Shorty was not in the Alamo Cafe, where the menu was part Chinese, part Kosher, part Tex-Mex. But while Cutler wolfed scrambled eggs and chili, Shorty came in.

"I seen your car out in the lot." He dragged out a bentwood chair at Cutler's table and sat down. "You ready to sell it, now?" Shorty kept his hair clipped close on top, it looked like dingy moss on a rock. "You should of took me up on my first offer. Market's down now."

Cutler drank Coke. "You said a thousand dollars."

"That was before. Best I can do is five hundred, now."

"Shit," Cutler said. "It cost nearly four thousand."

"Not you, it didn't." Shorty read the limp, dog-eared menu. "It was a birthday present — that's what you said."

"It's practically brand new," Cutler said. "Got less than two thousand miles on it."

A thin Mexican boy with skin like ivory and very black beard stubble came in a wraparound apron and took Shorty's order. Shorty told Cutler, "You gotta understand, I got a lot of overhead."

"You'll sell it for new," Cutler said. "It is new."

"Gotta remove the serial numbers, repaint it, fake new papers, new plates. You think that comes cheap? And what about the risk? The risk's worth something — believe it."

Cutler's stomach churned. "Seven fifty," he said.

"It's not even yours. It's your folks' car, isn't it? I mean, you're not even a legal adult, right?"

"Look who's talking about legal." Cutler tried to laugh. It was a despairing sound. "You don't care whose it is. You just want it and you want it cheap."

"By you, five hundred dollars is cheap?" Shorty said. "If you didn't need five hundred dollars, you wouldn't be here." He hitched forward on the little chair to wedge his wallet out of a hip pocket. He opened it on the worn silver-gray formica of the table top and thumbed out of it five one hundred dollar bills. He put the wallet away. He pushed the bills toward Cutler. "You gimme the keys to the car, it's yours. Your worries are over, kid."

Trembling, Cutler stood up. "I'm not that desperate. I'm not on drugs or something." A little square of paper with the cost of his breakfast scrawled on it lay by his plate. He picked it up, read it, slid a quarter under his plate, and went along between the tables to pay at the cash register. Tucking his change away, he went out onto the gritty sidewalk. To his right, past Ocean Front Walk, lay the brown beach. He thought he would go there and just sit and stare at the waves coming in. For the rest of his life? He went back into the Alamo Cafe, back to the table where Shorty sat forking down sauerkraut and knackwurst. He looked up, cheeks stuffed, chewing, eyes uninterested. Cutler pulled the keys out of his new jeans, held them up, and gave them a little shake so that they jingled. He was so near crying, he could hardly choke the words out. "Add another hundred, and it's yours."

"That's an Oregon plate," Shorty said, and wiped his mouth with a paper napkin. "Zero six three, apple baker mary. I made a note of it the first time we talked. I can trace the owners, tell them where it is, tell them where you are. You're in no position to bargain, baby."

"A lousy six hundred bucks," Cutler said. "Come on."

"Don't cry." Shorty reached for his wallet again, laid five bills on the table top again, one at a time, paused, sighed, and pulled out a sixth bill. He held onto it and looked up at Cutler. "I shouldn't do it," he said, "but you caught me in a generous mood, kid. I like you." He slapped the bill down on the others. Cutler snatched them up. "Hold it," Shorty said. "The keys?"

Cutler dropped the keys into Shorty's sauerkraut. "Hey!" Shorty said.

"Fuck you, Jew," Cutler said, and walked out.

The money didn't last long. He went back to the whorehouse motel because he didn't know where else to go. The unit had a cramped little kitchenette, but he didn't know anything about feeding himself. Food had been set in front of him, breakfast, lunch, dinner, all his life. By his mother, or by the women she hired when she was too busy working. One of these, a lumbering Swede, with a scrubbed, rosy face, had shown him a few things in the kitchen. But when Lorraine found out, she scolded the woman. She said strictly to Cutler, *Cooking is not man's work.* Cutler was ten years old. What did she mean? *People will think you're not normal,* she said. *Now eat your supper.* So lost in Los Angeles, he ate at MacDonald's, Taco Bell, Colonel Sanders.

And the money went. He didn't think about what he would do when it was gone. He didn't look for work. What was he equipped to do to earn a paycheck every week? Anyway, working was for those without beauty, brains, talent. He was meant for better things. He looked in the mirror. Maybe the movies. He had nightmares and began to be grateful to the whores bringing noisy drunks to their rooms at all hours. To be awakened from those awful dreams by anything was a blessing. Daytimes he spent at the beach, in tight little shiny red swimtrunks, lying on a towel, reading, soaking up the sun. A bus that passed the motel went straight on out to

Venice. He caught it early every day. If you took that bus now, jigs would cut your head off, but it was safe then.

So was the beach safe, even with the ragged, bearded hippies with their blue donkey-beads, pot-reddened eyes, guitars, tambourines, hand-lettered poems blowing in the wind. Once or twice, they had included him in parties that seemed to spring up for no reason, handing him bongo drums to beat, or a wooden flute to tootle on, while some of them sat in a circle, singing, playing, clapping hands, and others danced on the sand among the candy wrappers and soft-drink cans. He recalls a pudgy girl in a granny dress, a grubby baby straddling her hip as she danced, her long hair swirling. And a boy with black greasy curls and fish-white skin turning round and round to the music, face up to the sun, eyes closed, arms held straight out, ecstatic, wearing nothing but piss stained jockey shorts.

These types were not for him. But neither were the young men who watched him steadily through sunglasses, and now and then got up nerve to change their carefully marked out places on the sand and come and fussily lay out towels and sandals and cigarettes next to him. He thinks "young" but they weren't really, not most of them. They were middle-aged and had starved and exercised and sunned themselves to keep a young look. It didn't work. Asses flattened, muscles grew stringy, elbows pointy, skin lost luster, and hair receded at the front or bald spots developed on top. Those that worked up the courage to speak at all bored him with their nervousness, silliness, cowardice. Those few that came, stood over him, shutting off the sun, and said in four letter words what they wanted of him turned his stomach.

Riding home at twilight on the bus, shivering a little in his thin shirt and jeans because the air grew cold so suddenly here, he frowned to himself. He wanted sex, all right. But not with any of these. He kept thinking of Warren Fisher, his art teacher in Portland. He had treated Warren badly, always half-teasingly, half-menacingly threatening to expose him if he didn't give Cutler presents. Never money, but gifts. On the rattling bus, he took off the wristwatch Warren had given him for his seventeenth birthday and held it in his palm, gazing at it. It hadn't occurred to him to sell the watch. It was a gift of love. He had sold the car instead. What his mother gave him never meant anything.

But he did sell the watch when the money from the car was gone. And then, when a small-voiced man, deeply suntanned but with gray hair on his meager chest, came and stretched out nearby and ventured the usual empty conversational gambits about suntan lotion or riptides or aerobic exercises, Cutler laid down his book, leaned up on an elbow facing the man, smiled, took off his sunglasses, and said, "Can you lend me sixty dollars?" That was the amount he needed to keep his room at the motel. The man took him to bed in a dead quiet apartment on a West Los Angeles side street, fed him a salad full of beansprouts for lunch, drove him around to meet his roommate, a short blond youth who worked in a camera store, then drove Cutler to the motel, handed him three twenty dollar bills, and said, "When will I see you again?"

Cutler saw him again, and many like him. Mostly

what happened was all right, sometimes he disliked it, and a few times he had to fight and run. Now and then, a man refused to pay him when it was over. Cutler learned to get the money first. Some were sentimental, fell in love with him, moved him into their places. One of these, Hal Something, taught him to cook. But most of them couldn't afford him. Short of pocket money, he would go out and hustle. This made them jealous and possessive. They started laying down rules, issuing orders, reminding him of his mother. If they owned something worth selling, a good stereo, television, microwave oven, he sold it and went his way.

Then he met Ralph Pullen. Almost four years to the day after he'd come to L.A. Not on the sand at Venice. Cutler had given that up in favor of the Sea Shanty. He remembers the moment now as if it had happened last night. He'd been avoiding the pleas of a bald man with cornflower blue eyes framed by hornrims, had played pool just to keep out of the man's way, and he was moving around the table to line up his shot when, at the far end of the long room, the door opened, and a man walked in whose appearance made Cutler's heart give a sudden thump. He almost dropped the pool cue. It was Warren Fisher. Joy welled up in him.

But of course it wasn't Warren Fisher. Ralph Pullen was a little taller, slimmer, younger. But he wore the same kind of beard that boxed in a mouth too shapely and sensitive for a man. He had the same ready smile, and gave it to Cutler when Cutler managed to catch his eye in the back-bar mirror. Pullen lived in a split-level ranch style house in Van Nuys, was recently separated, and fighting with his wife over the house. Two small boy children came to spend weekends. Pullen edited books for a publisher called Brackett House in the west valley. Cutler made him happy. Pullen fed and clothed the boy and, sex apart, asked nothing of him, not even to take out the trash. Cutler felt secure, a good feeling for a change. Pullen was easy to get along with, amusing, and a good listener.

"That's quite some four years," Pullen said. "Why don't you write a book about it? You know how to use a typewriter—you said you wrote for the school paper. Write me a book, Darryl. And don't forget the sex scenes."

So, at Pullen's white electric typewriter, in Pullen's handsome den, with its glossy desk, rows of books on shelves, sliding glass doors looking out on a red-tiled patio with an avocado tree, while Pullen was away at work, and on weekends when he'd taken the little boys off to Disneyland, Marineland, or the zoo, Cutler started and finished *Lonely in the Night,* with a lot of help from Pullen. The things that happened to the boy in the book made Cutler cry sometimes, and he didn't like it when Pullen changed the title, but he liked the check for a thousand dollars. And he liked being a writer. He wrote a letter to Miss Frolich, his journalism teacher at the high school in Portland, to brag about his novel—leaving out mention of sleazy Brackett House, of course. But he never mailed the letter. Miss Frolich would tell his mother, and his mother would come find him, or send someone. He was no longer a minor, but she would punish him about the car. She would have him locked up. He knew her.

"You said you were stopping at ten." Moody's

voice is sharp with reproach behind him. Cutler jerks with surprise. For a few seconds, he doesn't know where he is. The typewriter, the draftsman's lamp over it, the desk and papers make him think he is back at Pullen's. He is confused. Moody scolds, "I was to have your company an hour before lights out. Wasn't that our understanding?"

"Of course." Cutler switches off the typewriter and gets stiffly to his feet. He shuffles papers with typing on them, as if putting the night's work in order. They are old pages. He isn't getting anywhere. He never will, with Pelletier only a teasing image in his memory. It's Pelletier in the smooth, sun-toasted, hard-packed flesh he has to have. "Forgive me?" Cutler goes to Moody, and gives him a quick hug. "I get absorbed and forget the time."

"Hmm." Moody detaches himself, steps to the desk, frowning. "Don't leave these out here. Someone might see them." The books have Cutler's name on them, and there's no mistaking that they're gay. "You know I'm proud of them, but it wouldn't do." He winces a smile. "Would it?"

Cutler stretches to stow the books at the back of the closet shelf, and shuts the closet door. He turns to find Moody examining the typed sheets, squinting because he hasn't his reading glasses with him. He says, "Still at page nine?" He drops the papers back on the desk. "I passed your door, going to the bathroom, several times tonight. I didn't hear the typewriter."

"Thinking first," Cutler says, "typing last." He puts an arm around the old man and steers him into the hallway. "I'm sorry it's taking so long."

"Perhaps your mind is divided." Moody unexpectedly turns for the kitchen. "I'm hungry. One of those grilled cheese sandwiches of yours on that lovely sour rye bread — would that be too much trouble?"

"No trouble at all," Cutler says, "but last time you only nibbled at it. You said it was too rich, remember?" He switches on the kitchen lights. Surfaces gleam. He helps Moody onto a chrome and wicker chair at the table, opens the refrigerator. "How about quiche? That will lie easy on your stomach."

"Like a lump of ice," Moody says. "I told you what I wanted. You'd fix it soon enough for that beach boy who came in today, looking for you."

The chill from the refrigerator seems to reach out and clutch Cutler. He can't breathe. He stares at Moody for a moment, then bends to bring cheese out of the refrigerator, mayonnaise, butter. He says lightly, "What are you talking about?" and closes the refrigerator door.

"Fargo must have forgotten to tell you. She has so much work to do lately, doesn't she? She was all alone downstairs — Suzie at lunch, Bob at the postoffice, Lester making deliveries. And in comes this blond, barefoot, blue-eyed surfer, asking for Darryl Cutler. You were at the supermarket."

"Fargo's making it up." Cutler lights the grill, cuts pats of butter onto it. "Why not? There were no witnesses." He smears slices of bread with mayonnaise. "She wants you to get rid of me. So she can inherit the business. I'm an upstart. She's the one who's been here longest."

Moody looks ashen. "She told you this?"

"Not in so many words." Cutler grates cheese. "But

she's hardly subtle. It comes out in a lot of ways."

"She doesn't know what we are to each other."

Cutler sets the grater in the sink. "She guesses."

"She goes," Moody says. "First thing tomorrow."

6

In the dark of his room, Moody says from the bed, "I won't sleep tonight. I know I won't. Thinking of that bitch. Imagine. After all I've done for her, all these years. Grasping females. They're all alike."

Standing in the doorway, the hall light at his back casting his shadow into the room, "Forget it," Cutler says. "I'll get you a sleeping pill."

"No, no. They make me feel awful the next day. I'll be all right. I'll think pleasant thoughts, won't I? That was always mother's prescription for insomnia. Think pleasant thoughts. I can hear her sewing machine whirring away. I can see her as clearly as if it were yesterday. In the speckled light from the front window through the lace curtains. I remember how those curtains used to smell when I'd put my face in them, peering out. That queer, dusty smell. It was a treadle sewing machine. You wouldn't know about those, would you? Too young. Under the machine, a wrought iron rectangle you rocked with your feet. Better than those electric ones that came along. So dangerous."

"Good night," Cutler says.

"She made all her own clothes in those days," Moody says. "Mine too. Shorts with two rows of big white buttons. Playsuits, they were called. Little straps over the shoulders." His words begin to slow and fade. The oxygen hisses. "The one I loved best was bright yellow, dandelion yellow. Did you play games with flowers? I suppose not. So sophisticated, children, by your time." He sighs. "Rub another child's chin with a dandelion. If the color came off, it meant he loved butter. And when they went to seed—blow all the fluff away in one breath, and you'd get your wish." Another sigh, a long pause. Is he asleep? Not yet. "Hollyhock dolls. Did you make those? Pick a hollyhock and leave half an inch of stem, turn the flower upside down, and pick a hollyhock bud and stick it on the stem for the doll's head. Pretty skirts." Sigh. "Such pretty skirts." Moody snores.

Cutler steps backward into the hall and softly closes the door. In the bathroom, urinating, he frowns at the window. It is wide open. He zips his fly and lowers the sash so that the opening is only two inches, as it's supposed to be. He flushes the toilet and lowers the seat so Moody will get no rude surprises in the night. Cutler frowns. The seat is smudged. He touches the marks. Dust, grit. How did that happen? He wets a cellulose sponge and wipes the smudges off. He rinses out the sponge in the basin, puts it away, brushes his teeth, and leaves the bathroom, switching off the light.

He reaches for the knob of his bedroom door and stops. Who shut the door? It was open when he left the room with Moody for the kitchen. What is going on? Bathroom window open, smudges on the toilet seat beneath the window? Someone has broken in. Moody has been predicting this for years. Everyone on the street except customers Moody sees as drugcrazed muggers, car thieves, house-breakers. *We'll be murdered in our beds,* he says. Heart knocking, mouth dry, Cutler tiptoes to the stairs. The phone up here is beside Moody's bed. He won't upset Moody until he has to. He starts downstairs, careful of the treads that creak. He halts. A thought flickers in his mind. He turns back.

He pauses outside his door. Light shines under it from inside. That isn't permitted by Moody—except for the office at night, a room with no one in it is never lighted. Cutler is trembling, half with fear, half with excitement. More than excitement. Joy. He turns the knob and eases the door open. Chick Pelletier sits shining on the edge of Cutler's bed—blue tanktop, yellow running shorts. He has folded back the bedspread and opened the bed. He has a foot up on his knee and frowns and bends close, examining the dirty sole of the foot. He glances up for a moment at Cutler.

"I got a splinter from that damn ladder," he says.

"Still annoying Wrigley by going barefoot?"

"Wrigley kicked me out. Without shoes. Without anything. Had to hock my watch. I can't see it, but it stings." He sticks the foot out at Cutler. "Can you see it?" Cutler glances across the hall at Moody's closed door, comes into his room, closes his door. He kneels, takes Pelletier's foot, and kisses it. "Let me look." The splinter is dark, long, sharp, but just under the skin. Cutler rises. "I'll get a needle and disinfectant."

"In the bathroom? I'll come with you."

"All right, but quietly. He's just across the hall, and he wakes up easily."

"Why didn't you give him Seconols? There's a barrel of them in the medicine chest. I looked."

"I didn't know you were coming," Cutler said.

"Oh, yes, you did." Pelletier hops on one foot, grips Cutler's shoulder to steady himself, and whispers close to Cutler's ear, "I hate pain. If you hurt me, I'll scream."

"If you scream," Cutler murmurs, cautiously opening the door and peering out, "we'll both be on the streets. Come on—and don't play games."

Pelletier sits on the closed toilet, Cutler kneels and washes the dirty foot. He dabs the wrinkled pink skin around the splinter with disinfectant. Working very gently with a needle, he exposes the end of the splinter. He draws it out with tweezers. "Is that it?" With a grimace, Pelletier takes it in his fingers and examines it. "Ugh."

"I didn't hurt you"—Cutler gets to his feet, finds a tin box of Band-Aids, crouches, tapes a Band-Aid across the place where the splinter went in—"did I?"

"Was there blood? I faint when I see blood."

Cutler laughs. "No blood." He puts everything away. "But there was damn near bloodshed because you came into the office today. I had to talk fast to explain that away."

"I thought the old hag would make trouble." Pelletier holds out the splinter. "Get rid of that, will you please?"

Cutler takes it. "I thought I'd have it mounted."

A floorboard in the hallway beyond the closed bathroom door creaks. Moody calls, "Darryl? Where are you? There's someone in this house."

Cutler freezes. He looks at Pelletier, who grins up at him. Cutler grabs his arm, pulls open the shower door, pushes him into the dark there. "Stand in the corner," he says. He flushes the toilet, counts three,

opens the door to the hallway. Moody is just outside it, in his pajamas, his hair rumpled from having pulled the elastic off in panic.

"I heard voices," he says. He is trembling, pale,
and props himself against the wall, having trouble
breathing. "Men talking. I told you we'd be robbed."

"I didn't hear anything." Cutler switches off the
bathroom light, steps out, takes Moody's arm, stands
with him quietly, pretending to listen. "I don't hear
anything. You must have been dreaming."

"It was real, I tell you." Moody shakes his head.
His pajamas are dank with the sweat of fear. "For
a minute I thought it must be your radio, but I
looked into your room. The radio's off. And then
I heard them talking again."

"Come on." Cutler picks the frail old man up in
his arms. "Back to your room." He carries Moody
along the hall, sets him down as carefully as if he
were glass. "Now, lock the door from inside. I'll go
have a look."

"They're not downstairs. They're up here."

"Then it will be the spare room." It is filled with
shop supplies, paper, ink, outdated files. "I'll look."

"Don't be foolhardy," Moody says. "They'll kill
you. Then what will become of me?" He turns. "I'll
telephone the police."

"Don't do that," Cutler says. "Lock your door. I'll
be back in a minute. I won't take any chances. I
promise." He pulls Moody's door shut. "Lock it." He
hurries along the hall, noisily slams open the storeroom door, switches on the dim light, knocks a few
boxes around, comes out, shutting the door hard.
He runs along the hall and downstairs. He tramps
noisily through all the office rooms and runs back

up the stairs. He raps Moody's door, panting. Moody peers out with a look of childish fright. "It's all clear," Cutler tells him. "Not a sign of anybody." He takes Moody's arm, helps him to his bed, eases him down. "Your imagination's working overtime. He draws the covers up to Moody's trembling chin, leans across him, finds the oxygen tube, and arranges it for him. He puts a kiss on Moody's damp forehead, gives his shoulder a squeeze. "No one's going to harm you. Not with me here."

"No, no," Moody says with a weepy try at a smile, "of course not. I don't know why I get so frightened." He clutches Cutler's hand. "I keep remembering things."

"This time," Cutler says firmly, "I am going to get you a sleeping pill." In the bathroom, he murmurs, "Just a few minutes more."

From the dark beyond the rippled glass door, Pelletier says brightly, "I could take a shower."

"Don't you touch those faucets." Cutler tips two red capsules into his palm from an amber colored plastic container, sets the container back, closes the medicine chest. "The plumbing in this house sounds like a Jamaican band." He runs water into a glass. Pipes rattle. "See?"

"I have these idle hands," Pelletier says.

"Shall I tie them behind you?"

"I don't go for that bondage shit."

"I'm sorry he's acting up." Cutler switches off the light. "I'll be back as soon as I can." He closes the bathroom door. Moody accepts the pills meekly, washes them down with small-child gulps of water, lies back with a weary sigh. "Stay with me," he says. "I'm afraid." Cutler sits on the edge of the bed, places the glass on the night stand, turns off the lamp. A soft glow from the offices downstairs comes through the open door. Moody takes Cutler's hand. His touch is cold. "I'm going to die soon. Promise me you won't bring some trashy boy to live here. Mother would hate that."

"You and I are going to be together for a long time yet," Cutler says. "Just the two of us."

"Promise me," Moody gasps. "Give me your — solemn word." He coughs feebly. "Death won't part us?" His grip is insistent. "You'll be faithful, always?"

"I promise," Cutler says, and kisses him on the mouth.

He kisses Pelletier on the mouth. Drowsily, clinging. They have been here naked in his bed in the dark for hours. It seemed that Moody would never fall asleep. In fact, the pills did their work quickly. It seemed forever only because Cutler wanted so feverishly to be here. What if he returned to the bathroom and Pelletier was gone, out the window, down the ladder, into the night? But Pelletier was there, as eager as Cutler was — his actions showed that. Not his words. There was no time for words, no need. Cutler breaks the kiss and murmurs against Pelletier's ear, "I want this to last forever. I don't want it ever to be morning."

"It will be." Pelletier moves suddenly, wide awake and brisk. He sits up, puts his feet on the floor, shakes two cigarettes from the pack beside the clock whose red diodes spell out two-twenty. He hands Cutler a lighted cigarette over his shoulder. "And you have to make up your mind."

"When it comes to you"—Cutler caresses Pelletier's smoothly muscled back, pale in the window light—"I don't have a mind."

"You said he was dying." Pelletier leans forward, elbows on knees, and talks to the shadows in the room. "You get his insurance. You get the property, the business."

"He is dying," Cutler says. "It drags on. He's been failing slowly for months. You think I like it?"

"How much insurance?" Pelletier says. "This old house isn't worth much. How about the lot? What does the business bring in?" Cutler gives him figures, and Pelletier whistles softly. He smokes for a minute silently. Then he says, "I read someplace that if we don't like things, we change them. When we don't change them, it means we really like them, whether we know it or not."

"I told you I was writing a screenplay," Cutler says.

"Bullshit," Pelletier says. "You asked me to live with you. Where? In the shower, for Christ sake?"

"I'm waiting," Cutler says. "It's worth waiting for. I've invested six long years. I've worked my butt off. I'm not throwing that away. Would you? Look, I'll rent you an apartment. We can meet there. I'll buy you clothes. Whatever you need. A new watch. Shoes?"

"Meet when? He's got you on a leash. You were going to get a house in Cormorant Cove. Did I want to come live with you in Cormorant Cove." Pelletier stands and faces Cutler. In the soft light, he is so beautiful Cutler can't catch his breath. Pelletier says, "I remember every word. I remember you walking into the Sea Shanty, just how you looked. I never saw a man so stunning. I remember every move you made, everything we did together. I couldn't get you out of my mind. Couldn't sleep. Couldn't eat. Wrigley didn't throw me out. I couldn't stand him anymore. I left. I had to find you." His laugh is small and self-mocking. "It's called love. I read about it someplace."

Cutler feels ready to faint. "Yes. I know."

"Oxygen, you said. He has to breathe oxygen. From a tank? Like on *General Hospital*?" Pelletier crouches to find his shorts, and pulls them on. Watching him, Cutler feels a pang of awful loss. Pelletier thumps barefoot to the room door. "I want to see."

"No." Cutler lunges across the bed. "He'll wake up." He gropes on the floor for his denims. "He'll see you."

"If he didn't have it, what would happen?"

"He'd suffocate." Cutler finds the jeans, fumbles into them. "Choke to death. His lungs would collapse." Cutler zips his fly. "I don't know exactly. All I know is, he has to have it to stay alive."

"Right." Pelletier opens the door. "Come on."

"No." Cutler catches his arm. "I killed someone once. That's enough. You never get it out of your mind."

"Who said anything about killing?" Pelletier tilts his head, blinks, smiles faintly. "Not me. Is that what you've been thinking about? Killing the old fart?"

"Come back to bed," Cutler pleads.

"Nobody's going to kill anybody." Pelletier gently pries Cutler's fingers from his arm. "There's just going to be an accident, is all. Nothing anybody could help."

*   *   *

"I don't know how it could have happened." The scratches of Moody's nails down Cutler's arms are deep, and still ooze blood. They sting, and he wants to rub them. He does not. He has put on a plaid flannel shirt to hide them from the doctor, who is on hands and knees beside Moody's body, which lies on the floor between the bed and the wall. The tube from the oxygen tank is twined around Moody's arm. The elastic is not around his head. The oxygen tank has fallen over. "I check on him in the night. I was in here at three." He will never forget the look in Moody's eyes as he pushed the pillow down on his face. "He was sleeping then. He'd asked for Seconols. He was restless earlier. I didn't like giving them to him. They always made him logy the next day. But he insisted."

"No harm in that." The doctor is youngish, trim and muscular. His skin glows with health. He is homosexual. That's why Moody chose him. He gets to his feet. The space is narrow with the body lying there, and awkward to get out of. The doctor takes a long, teetering step. "It's too bad. Tragic. But" — he squeezes Cutler's sore arm sympathetically — "it couldn't be helped."

"I ought to have heard the tank fall," Cutler says.

"Stop blaming yourself." The doctor glances appreciatively around the room. "You gave him the best of care. His condition didn't warrant nurses around the clock. I wish all my elderly patients were looked after the way you looked after Stewart."

"He has on fresh pajamas," Cutler says. "The sheets and pillowcases are clean. I bathed and shaved him every morning. I trimmed his hair every week, his nails. I —"

The doctor stares. "Are you all right? Let me give you a shot. Just a mild sedative. Till the shock wears off. Roll up your sleeve."

"No." Cutler in a panic takes tight hold of the cuff of the flannel shirt. "I'm all right." He gazes at the motionless frail form on the floor. "He was fussy about his food, you know. I had to keep thinking up new recipes to tempt him. It wasn't easy, sometimes."

"You kept his weight up," the doctor says.

"You'll tell them about the fresh pajamas, will you?" Cutler says. "The clean sheets?"

"Tell who? A coroner's jury?" The doctor smiles and shakes his head. "There's no need for an inquest." He steps to the telephone. "Which mortuary shall I call?"

"What? Oh, the ones who scatter the ashes at sea," Cutler says. "He wasn't religious, and he had a horror of being nailed up in a coffin underground. What do they call themselves — Evening Star? He bought a membership."

"Can you find the papers?" The doctor holds the receiver.

"Excuse me." Cutler reaches past him. The doctor steps aside. Cutler opens the drawer of the bedside table, rattling lamp and water glass. Insurance, car registration, house tax, and other forms lie there in a rubber band. Cutler's hands shake. To keep the doctor from seeing this, he turns away and thumbs through the folded forms. He pulls out a blue one with a sea, ship, star motif in white. He gives it to the doctor, and pushes the bundle back into the drawer. The doctor unfolds the form, finds the telephone number, punches it out on the instrument.

When he has given Evening Star the information they ask for, he hangs up. And Cutler says, "Can I put him back on the bed? He wouldn't like strangers to find him lying on the floor."

7

Quinn says, "Great view."

The window he is looking out of is one of three big panels just installed. The strips of brown tape that they wore on the delivery truck still cross them. Putty shows white around the aluminum frames. There is a smell of putty. Until this morning, sheets of plywood covered the holes where the sea had smashed out the windows, and the room was dark. Now it is dazzling with sunlight.

The floor under Quinn's rope sandals is new plywood. The whole room slumped toward the beach when the real estate woman showed Cutler and Pelletier the house six weeks ago. Now the room is propped on new prefabricated concrete and steel posts, and the broken floorbeams and the broken and water-warped floor have been replaced. If they keep their word, the carpet installers will come tomorrow.

The work on the house was noisy and went on and on. Even now the deck in front and the staircase leading down to the beach have still to be replaced. And the beach below the house is strewn with broken lumber, ragged slabs of stucco, torn and sea-stained plasterboard, rusty chicken-wire, scraps of tarpaper, torn cement bags half buried in the sand. But the house is livable again.

It was the only one left along this stretch of beach not so thoroughly smashed by the winds and tides of the spring storms it had to be demolished. None of the owners had nearly enough insurance. Most had the wrong kind. They are not going to rebuild. The film animator who owned this place never wants to see the ocean again, and is taking a deep loss to unload it and buy safety somewhere far inland.

The real estate woman was past forty, with big breasts bulging a tight sweater, long blond hair, and blue eyes that showed a lot of white and seemed never to blink. After every speech she made them about the house, she handed them each another card, like a Las Vegas dealer. Cutler had seen a lot of Las Vegas dealers since Moody's death — Pelletier loved Las Vegas, tossing money away, mocking the costumes of the showgirls, sneering at the tawdry old comics. When they had got the real estate woman to leave, Cutler and Pelletier stood on the road shoulder by the Porsche and gazed down at the broken house, the sea sparkling beyond.

"It's not Cormorant Cove," Cutler said.

Pelletier shrugged. "It's a short walk."

They had priced the two places for sale in Cormorant Cove. One was tagged a million two hundred fifty thousand, the other eight hundred fifty thousand — and that one was smaller than this. Moody had saved a lot of money, but not that kind. Settling into the Porsche that Moody's life insurance had paid for, Cutler smiled to himself. Those storms had brought him luck. Again. As when they had chewed up this road, giving him an alibi for reaching home late after taking the pages to Quinn, so he could stop at the Sea Shanty, where he met Pelletier. And now this house, so cheap that taking it seemed a crime, the kind of house he had coveted, seated on Quinn's deck that afternoon, drinking Quinn's expensive gin. Cutler started the engine. Pelletier dropped into the passenger seat and slammed the door. Cutler released the parking brake and glanced at Pelletier.

"If you don't like it, we'll keep shopping around."

"It's okay," Pelletier said.

And now he has the home he craved, and Quinn is standing in it, drinking Cutler's expensive gin, and admiring the view. More is missing than carpet. The only articles of furniture are stools at the breakfast bar, and the bed he shares with Pelletier. Two bedrooms and a bath are below, and only half painted. He has dreamed that one day, when all is ready here, he will stop by Quinn's in the Porsche and invite Quinn and Veronica for cocktails and dinner. He has never been sure he could work up his nerve to do it — Quinn still frightens him — but Cutler has savored the dream. It would be some kind of triumph.

What kind? His mother's voice is sour inside his head. *He earned that house of his with his talent and intelligence and hard work. How did you get this? By murdering a helpless old man who trusted you. And you're proud of that, are you, little boy?* Cutler can see her mouth, its way of turning down at the corners in loathing and contempt. Had she ever felt anything for him but loathing and contempt? He shakes off her memory. He worked for this — God, how he worked! Moody was dying anyway. Moody meant him to have his money. Cutler wants to run downstairs and get the will, the insurance policies and wave them in her face. That would show her.

"Something the matter?" Quinn says.

66

"What? Oh — no, sorry." Cutler gives an unsteady laugh. "Just thinking about all the work still left to do here."

He was outside and below an hour ago, trying to clear away the mess the builders left. The painting was what he ought to be finishing, but he hated the fumes, and the day was too fine and bright to waste indoors. The best he had been able to do outside was stuff torn cement and plaster wraps into big trash bags, which he stored against the side of the house. He needed a sledge hammer to break up the cracked slabs of old stucco, but he was doing what he could by jumping on it, when a shout stopped him.

The sunglare off the new stucco of the house front had half blinded him when he turned to look. But he didn't need to see the features of the man down on the beach in jockey shorts, kicking into corduroy trousers. The man's barrel body and big head told him it was Quinn. He had just waded out of the surf and water streamed off his hairy hide. He bent to pick up belongings from a handkerchief and stuff them into his pockets. He shook sand off the handkerchief. Drying his hair with it, he came up the sandy slope, drops sparkling off him, trousers darkening from the dampness of the undershorts. He pushed the handkerchief away and frowned.

"Darryl Cutler, isn't it? What are you doing here?"

"This is a dangerous place to swim." Cutler held out a hand. "The bottom drops off. There's an undertow."

"So they tell me." Quinn shook his hand. "I forget. The urge comes on, I'm in the water. No matter where, no matter when, day or night." He wagged his head glumly. "Once you could skinny dip. Too many people now."

"I'm one more," Cutler said. "This place is mine. I was going to invite you over when I get it fixed up."

"That so?" Quinn eyed the house with sharp interest. "What happened to Stewart's place? Did you sell it?"

"Oh, no. But he planned to move to the beach when he retired." Cutler smiled, careful to put a touch of melancholy into it. "We spent every nice weekend and all our vacations at the beach. I love it too." He glanced up at the house. "I did a lot of living for Stewart at the end. It got to be a habit. Maybe I'm living out his dream."

"I walk along here pretty often. I've been wondering if anybody would take a chance on this wreck." Quinn's big brown foot in its rope sandal dug at a splintered two-by-four half buried in the sand. "I hope you got it cheap."

"For beach property, I guess so," Cutler said, "but the repairs cost plenty, and they're still not finished. They have to put the deck back. It will be really nice, then. It will be worth it."

Quinn grunted. "Pray for calm seas," he said.

"This house was the survivor. Come in, will you? Have a look." Cutler glanced sunward, squinting. "It must be just about time for a drink." He had bought Beefeater gin, to be ready for Quinn when and if he ever worked up his nerve to ask him here. He climbed the slope beside the house eagerly, Quinn stepping heavily behind him. Things couldn't have worked out better. Pelletier wouldn't be back as long as there was a chance he'd have to work on the house. Pelletier was like himself when young— work was for others. Cutler showed Quinn in at the kitchen door. The kitchen was great, all newly fitted before the storms struck, and the storms hadn't touched it. It had everything — microwave and convection ovens, rotisserie, grille, six-burner deck, double steel sinks, cutting boards everywhere. And the ceiling was nothing but skylight. "Martini?"

Now, holding what is left of that martini, Quinn says, "Stewart went sooner than you thought. I remember you telling me he had years yet, that emphysema took its time."

"He'd had one collapsed lung episode." Cutler tries to let no alarm sound in his voice. "He couldn't go for long without oxygen."

"I remember that tube he wore." Quinn looks out at the beach, where small birds on spindly legs hurry along at the edge of the surf. "I remember the oxygen tank beside his bed."

"Yes. Well, somehow in the night, in the early morning, the tube came off. He could be a restless sleeper. Then breathing grew difficult for him. He woke in a panic and clutched around in the dark for the tube. Somehow it got wrapped around his wrist. Then he fell out of bed, pulling the tank over. That's how the doctor reconstructed it."

"You didn't check on him at night?" Quinn turns.

Cutler takes Quinn's glass and moves up the large, empty, sunbright room, toward the kitchen. "I haven't slept a night through in months. Yes, he was fine at three o'clock."

"Suffocation? Would that be what killed him, then?"

"You researching for a script?" Cutler rinses the glasses under the swing tap at the sinks. "I don't really know."

"Sorry. That wasn't very sensitive," Quinn says. "It looked heavy, that tank. Why didn't you hear it fall?"

"I ask myself that over and over." Cutler dries the glasses and fills them with ice from a big, sharp-cornered refrigerator. "When you live with an invalid, you're always listening, even asleep."

"Did it fall on him? Did his body muffle the noise?"

Cutler measures Beefeater into the glasses, over the ice, gently. "Possibly." He recaps the gin bottle, uncaps the vermouth, inches vermouth into the glasses, recaps the vermouth. The rim of each glass he rubs with lemon peel. He drops in olives, carries the glasses back down the living room, puts one into Quinn's hand. "How's Veronica?"

"Fine, thanks. If you're going to live here, what's going to happen to the rooms over the shop?"

"I'm renting them out as offices."

Fargo had said, "You're what?" Responsibility hag-rides her. She supports sisters and brothers-in-law galore, with their offspring. The grownups are able-bodied, but she needs them to need her, Cutler supposes. And they sense that need, and act shiftless and unemployable to satisfy her. "I thought, since you're moving to the beach, Ernie and Joy and the kids—they'd just fit up there."

"The rents will total four thousand dollars," Cutler told her. "Can Ernie and Joy pay four thousand dollars? Not from what you've told me about them. Isn't Ernie the one you just paid off twelve traffic citations for? The jailbird?"

"He was in jail overnight," she said indignantly. "Only until the bank opened in the morning."

"Your bank, of course," Cutler said.

"He's had a run of bad luck." She blinked back tears. "A lot of men are out of work today. Jobs are scarce."

"His kids will scribble on the wallpaper," Cutler said.

"You're meaner than Mr. Moody," she said. "After all he left you, I'd think you could be a little more generous. He didn't leave me a thing, and I was with him for twenty years. Working like a slave." Now the tears ran, inky with mascara. She jerked open a desk drawer for tissues, dabbed at the tears, blew her nose, blinked furiously. "But then, I was the enemy, wasn't I? I was a woman." She banged the wadded tissue into a waste basket. "Oh, what I would have given to trade places with you."

"No you wouldn't," Cutler said. "You could walk out at five. I had to feed him, watch TV with him, put him to bed. In the morning I had to bathe and shave him, feed him again. I had to clean the apartment, do the laundry, the shopping, drive him to the doctor. It was romantic as hell, Fargo. Glamorous, right? The life of a kept boy? Acapulco, the Riviera? Just one round of pleasure."

"I'm sorry." She sniffled, got another tissue. "But it hurts to be ignored. I gave him all my loyalty, and —"

"And he gave you a paycheck," Cutler said. "That's life."

"Not for you," she flared. "You're driving a Porsche — when that snotty boy isn't driving it." She pinched her nose angrily with the tissue. "I suppose he's going to live with you in your fancy beach house."

"Watch your mouth, darling." Cutler said. "Jobs are scarce, remember. You're right — I'm meaner than Mr. Moody. So you keep smiling." Grinning hard, he pinched her withered cheek. "There's a good girl."

With his fresh drink, Quinn sits cross-legged on the bare floor, still gazing out at the beach, the sea. "You going to have a chance to write, now? You said nursing Stewart didn't leave you time."

"I've got a screenplay started," Cutler says. "When I finish it, will you look at it?"

"Any time," Quinn says.

"That's very generous," Cutler says, and hears the Porsche roar to a halt back of the house, scattering roadside gravel. Pelletier only recognizes two speeds, breakneck and full stop. The car door slams. Footsteps run.

Quinn asks, "Fargo still there? Will she be looking after the business?"

"She always did." Cutler eyes the kitchen door. "Stewart liked to give me the credit, but that was sentimentality. I'll go in a couple days a week."

The kitchen door bangs. "Let's fuck," Pelletier shouts. "I'm horny as a goat. Look." His hands move to his fly, but then he sees Quinn, loses his smile, and says, "Oh, shit."

"This is Phil Quinn," Cutler says evenly. "The screenwriter. We're neighbors." And to Quinn, "Chick Pelletier, my house mate."

Quinn pushes heavily to his feet.

"Don't get up," Pelletier calls. "Nice to meet you. Darryl's told me a lot about you. All good stuff." He opens a cupboard for a glass. "What are you drinking?"

Quinn avoids Cutler's eyes and trudges toward the kitchen. Without looking at Pelletier, he says, "You have mine," and sets his martini on the breakfast bar. "I have to go. Work to do."

"Don't rush off on my account." Pelletier rolls his eyes at Cutler. "I won't interrupt. I'll go out on the beach."

But Quinn is out the back door, rope soles crunching sand. Pelletier grins. Cutler moans, "Oh, boy," and dives after Quinn. When he rounds the house corner, Quinn is thumping down alongside the house, big frame jolting with each step. Cutler hurries after him. Quinn jogs toward the wet, kelp-tangled margin of the shore. When he reaches it, he veers back in the direction of Cormorant Cove. "What's the matter?" Cutler calls. "Wait a minute." He puts on a burst of speed and catches up to Quinn. He doesn't touch him. He gets a little ahead of him and turns to face him, walking backward. "I don't understand this."

"Oh, don't act stupid." Quinn still won't look at him. He looks out to sea and digs sunglasses from a pants pocket. He wires them over his big ears. "Of course, you understand."

"So I'm gay," Cutler says. "I can't change that."

"That's got nothing to do with it." Quinn doesn't break his stride. He keeps marching. Cutler keeps walking backward, trying to see through Quinn's lenses. Quinn says, "Stewart's money paid for that place. All that smoke about living out his dream of retiring to the beach someday—I'll bet he never figured a dirty little trick like that into it."

"I'm not a monk," Cutler says.

"You're an idiot," Quinn says. "He'll jack you out of every dime, and leave you with nothing but herpes."

"You don't know him," Cutler says.

"I know his type. The beach is alive with them." Quinn halts, drops his disgust, becomes a friend. He grips Cutler's shoulders. "Get rid of him. You owe it to Stewart. Find some nice guy with a job and a bank account, someone your own age."

Cutler opens his mouth to make a scathing remark about Veronica, who could be Quinn's grand-daughter—but he says nothing. Quinn plainly doesn't make the connection himself. He barrels on:

"You know who this kid reminds me of? That teenage blond bitch that married Irv Liebowitz and destroyed him—one of the best men that ever lived. Identical twins."

"He's harmless," Cutler says. "You'll see."

8

Pelletier eats breakfast in silence. Waffles with strawberries and whipped cream. On the deck, at a white enamel metal table, seated in very small white shorts on a chair of shiny metal tubing and white webbing. The plate off which he eats is white, white the porcelain handles of the knives, forks, spoons. He is reading *People* magazine. The putative doings of movie actors, rock singers, soap-opera stars, their couplings and uncouplings, absorb him. Cutler comes out onto the deck with the glass coffee pot and refills Pelletier's white porcelain mug. Pelletier looks up.

"How's your script coming?" He tries to light a cigarette. The lighter is platinum. He wanted a platinum lighter. He got a platinum lighter. "When do I get to read it?"

Cutler hums noncommittally, fills his own mug, sets the pot down, sits himself down. The wind turns the pages of the magazine, hurriedly, as if looking for something. Cutler picks the magazine up. "Paul McCartney?" he says. "How can they arrest Paul McCartney? Do you know how much money he makes? A million dollars a week."

"Dollars don't impress Canadians," Pelletier says. "Theirs aren't worth that much. We should go there. Montreal. They have the best restaurants in the world." The wind lets the lighter flame stand for a second, and Pelletier can light his cigarette. He tucks the lighter into his shorts. Cutler envies the lighter. Pelletier slurps coffee and says, "I leave you alone to write. Like you asked. But I'm getting sick of poker."

"I should think so." Pelletier spends his days in vast poker parlors in Gardena, the airless hush of thick carpets, thick curtains, artificial light, cigarette smoke. Cutler doesn't know how he can stand them. Pelletier has dragged him there a few times. They give him the creeps. Not just the places—the people. Leathery men in purple satin cowboy shirts and polyester suits, women with rumpled faces, whiskey voices, liver-spotted hands. "If you want to throw money away, what's the matter with Santa Anita? At least it's outdoors."

"Horses don't know what they're doing," Pelletier says.

"Neither do poker players," Cutler says.

"I asked about the script." Pelletier wipes whipped cream off his chin, lays the napkin down. "When are you going to finish? I want to be in *People* magazine."

"We'll go to Montreal," Cutler says, "as soon as I can get plane tickets and hotel reservations." He blinks at the blond boy. "You've been there before."

"What kind of name do you think Pelletier is? Polish? I was born there." He gazes bleakly at the clean morning sunlight sparkling on the sea. He smokes, flicking ashes that the wind makes vanish. He drinks coffee moodily. "We can look up my dear *maman*." He gives Cutler a wry, woebegone smile. "Between drinks, between tricks."

"What about your father?" Cutler says.

Pelletier grimaces and stands up. "Who?" he says, and bumps on bare heels down the steps from the deck to enter the bedroom. Cutler rises heavily and gathers up the plates, mugs, utensils. He carries them into the house, where it is dim and cool compared to the weather on the deck. He is rinsing the shiny beaters he used to whip the cream, when he hears Pelletier's steps behind him, and says from his heart, "I wish you'd stay here today."

"Look me over," Pelletier says.

Cutler stops the water running, lets the beaters rattle into the sink, picks up a towel, and turns, drying his hands. Pelletier is not in his poker playing duds, with the Stetson perched on the back of his head. Instead he wears a poplin suit, oxford shirt, knit tie, all new, all blue. They make his eyes seem bluer than ever.

"Recognize me?" Hands on hips, he makes a full turn.

"What do I get if I guess right?" Cutler says.

"Tickets to the premier. I'm going to see my agent. Somebody has to get me into pictures."

Cutler scowls and swears. He sits at the word processor in the downstairs room he has outfitted as a place to write in. It is like Pullen's den in Van Nuys, except that instead of an avocado tree shading a patio scattered with kids' toys, the view here is of sand, surf foaming around rocks, glittering ocean, wheeling gulls, freighters smoky on the far horizon. He has installed bookshelves and filing cabinets of sleek Scandinavian teak, empty except for stacks of film scripts he has lugged home from Moody's. He studies these, trying to learn the form. Maybe he has learned it. He has. But he still can't get words into the computer. His forehead is sweaty from the effort. He is close to panic.

Pelletier means what he says. He always means what he says. *Nobody tells the absolute truth. I do. It makes people furious.* Cutler is furious. Why isn't the money for gambling enough, the beach house, the Porsche, trips to New Orleans, Acapulco, handmade shoes, the best restaurants, the best of everything? *I want to be in* People *magazine.* Jesus. Cutler stands sharply, the leather desk chair wheeling softly away behind him across the carpet. Disgustedly, he switches off the word processor and snorts a laugh at himself. He hated that sneer of Pelletier's whenever the matter of the screenplay came up. *Bullshit.* Cutler determined to put a stop to it. Setting up this office, and sending Pelletier off to play so Cutler wouldn't be disturbed at his writing seem to have done it.

But Pelletier is short on patience. Moody was a romantic, and would have waited forever. Pelletier is a realist. Holding the completed script in his hand will convince him. Nothing less. But Cutler can't produce. He doesn't know why. He thought what he needed was freedom, and he has freedom now. Yet he can't write. Wrong. He doesn't dare. The only scenes that seem to want out through his fingertips on the quiet white keys of the word machine are those that wake him screaming from nightmares. He must not carry those with him by day. They will drive him crazy. He wishes to God he had never pretended—to himself, to Moody, to Quinn, and worst of all to Pelletier, that he could write.

If another pretty boy he had picked up had said to him what Pelletier said to him this morning before he drove off in the Porsche, Cutler would have dismissed the notion with a laugh. Around here, everybody is an actor, everybody has an agent. But he can't laugh Pelletier's words off. Pelletier more than means them. Cutler slides open the glass panel, steps outside, climbs the stairs to the deck. In the long living room, he crouches to sort among the stacks of videotapes Pelletier has brought home — every movie he could think of. It is not movies Cutler wants. Here is what he wants. He ejects the tape that lies in the machine, and fits this one into it, and closes the compartment.

The remote control for the television set and VCR lies on the sailcloth cushion of the white wicker couch. He sits beside it, picks it up, works it. Flickers and skids appear on the screen, then the image clears. A commercial for a softdrink. Teenage youngsters in shorts and tanktops romp in woods beside a stream. Their taut, suntanned skins glow with health. Their teeth and eyes shine. Each is equipped with a can of the sponsor's soda from a tub of sparkling ice. Pranks are afoot. A blond boy is flung backward, laughing, into the stream. After a big splash, he surfaces, grinning, shaking water out of his yellow hair, and holding aloft his softdrink can in triumph. He is Chick Pelletier.

The screen flickers, numbers flash past, electronic confetti, white lettering in a corner, code words, and Quincy appears, face creased with compassion. The camera pulls back. The body of a teenage girl in a cerise swimsuit floats face down in a backyard swimming pool. Men kneel beside the pool to lift the body out. A party of teenagers stands back from the pool, wearing frightened faces. The camera pans the faces. One of them belongs to Chick Pelletier. There is a sharp cut, and the same clutch of youngsters stands in a schoolyard talking excitedly, then breaks up when Quincy appears. Pelletier's hair gleams before he disappears with books through a brickframed doorway.

Cutler knows what comes next. Pelletier in a starchy, stripy uniform, cute little cap, selling hamburgers and fries in a shop of shiny orange formica. With a half dozen other pretty youngsters dressed the same. They all smile ruthlessly. They sing a jingle. Cutler does not hear it. He has left the sound off. They don't sing it, anyway, Pelletier has explained. Professionals sang it in a recording studio before the commercial was shot. The actors only mouthed the words. Tricky. It took them two days to get it right. The screen goes gray and snowy. Cutler thumbs the switch, drops the remote control unit, and reaches for the telephone.

Ralph Pullen has changed, grown thick through the middle and lost a lot of hair. He no longer has the neat beard and mustache. His clothes look expensive and fit him well but his skin is too white, as if he never saw daylight. Behind him, outside Cutler's kitchen door, stand two boys in their teens. Beyond them a silver Volvo is parked at the road's edge. "Since it's the beach," Pullen says, "I thought I'd bring the boys."

Cutler wears an apron. He has been cooking. "It's not that big a chicken," he says, and shakes Pullen's hand.

"They had burgers in the car," Pullen says. "Boys—you remember Darryl? From the old house, in Van Nuys?"

The boys give him rehearsed smiles and limp handshakes. They come indoors with their father and stand around dumbly for a minute while Cutler sheds his apron and mixes martinis, then wander out to the deck, where Cutler has set the table for two for lunch. Cutler gives Pullen a glass and carrying his own glass leads Pullen out there. He tells the boys:

"There's a volley ball setup in the locker down below. Interested?

The boys may or may not be interested, but they go down the stairs obediently. Seated at the table with their father, Cutler hears them rattle in the locker. They look dejected, hauling the equipment down the sandy slope. One of them turns and calls back:

"Can we swim here?"

Cutler cups hands around his mouth and calls, "Too dangerous. It's deep, and there's a bad undertow."

Their heads droop, they kick on down the sand, and begin trying to set up the volley ball net, going about it with exaggerated clumsiness. Cutler turns his back. Pullen knows better than to watch. Cutler lifts his glass and gives Pullen the hint of a smile.

"Thanks for coming." He sips his martini.

"Nice of you to ask me." Pullen sips his martini.

"I stole your typewriter," Cutler says. "I want to give you a check for that before you leave today."

Pullen shakes his head, shuts his eyes, waves an open hand as it to fend something off. "I used you while I needed you and when I didn't need you anymore I threw you out. I got off easy." He laughs morosely to himself. "You earned the typewriter.

And anything else you chose to take. You saved my life, kid. Did you know that?"

Cutler stares. "I thought it was the other way round."

"No. I was ready to kill myself when Caroline left."

"You didn't act it," Cutler says. "You seemed happy."

"Once I found you, I was." Pullen smiles. "The truth." He looks away and is quiet. The boys have got the net up. When Pullen turns his gaze on Cutler again, his eyes are dull. "In case you were thinking of it, don't get married. Never make someone else so important in your life you can't make it on your own. Remember—hell is other people." He tries to lighten up, sits straighter in the chair, gives a short, unconvincing laugh. "Do you know who it was who said that? I can't find anybody who knows who said that."

"She came back," Cutler says. The neighborhood was a quiet one. He heard the sound of her key in the lock, the front door opening. He was sitting in that pleasant study of Pullen's, typing away at another novel. The last one. He never got to finish it. He didn't figure Pullen coming home only an hour after he'd left. Cutler switched off the machine, and got up to go look. She was carrying a suitcase and a garment bag, and she stopped when she saw him. Bewildered.

"Who are you? What are you doing here?"

"Some work for Ralph—for Mr. Pullen, " he said.

"That's Darryl." The boys came up behind her, lugging cartons in their small arms. Bright clothes lay folded in one carton, bright plastic toys poked out of the other. "He's always here."

"Oh, yes?" She studied Cutler for a few seconds, then passed him, making for the bedroom. He hurried after her.

"Let me take those for you," he said.

She marched on. "You were typing when I drove up. Perhaps you'd better get back to that."

"Was he expecting you?" With a sinking heart, Cutler watched her cross the bedroom and roll open the closet door. Her back went rigid. His clothes hung in the section that had been hers. Cutler said, "He didn't tell me you were coming."

"He didn't know. It was a sudden decision." She pushed his clothes aside, the metal of the hangers clashing, and hung up her garment bag. She faced him, witchy—black-haired, spindly, dried out. "Are you living here?"

"Temporarily." He edged past her and began to load his arms with shirts and slacks. "I just used this space because the boys come on weekends and their room—"

"There's a closet in the den," she said coldly.

"It's full of office stuff," he said. "Look, I'm getting everything out. I'm sorry." He was sweating and his hands shook. He dropped a sweater. When he stooped to retrieve it, hangers slipped from his grip. He didn't own many clothes. At that moment, it seemed like a whole men's department. He grabbed up the bundle any which way he could, and fled with it. He dumped the clothes on the leather couch in the study, picked up the phone and dialled Brackett House. While he waited for Pullen to answer, Cutler saw Caroline pass on her way out to the car. He could see the hood of the car from the side window, in leaf-dappled sunshine.

"Your wife is here," he said into the phone.

"You're kidding," Pullen said. "What does she want?"

"She brought her clothes," Cutler said. "She brought the boys, and they brought their clothes. I think she's moving back in."

Pullen let out a whoop of joy. It was loud in Cutler's ear, and he winced, and held the phone away from him. Pullen babbled with excitement. "Put her on. Where is she? Call her. Go get her. I want to talk to her. Oh, boy."

"What do I do?" Cutler said.

"No, don't call her. Don't tell her you told me. I'm on my way there. Right now."

"What about me?" Cutler said, but the phone only hummed.

Above the sigh of the sliding and retreating surf, the cries of gulls, the whoosh of cars up on the highway, there is the slap of the volleyball now, the boys arching it back and forth across the net. Sipping his martini, Pullen watches the boys. As if he had been doing it for a century, and would be doing it ages hence. Like a statue.

"You were happy that day," Cutler says.

Pullen's laugh is without cheer. "Happiness doesn't last. Dissention lasts." He sits up, knocks back the rest of the drink, holds the glass out that now contains nothing but ice and a limp twist of lemon. "Please sir — I want some more."

"If you like." Cutler glances at his watch, takes the glass. "Lunch is ready. I thought we'd have wine with it." He gets up and takes the martini glasses to the kitchen.

Pullen trails after him. "You live alone?"

"It only feels that way." Cutler sets the glasses in the sink. He opens the refrigerator, pulls out a slim pale green bottle of pinot blanc, closes the refrigerator, hands the bottle and a corkscrew with a white porcelain handle to Pullen. "It's different than it was with you and me. I never loved you. Didn't know how. I was too young."

"And now" — Pullen peels leaden wrapping off the neck of the bottle and works carefully at inserting the shiny screw into the cork — "you're older. And it hurts, right?"

"I send him away so I can write," Cutler says.

The bottle between his thighs, tugging with the corkscrew, Pullen regards the long, handsome room. "Nice place. Expensive. Yours, yes? Right. So you've got it made, kid. You said on the phone" — the cork comes out with a gentle pop — "you needed my help." He straightens, flinching a little, as if maybe his back hurts. He sets the dewy bottle on the counter, and carefully twists the cork off the screw. It squeaks. "I'm not an accountant, and I'm sure as hell no marriage counselor." He lays the corkscrew down, and taps the cork lightly into the bottle with the heel of his hand. "What does that leave?"

"Writing." Cutler pulls a loaf of salt bread out of a warming oven, sets it on a cutting board, slices it. "You taught me how once." He tucks a napkin into a basket, nestles the bread slices in the napkin, and folds it over them. "I can't seem to remember." Plates of lettuce, tomato, avocado stand on a counter. He douses them with dressing. "I want you to teach me all over again."

*　　*　　*

It is late. The surf shifts with a sound like heavy silk. Coolness breathes in through the open panels of the dark bedroom. They lie naked. Pelletier sighs and stretches. "Oh, man—you do that so good." He leans up and reaches across Cutler for cigarettes and lighter. In the glow of the lighter flame his look goes from dreamy to serious. "We better forget Montreal." He sets a cigarette in Cutler's lips. "Hoffy's been try- ing to find me. Pissed that I didn't keep in touch. He's going to get me work."

"I knew he would," Cutler says bleakly.

9

The house is a glass-fronted box perched on slim steel legs up a steep slope in the Hollywood hills off Cahuenga pass. Cutler sees the house from below, first, by peering up from the Porsche as it winds along twisting Woodrow Wilson drive, among brush and rock and strands of ragged eucalyptus trees. The glass front of the house catches the morning sunlight, but dustily. The folds of the closed curtains inside the glass hang crooked. The look of the place saddens Cutler.

Pullen has sketched him a rough map, and Cutler finds his way up steep, pot-holed little trails with names like Fern and Goodview to Pullen's mailbox, Pullen's silver Volvo parked beside it. An old red setter sleeps in the shade of the car. He raises his head to watch as Cutler parks the Porsche, but he soon judges that he needn't move, and puts his head down between his paws again, and closes his eyes.

Cutler switches off the engine of the Porsche, and gets out of the car into surprising quiet. The roar of traffic rushing through the pass below is a whisper up here. The rustle of wind in the tall trees is louder. A mockingbird sings. Cutler glances up to spot the bird and sees a squirrel on a branch instead, watching him with bright eyes, tail jerking. A rickety bridge of redwood planks crosses to the door of the house, from which rain and sun have flaked the varnish and bleached the stain in streaks. Before he can rap on the door, it opens.

Pullen stands there in what looks like a brand new bathrobe. Dark brown velour with bands of paler brown. He is barefoot. Cutler thinks the robe is all he is wearing. Except shaving lotion. The smell of it is so strong it suggests Pullen has emptied the bottle over himself. Pullen smiles and sticks out his hand. But his eyes are frightened, and the hand when Cutler takes it is clammy. Pullen starts to say something, his voice cracks, he clears his throat self-consciously and starts over again. Trying for casualness, sounding nervous.

"Well, you found the place. Not easy, right?"

"I was glad I had the map." Cutler looks Pullen up and down and apologizes. "Sorry if I'm too early."

"What?" Pullen acts as if he would blush if he could. He pretends to read his watch. "No. You're right on time." He looks down at himself, runs hands on the new velour. "You mean, I'm not dressed. Well I" — he breaks off, reaches Cutler's hand again, draws him indoors — "I didn't think we had to be formal. It's a day off from the office for me. I didn't think you'd . . . " He peers in the long, shadowy, curtained room at Cutler's face. "Didn't think you'd be embarrassed."

What Cutler is, is surprised and disgusted. But he says, "No way. Hey. It's your house. Be comfortable. That's fine." He walks on past Pullen. The room is cluttered. Magazines and books litter furniture and rugs. The mess is diversified by boxes of electronic games and by record albums, by empty softdrink cans and pizza tins, crumpled socks and T-shirts, gym shoes, a guitar, a tennis racquet. There is a locker-room smell. "You didn't say she'd left you again."

"It happens." Pullen shrugs. "But it's never final." He tries for a rueful, comic face and doesn't manage it. "She can't live with me and can't live without me."

"She doesn't take the boys anymore?"

"They give her an excuse to come flocking back," Pullen says, "without letting me believe I'm the reason."

"And you said you weren't a marriage counselor."

"That's my shrink talking," Pullen says. "Not me." He has been standing gazing at Cutler as if Cutler were a handsome piece of consumer goods in a show window Pullen is afraid to price. Now he gives his head a little shake and forces a smile. "Well." He rubs hands together briskly. "I promised you breakfast, didn't I?" He turns and starts off, saying over his shoulder, "I'm no gourmet chef like you. That was a lunch to remember." He thumps down a shadowy hallway, robe flapping. He is a little bow-legged. "But I can scramble an egg, and I don't always burn the bacon. Woops!" He dodges. "Watch out for the skateboard." He opens a door to a kitchen filled with sunshine. "Come in, sit down."

The table in the eating alcove is white wrought iron with a glass top imperfectly sponged off. A film of greasy dust lies on the stove and counter tops. Dishes are heaped in the sink. Plants hang in pretty pots and look in need of water. Cutler shifts yesterday's *Times* off a white wrought iron chair and sits down. Pullen rattles glasses, ice-cubes, bottles, punctures the top of a tomato juice can, fumbles at slicing a lemon and, sweating from the effort, presents

Cutler with a bloody mary, a dribble of Worcester-shire sauce streaking the outside of the glass.

"Thank you." Cutler tastes the drink. The vodka ratio is so high the fumes make his eyes water. Pullen is trying to get him drunk. Pullen has mistaken Cutler's reason for telephoning him, inviting him to the beach, and agreeing to come here. He stands with his glass now, smiling down at Cutler, plead-ing with his eyes. Cutler says with raised brows and the faintest trace of a smile, "Breakfast?"

Pullen jerks. Tomato juice runs down his chin. "What? Oh, yeah, sure." He turns away, busies him-self with frying pans, sausage, eggs, the crackly wrap-ping of a loaf of bread. "And writing, of course. And writing." He sounds sarcastic.

"That's what I came for," Cutler says. "I've got a wonderful break—somebody who can really make it happen for me in the picture business. But I can't get a script. I have to write a script. And I don't even have an idea."

"Idea?" Pullen snorts. "When did you last see a movie with an idea in it?"

"You know what I mean—a story. It has to have a lead part in it for a kid just out of his teens."

"Can he dance?" Pullen slices up a potato on a cutting board with the same grace he used on the lemon. "Put dancing in it. Put drugs in it. Wife-beating, lesbian friendships, a dear old man dying of cancer. Set it in St. Tropez. A divorced husband kidnaps his own kid." Pullen dumps the chunks of potato into sizzling grease. "And the only place to go is outer space, with beep-beep robots and people covered in long fur."

"I'm serious," Cutler says.

"'Serious' doesn't sell tickets." Pullen drops slices of bread into a scorched toaster. "Who is this kid just out of his teens?" He turns and regards Cutler. Bitterly. "Your lover?"

Cutler says, "You used to have some rules about writing. Something about A, B, C. I can't remember."

Pullen pushes down the lever on the toaster. "A is a character who wants C." The toaster buzzes. "And B is what interferes with his getting it. How he gets over, under, or around B is the story. In pretentious novels he fails. In good novels he succeeds but it doesn't help. In movies he succeeds and everything is okay." The bread pops up untoasted. "Damn." Pullen downs the lever again, the bread pops up again. Cutler rises, takes the slices out of the toaster, picks up the toaster, and turns it upside down over the sink. Burnt crumbs shower out of it. He slaps its bottom. More crumbs. He set the toaster back in its place, drops the bread slices into the slots, and pushes down the lever.

"It will work now," he says.

Pullen catches hold of him and kisses him. Awkwardly. He presses Cutler back against the counter. The shaving lotion smell is overpowering. Under the robe, the man's want is stiffly defined. He mumbles damply against Cutler's ear, voice trembling. "Let's forget the play-acting, okay. You didn't come for breakfast, you didn't come for talk."

"Oh, but I did." Cutler pushes him away, returns to the table, picks up his glass. "Sorry about that." He empties the drink into the sink, holding back the ice cubes. The can of tomato juice stands on the counter. He pours tomato juice into his glass, sets the can down, lifts the glass to a rigid-faced Pullen, and gives him a big smile. "Here's to nutrition," he says, "and to A, B, C." He drinks, stops smiling, sets the glass down with a click, and moves to the door. "And to never trying the same shuck on the same victim twice, okay?" He starts down the dark hallway.

"Oh, wait, listen, stop, don't go." Pullen's bare feet thump after him. "I'm sorry. I didn't mean to—"

Cutler stumbles over the skateboard and falls. It is a bad fall and knocks the wind out of him for a minute. And the sense. He lies on gritty carpet unable to move. He is dimly aware of Pullen on his knees beside him talking. "Oh, God. Hey, are you all right? Darryl? Darryl?" Pullen's hand shakes Cutler's shoulder. "Oh, Christ." Pullen stumbles to his feet. Light goes on in the hallway. "Oh, Jesus. Blood."

"Blood?" Cutler hears himself mumble. Feeling begins to return. He makes a try at getting up off the floor. He doesn't coordinate. He must have banged his head. "What blood?"

Pullen kneels beside him on the floor again. The robe has come open. Cutler was right. The man is naked under the robe. He turns his face away. Pullen lifts one of Cutler's wrists. "You cut your hand. It looks bad. Can you get up? Here. Let me help you."

"I'm all right," Cutler grunts. He pushes to his hands and knees. He sees blood soaking dark into the carpet. He sees a shattered clear plastic box on the carpet, the sharp pieces sparkling in the light. He lifts his left hand, turns it, stares stupidly at it. Two deep cuts across the heel of that hand and blood runs up his arm. He totters to his feet and gives the box a savage kick. "What the hell is that for?"

"Something of the boys'," Pullen says. "Chess pieces? Poker chips? They never pick anything up. Come on." He puts an arm around Cutler, which Cutler angrily shakes off. "Let's go to the bathroom — all right? Have to bandage that hand."

You're so careless, his mother scolds inside his head. *Can't you watch where you're going? You're not a baby, anymore, just learning to walk, you know. You're a big boy. When are you going to grow up? You don't see me falling down all the time, do you?* He is in the gaunt bathroom of some old Portland sidestreet house. He sits on a closed toilet, oakwood, cracked, the toilet tank high above, chain dangling from it, clotted with white paint. He has scraped a knee. She crouches before him, smearing on iodine. *Stop that crying. You're supposed to be a boy, not a blubbering little girl. Of course it stings. It's supposed to sting.*

"Shut up," Cutler says. He is sitting now on a closed toilet seat sleekly white in a bathroom that ought to be sleek but is strewn with damp, crumpled towels and dirty underwear leaking from an overloaded hamper. Pullen crouches in front of him, wrapping gauze around and around the hand that won't stop bleeding. He looks puzzled and hurt. "What? I didn't say anything. Darryl, this isn't working."

"I've ruined your new robe," Cutler says dumbly.

Pullen glances down. "Oh, shit." He stands and strips it off. "Listen, couldn't be helped. Not your fault." He drops the robe in the bathtub. "Look, I'm calling the paramedics." He starts naked out of the bathroom, and Pelletier is standing there. Pullen yelps. "Who are you?"

Pelletier points at Cutler. "Ask him." He looks Pullen up and down. "Fell out of bed, did he?"

Cutler feels dizzy and sick. "I thought you fainted at the sight of blood," he says. There is blood aplenty. It has soaked the gauze wrapping of his hand. It has formed a blotch between his feet on the shag bathroom carpet. "Let the man by. He wants to get me help."

"Only my own blood." Pelletier steps back, so Pullen can pass him. Pullen goes. "I needed the car." Pelletier leans in the doorway, regarding Cutler as if he weren't bleeding to death, or rather as if that fact does not interest him. "I called Moody's, which is where you told me you'd be."

Cutler's head swims. He shuts his eyes. "Car for what?"

"Hoffy called. Audition for a commercial. So I phoned you to bring the car home, and you weren't there, and Fargo didn't know where you were. Nobody knew. You want to open your eyes and look at me?"

Cutler opens his eyes. His vision is blurry. "So how did you get here? Taxi?"

"Limousine," Pelletier says. "I thought you were crazy about me. What's that old man got I haven't got?"

"How did you find me?" Cutler sounds to himself remote, faint, an echo in his own ears.

"His business card was lying on your desk. Home address written on the back. 'Thursday, ten A.M.' Right? I didn't think you'd do it in his office."

"We didn't do it anywhere," Cutler says wearily. "He had the wrong idea, and so have you."

Pullen comes back. He has put on a T-shirt and clean bluejeans that are too tight. He balances on this leg, that leg, to pull on grubby, elastic-sided canvas shoes. "They won't come. They say we have to drive to the emergency room at the nearest hospital."

"It's all right." Cutler draws a deep breath and tries to get up off the toilet seat. He hasn't the strength. He looks at Pelletier. "Chick's here now. He can drive me."

"Sorry about that." Pelletier reads his watch. "Gotta go. Audition's in less than half an hour." He turns away.

"A limousine?" Cutler says. "Are you serious?"

"A Rolls-Royce." Pelletier's voice comes back. "If that doesn't get me the job, nothing will."

"That's insane," Cutler shouts.

"If I had my own car" — Pelletier is far off, now — "it would never have happened." And Pullen's front door slams.

The wind is brisk and cool, the sun warm. Plastic pennons, red, blue, yellow, flutter with bird-wing noises on wires between the tall, silver light posts of a car sales lot. Neat little sports cars glisten in the sunlight. Rows of them. Cutler remembers when his mother took him to pick out the Sunbeam, long ago, in gray, rainy Portland. He wanted one of the shiny toys so much it made an ache in his chest. He smiled so hard his face hurt. He chose a red one.

He wonders what color Pelletier will choose. And then he realizes that Pelletier is not with him. Cutler has wandered in a dream of adolescent motor lust among the glitter of spokes and the gloss of waxed enamel half a block by himself. He looks back. Pelletier stands at the edge of the lot, and appears to be sulking. Cutler raises his bandaged left hand to beckon him. The blond boy doesn't budge. Cutler returns to him, and Pelletier says:

"What did you bring me here for? You going to fob me off with some Japanese junk? You've got a Porsche, Darryl. I want a Porsche." His hair blows like a yellow flower.

"That was Stewart's life insurance money," Cutler says. "All of it."

"Get some more." Pelletier turns, crosses the walk, drops into the Porsche. He slams the door and switches on the tape deck. Loud. The sea wind takes the music and strews it across the car lot. Cutler crosses the walk that has a sifting of sea sand on it. "All right," he says. "You have the Porsche. I'll drive one of these."

Pelletier winces up at him. The music is too loud, and he has not heard. He switches off the tape. "Say what?"

Cutler repeats himself.

Pelletier sticks out a bored hand. "Keys?"

Cutler half-remembers something like this happening to him before. There was a gritty sidewalk that time too. Outside the Alamo Cafe. Shorty. Sauerkraut. But that was ugly. This is beautiful. Pelletier's smile is beautiful as Cutler detaches the car keys from his others, and drops them into the kid's palm. Pelletier gets out of the car, moving as if enchanted. He walks dreamily around the car, touching it. He tosses the keys dreamily in his palm.

"Do I get the pink slip, too?"

"I said it was yours, it's yours," Cutler answers. "We'll go to the DMV tomorrow and transfer the ownership to you. Soon enough?"

Traffic hurtles along Washington boulevard. A plaid-jacketed salesman watches across the acre of sparkling cars. Pelletier doesn't care. He grips Cutler's shoulders and kisses him hard on the mouth. "You are something else." He grins, and tosses the keys in his hand again. His eyes shine. "Really."

"Come on." Cutler takes his arm. "I want a red one."

10

The spring before his father died, the man turned up in Portland. In a new gold Continental convertible. With a young blond woman in dark glasses. It was a cold, gray Saturday, the hills around the city veiled in rain. The living room of the old frame duplex Cutler and his mother rented that year had a bay window. Outside it grew a big lilac bush where bees toiled in the blossoms when the sun shone. Not today.

His mother was at work. Cutler lay on the faded green plush padding of the windowseat and dully turned the pages of old comic books. He had smoked three stolen cigarettes and they had left him feeling a little sick. Whiskey was supposed to settle your stomach, and he had swallowed some, but it gave him a headache instead.

The hero in one comic book was muscular and wore only a fancy helmet and boots, a cape pinned somehow at the shoulders, and a swatch of cloth across his loins. There was a bulge there that fascinated Cutler. He stared at the drawing, and felt his mouth go dry and his heart begin to beat faster. He knew what to do to relieve the feeling. But he didn't want to.

Damn the rain. He threw the comic book across the room. All week long in dreary, droning classrooms, he had dreamed about the coming weekend, when he could go back to the park again. Last week he had met a man there. Harvey. Cutler didn't know how old he was. His pale hair was thinning. Maybe he was thirty. Not muscular like the comic book hero. Too skinny. Quiet, with a frightened smile. Afraid to say what was on his mind. But Cutler understood. What happened to him in that man's scruffy car was wonderful. He was dying, dying for it to happen again. But the man wouldn't be there in the rain. There would only be the bare and dripping trees, the statues, the long wastes of soggy green lawn. Nobody.

Still, he couldn't rest here, thinking about it. He got off the windowseat and started for the back to get his raincoat. And heard a car door slam out front. Two doors. He returned to the rain-streaked window and looked out and saw the flashy car and saw a man and a woman climb the cracked cement steps from the street and come hurrying up the footpath. They kept their heads down because of the rain. He couldn't see their faces. Then their steps were hollow on the porch, and the doorbell buzzed back in the kitchen.

He was fourteen. That meant it was nine years since he had seen his father. But when he opened the door, which had a small panel of stained glass roses at its top, he knew the man. Looking into his face was like looking into a mirror—but in the far future. Cutler's face at that age was still pretty. His father's face was handsome. Ruggedly so. With deep creases down from the cheekbones. He showed dazzling teeth in an easy smile. His laugh was deep and easy.

"How about that?" he said to the young woman.

"He's yours all right," she said.

"Do you know me, kid?" Ransom Cutler said.

"You were supposed to send money," Cutler said. It was out of his mouth before he could stop it. Maybe the wonder was that he didn't say, *Yes, you're the son of a bitch.* Those were the only swear words he had ever heard his mother utter. "It was a bargain. You agreed to it."

"To send money," his father said, "you have to have money. May we come in? Is your mother here? This is Tammy Fancher."

The young woman smiled and held out her hand. She was so pretty she was unreal. Raindrops sparkled on her dark glasses. Cutler shook her hand. It was cold and damp and small. Cutler let it go and turned away. "My mother's at work. She works forty-eight hours a week. On her feet. In a department store. Because you never send any money."

"I've brought money," Ransom Cutler said. The front door closed. His footsteps and the footsteps of the young woman sounded in the hall. "Ten thousand bucks. How does that sound?"

Cutler stood on the worn carpet among the worn furniture of the rented living room and gazed at the man. He was poor at arithmetic, but it didn't sound like much for nine years. He shook his head. "I don't know. You'd have to ask her."

The young woman shivered and hugged herself. "It's cold in here." She sat on the couch and poked in her purse for a pack of cigarettes. When she lit a cigarette, the match flame shook in her hand. "No wonder you came to L.A."

"Some coffee would warm us up," Ransom Cutler said.

"She won't be home till five thirty," Cutler said.

"If you want to see her, you can go to the store. Women's wear." He swung away so they wouldn't see that he didn't own one, and pretended to look at his wristwatch. "I have to go now. To school."

"It's Saturday," Ransom Cutler said.

"Rehearsal for the class play," Cutler lied.

"Tammy's in the movies." Ransom Cutler smiled down at her. "If you come to L.A., she can get you inside the studio. You can watch how the professionals do it."

Cutler stared. "How could I get to L.A.?"

"We're on our way to Canada," his father said.

"I'm shooting some location stuff there," the young woman said. "Just a week."

"We'll pick you up on our way back," Ransom Cutler said. "Take you down with us. You can go out in the sunshine every day. Disneyland. The beach. The race track."

"Is that where you got the ten thousand?" Cutler said.

"Eighty-five thousand," Ransom Cutler said. "All in one day. It's quite a place, the race track." He took an envelope from his inside jacket pocket and laid it on the nicked coffee table. "It's a cashier's check. It won't bounce."

Cutler gazed at the envelope. "She'll think it should be more," he said.

The blond young woman stood up. She said to Cutler's father, "You talk too much. Come on, let's get out of here." She twined an arm around his and tugged. "What did you have to mention the eighty-five thousand for?"

"If I hadn't mentioned it to you," Ransom Cutler said, "you wouldn't be with me now, would you?"

He let her pull him toward the hall, the front door, but goodnaturedly. He grinned over his shoulder at Cutler. "We'll stop for you on the twenty-third. You have your bags packed." Tammy Fancher dragged him out of sight. The door opened. With a small shudder. It was swollen with dampness. Ransom Cutler called, "It's time you and I got to know each other."

Cutler went into the hall. "She won't let me," he said.

The two of them were on the porch now. His father detached himself from the young woman's grip. "Wait a minute," he said. He looked seriously at Cutler. "How old are you?"

"Just fourteen. She's got custody. She won't let me."

He waved a dismissive hand. "I'll charm her into it. You'll see." He grinned, and turned back to the young woman's clinging grip on his arm, and they went down the porch steps together, and hunching in the rain, scuttled down the walk. From the street, his father called back, "You be ready." And the car doors slammed.

The grandstands at Santa Anita are a vast cavern, cold, gray, gloomy. Too much metal—girders, seats, partitions boxing in the seats. Too much bare cement. The mouth of the cavern yawns northward, so no sun ever shines inside, and the air is clammy. The grandstands face a smooth dirt track, a vast oval of grass, green foothills sloping up to tawny, hulking mountains. Sunlight shines on white railings and on the gaudy silks of the jockeys. Sunlight glazes the sleek coats of the horses. Sunlight sparks off the long golden trumpet blown by a man in a red jacket to announce each race. But back up here, trash lies underfoot, crumpled tip sheets, waxpaper beer cups, gray cardboard boxes, hamburger wrappers, cigarette butts—and the sun never shines. Cutler shivers and stands up. "This is a waste of time," he says.

Pelletier hunches forward on his chair, elbows on knees, studying a racing form. Betting slips lie around his shoes. How much he has bet so far Cutler is afraid to ask, but all his picks have run out of the money. Folding the racing form, Pelletier rises. "Only two more races till Chick's Luck." He gives Cutler a grin. "How can I lose on Chick's Luck?"

Cutler steps out of the box. "You seem to have it down to a system." He looks for a way out, spots a high rectangle of sunshine. "Can't even see the horses from here."

"Go to the paddock," Pelletier tells him. "You can practically reach out and touch them there." He follows Cutler into the vast, sunlit room where the betting windows are open. Lines have formed—men, women, children anxious to throw good money after bad. Where do they find the clothes they wear— the awful plaid Bermuda shorts and Hawaiian shirts of the men, the bulging bluejeans and ruffled square-dance blouses of the women, the baseball caps, the Mexican straw hats?

Cutler shakes his head. But he finds himself searching the lines of bettors with his eyes. Looking for his father. Who never came back for him. And who died nine months after that stop in Portland. Tammy died with him. In the Continental Mark IV convertible. In a snowstorm, at night, in the San Bernardino mountains. They froze to death in their ski suits. Yet Cutler looks for him now. He has never seen a race track until today, but when he pictures his father, it is always here, winning all that money. Pelletier nudges Cutler's arm.

"Chili dog? Best in the west." He holds the garbagey looking thing out in a fluted eclaire paper and a wad of napkins. "You get down to the paddock that way." When Cutler accepts the chili dog, Pelletier points. "I'll place my bet"—cradling the chili dog in his hand at his mouth and gobbling it messily, he strays away—"and join you there." Cutler looks after him with an ache in his heart. He doesn't understand how the boy can grow more beautiful every day. All the same, he drops his chili dog untasted into a trash recepticle before he finds his way out and down.

The horses are not tiny and fragile as they look from the stands. They are tall, and steely muscles ripple under their handsome hides. Some of them, the race hasn't tired. They rear and toss their heads. They parade past between rail fences on their way to a long, shadowy shed, half below ground, where exercise boys walk them round and round to cool them out. The jockeys come trailing after, their dandy silks a bit rumpled. Kids follow them with autograph books, programs, pens. The jockeys sign without breaking stride. They are as tiny and fragile as they look from the stands.

When they have vanished, Cutler wanders the paths behind the grandstand, between lawns and flowerbeds, passing in and out of the shadows of gnarled olive trees whose leaves the wind turns silver. He is gazing at a green bronze statue of a jockey holding his saddle, when he senses Pelletier beside him.

"They look like dolls," Cutler says.

"They all marry huge blonds with tremendous boobs."

"That lets me out. Which loser did you bet this time?"

"I'm not going to tell you till he wins. Look, they're coming into the paddock for the next race." Pelletier starts off, his laughter drifting back to Cutler. "This I love — watching the jockeys trying to mount. They look like five-year-old girls at riding school."

In some cases, it is true. The horses are fractious. They wheel and rear, and the exercise boys and girls trying to hold them are not strong enough, don't weigh enough, to keep them in control. Men in suits or sports jackets help the jockeys mount, but sometimes the results are comical. The jockeys show no expression. And no one laughs at them. Except Pelletier. A jockey whose little boot has lost its stirrup and who has to scramble into the saddle, once he is there gives Pelletier a dirty look. He reins the horse around and aims it at Pelletier like a weapon. Pelletier's grin fades and he backs away from the fence, bumping into people behind him. The jockey jeers at him, yanks the horse around, and it dances away. Pelletier opens his mouth to jeer in return, but Cutler puts a hand over it and drags him away.

"That's my horse too," Pelletier says, "the six horse."

"Wonderful," Cutler says. "A twenty to one shot."

"You don't make money betting favorites," Pelletier says.

"You don't make money, period," Cutler says.

"Wait'll Chick's Luck," Pelletier says, and heads for the stands again. Cutler does not follow. Loudspeakers bellow across the sunlit lawns and flowerbeds. He will sit on a bench under an olive tree and listen. The six horse finishes a distant fourth. Pelletier doesn't come down afterward. He waits for the next race to finish. Then he comes. "I want you with me for this one," he says, and holds out his hand.

It is the last race of the day. The sun is in the west and losing warmth and the stands are colder and more cavernous now. The crowd has thinned. Wallets have been emptied. What reason is there to stay when you can't bet? It crosses Cutler's mind that he ought to set a limit on how much money Pelletier can lose in a day. But the thought passes almost as quickly as it came. How could he say it? What words would he use? Pelletier is sudden. He might just pack and leave. In the cold steel chair, Cutler sits and watches the horses wearing their big numbers amble around the track to the white toy-like starting gate away far off. Cutler reaches across and pulls the *Racing Form* out of Pelletier's hip pocket.

"You can't read now," Pelletier says. "They're going into the gate. The race'll start in a second."

Cutler grunts and finds the ninth race. Chick's Luck is a speed horse who has never run a race this long. He has finished in the money in nine out of eleven starts, but first only three times. The track announcer's voice echoes from metal horns overhead. "And they're off." Cutler folds the *Racing Form* and strains his eyes to see the toy horses toiling along the track on the other side of the vast oval.

"He's in front," Pelletier says, and stands up.

"And at the far turn," the public address system says, "it's Chick's Luck by a length, Sir Calico running second on the inside, and Longstem, followed by . . . " Cutler stands up so he can see. "And now, entering the final stretch . . . "

"He's pulling away," Pelletier punches the air.

". . . And here comes Main Chance on the outside. It's Main Chance and Sir Calico battling head to head for second place. Chick's Luck takes the rail, leading by a neck."

Chick's Luck is a little gray horse. The jockey in polka-dots whips him. Sir Calico and Main Chance are rangy bays. Main Chance's jockey almost lies along the horse's neck. His whip moves frantically. He pulls ahead of Sir Calico. Chick's Luck scrambles. The big bays stretch.

"And coming to the finish line, it's Main Chance by a head, Sir Calico second, and Chick's Luck . . . "

The roar of the crowd dies. Scuffling trash, they fill the stairstep aisles, and head for the exits.

"Chick's Luck, all right," Cutler tells Pelletier's back.

"But outdoors in the sunshine and fresh air, remember." Pelletier grins and claps Cutler's shoulder. "Hell, it's only money." He steps up out of the box. "Wait till tomorrow."

Cutler follows him. "How much did you drop today?"

Pelletier shrugs. "What — thirteen, fourteen hundred?"

Cutler can't speak. Not till they are in the car, inching along in traffic from the parking lots. His hands are damp on the steering wheel. He feels cold inside. He clears his throat and still sounds hoarse.

"We can't afford it," he says.

"Let's eat at Ma Maison tonight," Pelletier says.

Cutler strolls smiling into Moody's, and Fargo pounces on him like a bird of prey. Her ragbag blouse flaps and flutters like moulting feathers. Her fingers on his arm are like talons. She drags him through the bright room where the shiny presses whirr and the typesetting computer clicks, and where white paper gleams like snow. She pushes him ahead of her into the office marked PRIVATE and closes the door.

"You are destroying this business," she says.

"Hey." Cutler cajoles her. "Easy. I just walked in."

"Letting him write checks!" Behind the desk, she tosses cancelled checks into the air. "Have you added them up? Jewelry, camera, eight hundred dollar surfboard?" The checks drift and whisper to the desk. "Clothing. Not J.C. Penney—oh, no. Brooks Brothers, Silverwoods." Her claws scrabble among the checks. She snatches one, two, three, and holds them up. "Cash," she says, "cash, cash." She reads the checks. "One thousand dollars. Seven hundred eighty. Two thousand dollars."

"Just imagine if he had credit cards," Cutler says.

"It's out of the business account," she says. "How can you do that? I couldn't even meet the payroll last Friday. I had to pay Lester out of petty cash." Her glance lights on another check, and she picks it up. "Limousine rental?"

"He had to get to an audition," Cutler says.

"And that explains the new car?" she says.

"That explains it," Cutler says. "Back off, love."

"You pay yourself very well," she says. "What happens to all that money?"

"It isn't enough," Cutler says bleakly.

"It has to be enough," she cries. "I've got bills to pay." She grabs up a clutch of pastel-colored flimsies and waves them at him. "I juggle them the best I can, pay this one month, that the next. But it can't go on, Darryl." Tears form. She wipes at them, and her mascara smudges. "We're getting a bad credit rating. They warned me at the bank." She drops heavily into the desk chair, stares at the papers, dolefully shakes her head. "What would Mr. Moody say?"

"Why don't you snorkle out and ask him?" Cutler says.

She looks slapped, turns pale under her makeup for a second, then angry red. "He gambles, doesn't he — Laughing Boy? That explains all those checks cashed at Las Vegas hotels."

"Casinos." Cutler turns for the door. "Always a pleasure talking to you, Fargo."

"I know it's not." She looks mousy and hurt and helpless. "But please, Darryl."

He smiles placatingly. "He's getting work now. Commercials. TV. He'll have some money of his own."

"Thank God," Fargo says.

"Depends on your point of view," Cutler says.

11

Knuckles rap the metal edge of the open glass panel. Cutler blinks. Beside him, under a sheet and electric blanket Pelletier stirs, murmurs, but does not waken. Cutler pushes himself up on his elbows and squints. It is not yet daylight. The figure on the deck outside is vague. Cutler's mouth is too dry to talk with yet. Moistening it with his tongue, he glances at the bedside clock. The red numerals read four-fifty. He sits up, swings feet to floor, and mutters hoarsely:

"Who the hell are you, and what do you want?"

"Chick Pelletier?" The voice sounds young and lively. "Jesus. I'm sorry. Did I get the wrong house?"

Cutler reaches behind him without turning and gives Pelletier a gentle shove. "Somebody for you," he says. He paws a cigarette pack from the night stand and with numb fingers draws a cigarette from it and clumsily hangs it from his mouth. He uses Pelletier's platinum lighter to get the cigarette going, then holds the lighter flame high and peers at the open glass panel again. No use. He lets the flame click off. "Hell of a time for an appointment," he says.

"Tell him to go away," Pelletier mumbles, face in pillow.

"Chick Pelletier says to go away," Cutler tells the vague form on the deck. "And so do I."

The visitor steps into the room. "He wanted a surfing lesson." Cutler can make out the speaker's form, now. It is lean, muscular. The hair appears to be blond. He is wearing a thin, floppy jacket over a wet suit. "It's a business arrangement." He steps to the bed and yanks the covers off Pelletier's nakedness. "Hey, Ripper," the surfer says, "haul ass, baby. Time to shred some big ones."

"Fuck off," Pelletier grumbles into the pillow.

The surfer siezes Pelletier's ankles and drags him from the bed onto the floor. "Let's go, man. Surf's up." Cutler sees the shine of the stranger's teeth in the darkness. The stranger explains, "This is how he said I'd have to do it."

Face down on the carpet, Pelletier kicks feebly. "I changed my mind." He pushes groggily to hands and knees and lays face, arms, torso across the bed. The surfer grabs him around the chest from behind and hauls him to his feet. He says to Cutler, "You want to find something to cover his ass?"

Pelletier has bought an expensive wet suit. Cutler blows out air, wipes a hand down over his face, rises, gropes the thing out of the closet, holds it out to the stranger. Pelletier is hanging in the young man's arms almost as limp as the suit. His head droops, his breathing sounds as if he is asleep. "Sit him in that chair," Cutler says. "I'll put it on him." Kneeling, working Pelletier's feet and legs into the legs of the wet suit, Cutler is reminded of his life with Moody. He jerks the rubbery tough material. "Cooperate," he pleads. "Come on, Chick. End of joke."

Pelletier stands up, bumping Cutler backward so he sits on the carpet. Pelletier pulls the wet suit up his legs. His sturdy little cock stands straight out. This disconcerts Cutler and probably embarrasses the surfer, but it doesn't bother Pelletier. "I have to pee," he says, and walks out of the bedroom.

Cutler gets off the floor and goes to retrieve his cigarette from the ashtray. "Are they often like this?" he asks.

"Pretty much," the surfer says. "Teenage lazy. But if you want to surf, early is when you get out of the sack."

"How long will it go on?" Cutler sits down wearily.

"You know him," the surfer says, "I don't."

"Forever," Cutler says, "but only if I complain."

"I won't be here forever," the surfer says. "With what he's paying me, I can live in Hawaii half a year and Australia the other half. And I can't wait." He gestures at the gray deck, gray sand, gray ocean. "California breaks are okay for grommets. For me that was a long time ago."

Cutler stubs out the cigarette. Down the hall, the toilet flushes. Cutler would like to go back to sleep now. But he asks the surfer, "Do you win contests? Trophies?"

"Don't ask to see them. I cash the checks and travel light. Airlines would only lose them, anyway."

"You travel a lot?" Cutler asks.

"Name anyplace—I've been there," the surfer says. He goes to stand gazing out at the ocean. "He's gay, right? I don't think he'll keep it up. He'll hurt his little self."

"If you think he's afraid of anything," Cutler says, "you should drive with him sometime."

"The Porsche, right? A hundred and how fast?"

"I try never to look," Cutler says.

Pelletier bangs in the hallway. A shape looms through the bedroom door, the shark snout of the surfboard. It gleams darkly in the dawn's pale light. It brushes a lampshade, and the lamp rattles and totters.

"No seatbelts on that," the surfer says.

Cutler tells Pelletier, "He thinks you're a sissy."

Pelletier pushes the surfboard at the stranger. "Carry this," he says. The surfer steps aside and the board crashes to the floor. "I've got my own to carry." He goes out onto the deck. "Right out here." His shape shortens as he goes down the steps to the sand. His voice grows faint. "You want to be careful with that stick. Looks like it cost a bundle. You don't want to go slamming it down on floors."

Pelletier stoops for the board and grunts, picking it up. It is taller than he is.

Cutler asks him, "Are you a sissy?"

"I'll show you when I get home," Pelletier says, and carries the board outside.

Cutler smiles, stretches out, goes back to sleep.

He stands up to his chest in water and cries. He can hear his own six-year-old voice, shrill with terror. Where is this? His mother is beside him. Her bathing suit is of a harsh blue fabric. A blue rubber bathing cap with a wave pattern molded into it covers her hair. She holds in her hand a plastic lifesaver, green and blue striped. She has just pulled it off him, up over his head, and his arms and one ear sting where the wet plastic scraped them. Where is this? Is it river, lake, sea? She is angry at him. Her face — looking strangely naked without makeup, strangely young, as if she were another woman — is red with anger.

"Oh, stop that shrieking," she says. "There's nothing the matter with you. Look how everyone's staring. They'll think your mother is doing something awful to you." Her hand bites his shoulder. She shakes him so his teeth rattle. Mucus and salt tears run into his mouth. He reaches for the lifesaver, float, he doesn't know what to call it. But it is his safety. He doesn't mind the water if he can have it around his chest, buoying him up. But he is terrified without it. She holds it high, out of his reach. He looks up at it hopelessly and the sun strikes his eyes. She says, "You can't have it. If you have it, you'll never learn to swim."

"I can swim," he shouts at her. "I just don't want to."

"Don't lie to me." She raps the side of his head with knuckly fingers. "Come on, now. Look at all these other children. They're staring at you. They think you're a sissy. Look at that little girl. She's not as old as you are, and she's swimming — swimming, Darryl."

He looks around him through the blur of his miserable tears. Everywhere children are swimming. It seems to him hundreds of them, thousands, the whole world of children is swimming. They are all smiling as they swim. They are laughing. They are happy. He shuts his eyes and howls. And suddenly he is picked up by his waist. He is laid flat on his face in the water. Surprise makes him try to suck in air. Water rushes into his nose and mouth. He gags and coughs and splutters and struggles in the hands that hold him to get his face out of the suffocating water. He waves his arms. He kicks.

114

"That's the way," a man's voice says, "keep it up. Paddle, kick your legs."

He gets his face out of the water and screams.

"You're all right," the man's voice says. "Turn your head to the side." A big hand has hold of his skull, twisting it. "Keep paddling. You're all right. I'm holding you. Paddle. Kick your legs. Like a frog. That's it. Now, see? Nothing to it. You're swimming." The man lets him go.

He sinks. It is silent under the water. And slow. His small, skinny body in the tiny green and blue swimtrunks, turns over slowly, lazily, once, twice. He lies on sand and gravel. He looks up. The surface of the water with the sun striking it looks like thin pale brown leather. For a second that seems a long time, he is not frightened, simply dazed. He sees a man's hairy legs beside him. He sees his mother's pale legs. Then hands grip him and raise him up out of the water into the sunshine and the air and he sucks the air in frantically and chokes and sobs and struggles. He kicks the man in his struggles. The man holds him out, away from his body, and laughs with hard white teeth. He is a short, dark, muscular young man.

"Hey, take it easy, little buddy. You're all right."

"He'll never learn, he'll never learn," Cutler's mother is saying. "He does it on purpose. To shame me."

"He's just scared of the water," the man says. "Some kids are. Give him a break." Cutler has stopped crying to listen. He blinks watery eyes at the two adults. The man stands him in the water again. "You're not going to get him to swim by losing your temper with him."

"When I want your advice on child rearing"—Lorraine Cutler snatches Cutler by the arm—"I'll ask for it, thank you." To Cutler's relief, she marches for the shore, dragging him with her. She snarls over her shoulder, "You're nothing but a child yourself."

"And thanks for your help," the young man calls.

On the sand, Cutler's mother makes a punishment out of drying him off, rubbing hard, so that the towel becomes a rasp. "See the trouble you've caused? Humiliating your mother in public? Everywhere we go." Kneeling, she folds the towel with furious, jerky motions. She blinks to keep back angry tears. She snatches up the blanket, sending sand flying. "Why, I'd like to know?" She pushes a yellow plastic bucket toward him. "Carry that." It has a toy dumptruck in it, and a brown paper sack of sandwiches and cookies. He picks it up, sniffling. She drops the lifesaver over his head, around his neck, pulls rubber shoes onto her feet and, standing, wraps a flowered skirt around her and snaps the waistband.

Folded blanket and towel clasped to her front, she strides toward the paved space where windshields glare in the sunshine. Cutler trudges wanly after her. Without turning to look at him, she says, "We are going home. At least there the whole world can't see the way you treat your mother." Cutler stops and turns to peer back at the crowded water, hoping for another look at the young man. But the sun is too bright—he can't make him out. "Darryl," his mother calls sharply, and he trots to her. She holds the car door open and, as he climbs inside, raps his skull again with her knuckles.

116

"Damn," he says, and wakes up. Thrashing around in a dream, he has knocked his head on the bedside table. He sits on the bed edge. Sun glitters on the ocean. He shudders, and stumbles down the room to pull the curtains closed.

Cars are parked two and three rows wide along the road shoulder above the house. When he switches off the Celica's motor, rock music bellows up at him, so loud he wonders how the roof remains in place. He gets out of the car, slams the door, and walks back to the white painted wooden staircase that jogs left, right, left, down to the kitchen door. The music makes him wince. Through the racket, laughter penetrates, and shouts, not of anger but of high spirits. He hears the rhythmic pounding of feet. Dancing. The kitchen doors stands open. He steps inside. The roar is a physical force, like a blow in the chest.

Down the long, white room, against the sea glare of the three big glass panels, one of them open to the deck, bodies twist to the music, arms wave, long hair flies. The bodies are trim and near naked. The boys and young men wear floppy, flower-print shorts — "Surfers don't like bun-huggers," Pelletier has explained, "they think only girls have pretty buns" — the young women wear bikinis, about as much fabric to them as paper to postage stamps. Soft drink cans, beer cans, green, red, gold, glint in the light. The breeze off the sea does not let smoke accumulate, but Cutler smells burning marijuana.

Looking for Pelletier, Cutler starts to work his way down the room. Not everyone is dancing. The wicker and sailcloth couches and chairs are occupied. When a recording track ends, before another can take up, while the loudspeakers pour out silence, he hears talk. "Rincon, shit. It's like anyplace else on this dumb coast. Breakers maybe one day in five. Rest of the time, it's a pond. Australia, man. South Africa. Hawaii, the Backdoor. Don't talk to me about California." It is Saluto, the surfer who is coaching Pelletier. He lifts a lazy hand and his sunbleached eyebrows to Cutler in a laid-back greeting. Cutler gives him a nod.

The music crashes to life, and the dancers take up shivering and stamping again. Cutler pushes through the bodies that give off warmth like the sun they have soaked up all their young lives. A golden girl stops in the middle of dancing, opens her eyes wide, flashes glorious teeth at him. "Hey, beautiful—take off your clothes and stay awhile." Cutler twitches her a smile and moves on. Behind him, he hears her shout above the din, "What a hunk. Where did he come from?" And someone shouts the answer, "I think he owns this place."

Cutler steps out onto the deck, where the sun-burned young talk, gawk, neck. He pushes down to the lower deck. Surfboards lie underfoot, all colors and sizes, pointed, blunted, glassy with resin and wax, some with sharp fins. Surfboards tilt against the house wall. Others, footed in the sand, angle against the deck. Youngsters have gathered out here too, resting elbows on the rail, sitting on the rail, talking, laughing. A stocky redhead leans on crutches, one leg in a plaster cast. A boy who looks Polynesian turns his head to glance at Cutler, and Cutler flinches. Terrible things have happened to the boy's face. The boy looks away, says, "No, man. It's not worth it. Get rid of it. Look what a pointed stick did to me." Cutler, in his haste to get out of earshot, starts down the steps to the sand, and almost falls over a dark, short-haired girl seated there with a drawing pad on her knees. She has covered a page with sketches of surfers, nice professional work.

"Excuse me," Cutler says, and she shifts aside.

He has seen Pelletier—with a handful of volleyballers, knocking an orange sphere over a green net, sand spurting up under their bare feet. Out beyond them, half a dozen surfers ride the low waves with easy, almost absent-minded grace. The water keeps shifting colors, from green, to blue, to purple, and all shades between. Yards out in the surf, a young man has climbed the jagged rocks where cormorants, gulls, pelicans like to gather. Perched on the highest point, he shouts good-natured derision at the surfers as they curve past.

Cutler starts toward Pelletier, and frowns because he thinks he knows the slim, blond young woman jumping and lunging for the ball beside him. It is Veronica Quinn. It can't be, but it is. And here is brown, thick-bodied Phil Quinn, seated on the sand, arms clasping knees, among youngsters watching the game, cheering and jeering. Not all. Two directly behind Quinn lie face to face on a towel, and appear to be trying to melt into one another. Sweat shines on their copper skin. Cutler steps over them and sits down beside Quinn, who glances at him and raises thick brows.

"You're late," he says.

"I didn't know you were coming," Cutler says.

"Neither did I. We set out for a solitary walk along the beach, and ran into this." A beer bottle stands in sand between Quinn's feet, in their heavy sandals. Cutler pulls it up, examines the label, sets the bottle back.

"There's champagne," he says. "For you."

Quinn shakes his head. "Thanks. I want to go home."

Cutler moves to rise. "I'll get her for you."

"Don't try. When she's ready, she'll start for home. If I notice, I'll follow her." He drinks from the beer bottle, sets it down, wipes his mouth, nods toward Pelletier, who has gone sprawling, face down in the sand, to bat the ball upwards so a tall boy can whack it over the net. Quinn says, "A real beach bum. What did I tell you?"

"He's an actor," Cutler says. "I've got tapes to prove it. And Thursday, he films a new commercial." He has been watching Pelletier, and Pelletier suddenly senses this, looks for him, grins and waves. He says something to Veronica, and comes jogging over to Cutler. His muscles glisten with sweat, and he pants. He hikes up the waist of his loose, almost knee-length shorts, and pushes hair out of his eyes. He holds out a hand to Cutler, and pulls him to his feet.

"Come on up to the house. I want to show you something."

"You didn't say you were having a party," Cutler says.

"It's a farewell party for Saluto," Pelletier says, and starts up the slope of beach, tugging Cutler after him. "Come on, Mr. Quinn. You want to see this. It's great."

Quinn grunts and gets to his feet. "Veronica," he

shouts. He makes a big, beckoning motion. She stops and stares, and the volleyball comes over the net and hits her in the chest, and she sits down hard in the sand with a cry. She is not hurt. She means the cry for Quinn. It is a cry of indignation at having been distracted. Muscular boys lift her to her feet, and she calls to Quinn, "Go without me. I'm busy, Phil. We're winning, here." There is a ragged cheer.

Quinn joins Cutler and Pelletier, trudges with them up the sand, grumbling, " 'Golden girls and boys all must —' "

" 'Like chimney sweepers'," Cutler says.

" 'Come to dust'," Quinn says.

Pelletier cocks a puzzled eyebrow at them. "What?" Then he sees the dark girl with her sketch pad on the steps. "Hey, Melissa, when did you get here?"

She looks up at him for a second with dark, reproachful eyes, then watches her moving pencil again. "You thought I wouldn't find out about it, didn't you, you and Saluto?"

"You're crazy," Pelletier says, and climbs the stairs. He works his way through the gathered surfers on the deck, and past those gathered in the doorway. The music and dancing have ceased. A knot of youngsters has formed around the television set. An electronic game is in progress. There are whoops and squeals and groans. Pelletier leads Cutler and Quinn up the long room, and stops at the breakfast bar. Saluto sits alone on a stool at the bar, moodily drinking beer from a brown bottle, and staring at a statuette that stands on the bar. The material looks like bronze. The figure is a surfer in a half crouch on his board. When Saluto becomes aware of Pelletier and friends, he works up a wan smile. "It's supposed to be me," he says. "What do you think?"

It could be Pelletier, but Cutler says, "It's you."

"He's leaving it with me," Pelletier says, glowing.

Quinn runs a hand on the figure. "Nice work. Whose?"

"Melissa," Pelletier says. "The girl on the steps." He glances worriedly past Cutler and Quinn. "But don't tell her."

"No," Saluto says, "for Christ sake. She's pissed at me already for going without her. She'd kill me if she knew I was leaving this behind — her love offering."

Cutler says to Quinn, "He travels light."

Quinn turns away. "Back to the volleyball game. If I don't see Veronica win, she'll never let me forget it."

Supermarket doors slide open for him, he wheels a glittering wire cart out into sunlight, the doors clunk shut behind him. He blinks in the brightness, looking for the red Celica among the rows of cars that wait on the clean blacktop of the shopping center parking lot. He spots the Celica, and begins to push the cart toward it. He is eerily alone. Only two things move out here — himself and an immense stars and stripes that flaps in the sea wind atop a tall pole.

He stops the cart behind the Celica, digs keys from his jeans, unlocks the hatchback, loads sacks of groceries into the car. He slams the hatchback and tucks the cart out of the way. Looking around, he finds he is no longer alone. Shoppers have come from the market, drugstore, hairdresser, baker, florist, bookshop. All at once. They stream toward their cars. New sounds mingle with the flapping of the flag — voices, slamming car doors, whizzing ignitions. Someone taps a horn button. Cutler feels relieved.

The sun through the glass of the Celica has heated the red fake leather of the bucket seat. He winds down the window and closes the door. The red wrapping of the steering wheel is hot. He twists the key to start the little motor but the lane behind him is crowded. He has to sit and watch in his side mirror for a break so he can back out. It doesn't come soon, and when it does he joins a very slow inching of wheels toward the exits and the coast road.

A fast food place called the Copper Penny — Cutler calls it the Penny Dreadful — faces the road. And the first unit of the shopping center immediately behind it is a savings and loan office, topped by a digital clock that gives time and temperature — both wrong. Cutler has to halt and idle in front of this place, and as he does so its doors open and Pelletier comes out, a cowboy hat pushed back on his shaggy hair. Cutler beeps the Celica's horn and waves. Pelletier frowns, grins, comes jogging to the car in cowboy boots. He wears sunglasses, and in his hand is a savings passbook. He tucks this into a hip pocket, takes off the hat, pokes his head into the car.

"Been shopping?" he says.

"I thought you were filming," Cutler says.

"It's over." Pelletier makes a face. "Thank God. I mean, it's one thing to fill your smiling mouth with Amarillo Brand Chili at a backyard barbecue in Encino. But they keep making you spit it out. They say if you swallow it on every take, you'll start gagging."

"Charming," Cutler says. "Doesn't the grass get slippery?"

"They set buckets around," Pelletier says. "Yellow plastic, with water in them. Elegant, right?"

Cutler frowns past him at the doors of the savings place. "What were you doing in there? What's with the passbook?"

Pelletier shrugs. "Banking a check. Residuals."

"What for?" Cutler feels hollow. "Am I Wrigley? Do I keep you barefoot and pregnant?"

"A girl needs mad money," Pelletier says.

Cutler grows angry and reckless. "How much did you pay Saluto, really? Enough to live on for a year?"

The cars that idled between Cutler and the highway have driven off now. Behind the Celica, horns begin complaining. Someone shouts impatience. Pelletier pulls his head out of the window, straightens, takes a backward step, eyeing the cars. "The way he lives, probably. Five thousand bucks. Why not, Darryl? It'll be worth it to me. Every skill an actor learns is money in the bank." He puts the cowboy hat back on.

The horns honk. Cutler calls, "It was my five thousand. Did you ever think I might like to have it back?"

Pelletier winces. "It's so noisy here." He glances at the complaining cars again. He bends again, hands on knees squinting into the Celica. "I don't think I heard what you said, Darryl. I sure as hell hope not."

Cutler smiles stiffly. "Nothing," he says, and drives away.

12

He longs to be on land. The sky is blue, the blue
ocean calm. Tony Baron's yacht bears southwesterly
toward where the channel islands sleep low in the
water. Cutler has stood in the bow and studied them
for signs of life and seen nothing. Goats are said to
live out there, wild pigs, even beef cattle. He doubts
it. He stands now at the stern and gazes back at the
city, the wink of sunlight off a windowpane, the white
buildings and red roofs half hidden among treetops,
the mountains behind. He wishes he were back there,
sitting in some cool patio with a fountain, good food
on the table, big creamy margaritas to drink. Santa
Barbara is full of such places.

Out here it is hot and unforgiving. The deep water surging and hissing along the boat's hull only worries him. The farther the ship voyages, the lonelier
it all becomes. He searches the waves for a glimpse
of life. Once he saw the sleek, dark heads of swimming sea lions. But only once. Gulls followed the
yacht out from the docks but they turned back. At
first, everyone stayed on deck. A black fellow in a
ruffled, puff-sleeved shirt sang calypso songs for a
while. There was a cheerful jingle of ice in glasses.
Now two young crewmen, shirts off, arms across
their eyes, doze on a hatch cover. All the guests have
gone below, out of the sun.

But Cutler can't be easy down there. Even with
the talk and laughter, the sounds of eating and

drinking—the food was oysters, crabmeat, abalone, handsomely served—he could hear the straining of the old timbers and sense the strength and weight of the water against the hull. He wolfed his food and hurried back up the companionway, the tilting of the ship jarring first this shoulder, then that against the varnished planks, to emerge wincing into the sun-glare and the heat again. And the isolation. The flat miles and miles of nothing, stretching emptier with every moment that the ship bore onward. The way he felt he had felt only once before in his life, a long, long time ago. He had forgotten it.

After his father deserted them, his mother needed time to find her feet, and Cutler was too young to leave alone. She had driven him to the farm of her brother in Dakota. It was very different country from that around Portland where there were mountains, rivers, trees. Dakota was flat and empty forever. Like the ocean. A sea of wheat moved under the wind the way the ocean moved under the wind. *Amber waves of grain.* Nothing on the horizon, hour after hour. Now and then a crow, maybe. More rarely still a ragged line of poplars. A steeple. Then nothing again for miles and miles. And the farm, when they reached it, the bare board bleakness of the barn and outbuildings like the below-decks of this ship. They even creaked in the wind that blew there the way it blows across this flat blue emptiness, the same.

He turns his back to the land, and gazes along the glossy length of the ship. Once, of course, the wind meant everything out here, meant the difference between travel and doldrums to this very ship. It has two strong masts, but he has examined the tackle. Paint chokes the pulleys. Sails are gathered and tied along the sturdy spars, under which a tall man like himself has to duck to pass — but when were the sails last unfurled? If the ropes that hold them now were to be unknotted, if the lines were tugged, if the sails rose, wouldn't they rip away, rotten, hang in tatters, flutter useless in the wind? An engine thrums below decks. He turns, leans on the rail, looks down at the foaming, fanning wake the propeller leaves. If the motor jammed and no one could fix it, with shredded sails, wouldn't they be stuck out here forever, a painted ship upon a painted ocean? He doesn't like it.

"Feeling sick?" a voice asks. Cutler turns. The man beside him, small, bony, face crinkled like worn leather, is Tony Baron, screenwriter, an old customer of Moody's, one of those Moody romantically regarded as a friend, simply because they had said hello across a counter for years. Baron wears a yachting cap. "I've got medication for that."

"I'm not sick," Cutler says. "Don't you worry about the life boat? The chains are so clotted with paint — can you lower it, if you have to?"

Baron's mouth twitches. "We aren't sailing around Cape Horn in the dead of winter." He brushes a white mustache with a knuckle. "This craft is sixty years old, and never even lost a mast. Stop worrying."

"I'm happy to be aboard," Cutler lies. "Thank you."

"Thank Veronica Quinn," Baron says. "She wouldn't come unless I invited you. Phil wouldn't come unless she came. And it's Phil's going-away party, isn't it?" Quinn is off to Turkey with a film company. He is producer of this picture, as well as its writer. Veronica is not going with him. Baron gives Cutler an odd look, starts toward the aft companionway, turns back and stands, swaying a little with the motion of the ship, studying Cutler. "Do you miss Stewart?"

"Every day," Cutler says. "He would have loved this."

Baron blinks surprise, frowns, sadly shakes his head. "Jesus, you're right, aren't you? Funny about that. Failure of imagination. You connect someone like Stewart to his shop, as if he didn't have any existence apart from it. Hell, I could have invited him, plenty of times. You're right. He would have loved it. I'm sorry. What killed him?"

"Three packs of cigarettes a day," Cutler says.

Baron waves the idea away with a liver-spotted hand. "Smoking doesn't kill people. It's genes. All a matter of bloodlines. My forebears were Sardinian fisherman. Tough. My mother was ninety-eight when she died. I never remember seeing her without a cigarette."

Cutler says, "I don't know who my forebears were."

"English," Baron says. " 'Cutler'? They made knives."

Cutler studies the navy-blue, brass-buttoned blazer Baron wears. The breast pocket is flat. "You don't smoke."

"Why take chances?" Baron grins and turns away again.

Young people burst up out of a companionway, laughing. They surround him, almost naked. All are dark except Veronica and Pelletier, whose silvery hair shines. Veronica flings her arms around Baron, making him look brittle as a mummy, old as time.

"When can we swim, Tony? You promised we could swim."

Baron reads his watch. "When we anchor at Las Cruces."

A black actor from a television cop show looks over the ship's side. "It's a long way down," he says doubtfully.

Baron hauls a contraption of rope and wood from a locker and holds it up. "This clamps on the rail. You climb down."

Pelletier ambles back to Cutler. "Where have you been?"

"I didn't know you cared." The boy's trunks are minimal. No one is watching. For a second Cutler cups the cloth-packaged genitals in his hand. "Aren't you afraid you'll bust out?"

"I will, if you don't stop. Hey, isn't this great? Wow!" He grins around at sea, sky, ship. "Buy me a boat, okay?"

"Okay," Cutler says.

After they swarmed noisily down the rope and wood ladder to swim with cries of wonder in water green and crystalline among the big white drifting jellyfish of the island cove, and climbed, water streaming from their handsome bodies up the ladder again, the youngsters were sleepy and went below, leaving the lonely deck to Cutler again — and the crewmen once more asleep on the hatch cover. The sloop bore southwards. For a time, Cutler gazed up at the islands' crusty black volcanic cliffs, clumped here and there with struggling greenery. But he saw no goats, no pigs, no browsing cattle. No life.

At the last landfall, the long slender whiteness of the ship swung like a compass needle past the ragged tip of the lower island, Anacapa, and into deep water. The power of the Pacific impressed him, made him straighten and stand clutching the rail hard for a few minutes. The ocean put its shoulders under the yacht and lifted it as if it were a stick of driftwood. And yet this day was calm. *Sardinian fishermen.* He shivered in the sun. Why would anyone put to sea every day to make his living? This was his first time, and he knew already that the sea was no man's friend.

With the setting of the sun, it has grown chilly on deck. The black singer lays down his guitar and puts his ruffled shirt back on. The youngsters in bikinis get up and hurry below, to return in blowsy trousers and jackets of parachute cloth, sizes too large—the style right now. Baron has not lighted the deck. Running lights top the masts and point the bowsprit. Light glows from portholes below. But he keeps the deck dark because of the stars. The stars are numerous and bright out here. Seated on the deck, leaning on the rail, perched in rigging, everyone marvels aloud at the splendor of the stars. And falls silent. The red coal of a cigarette curves like a tiny comet from the ship into the sea. Out of the darkness, a young woman's voice scoffs:

"Nobody believes in ghosts anymore."

Tony Baron says, "Nobody believes in anything anymore."

"Aerobics," someone says. "Cocaine," says someone else.

"Just the same," Phil Quinn rumbles, "everybody has a ghost story. They may deny it, but they have."

A murmur travels the deck. Assent. Dissent. Cutler turns away, leans in the bow, eyes on the glow of Santa Barbara in the sky, the harbor lights reflected in the water. The ship's engine makes the deck hum under his feet. But they do not seem to be traveling. They seem to be standing still. He reads his watch. Only two minutes since he last read it. He sighs. He wants not to hear. No one knows ghosts as he does. Moody visits him, eyes filled with crazy fear. The mangled boy from Portland, clutching the shiny crash helmet. He almost dies of terror. This talk is kid stuff—scaring each other with second-hand spooks in a cellar. But he can't help hearing. The night is silent. The yacht is only ninety feet long.

"We thought we were done for. Then we saw lights through the snow, through the trees. And here's this lodge. A fire was burning in the fireplace in the main room. The kitchen was closed, but the owner's wife fixed us some supper. All the rooms in the lodge were filled, but one cabin was empty. And there was something strange about it. It felt as if it never got used. We were dog tired, and went to sleep right away, but later something woke me up, and I was scared. The storm was over. Not a whisper of wind or snow. And then I heard what had wakened me. A knock at the door. My watch said two thirty. I waited for my dad to make a move, but he didn't. The knocking kept on.

"What the hell, I was almost thirteen years old. Why couldn't I answer the door? The floorboards were cold. I opened the door. There was no one there, not a sign of anybody. It was bitter cold. I closed the door and went back to bed. I don't know how long it was, but the knocking woke me again.

I opened the door again. Not even footprints in the snow. It was creepy. My folks were still asleep, and I decided I'd dreamed the knocking. So I crawled back under my blanket again. But I couldn't sleep, and the knocking took up again. My folks didn't stir. I went to the window, unlocked it, pushed it up, stuck my head out. The knocking went right on. But there was no one out there, no one at all."

"A tree branch hitting the roof," someone says.

Quinn says, "There was no wind. And no tree branch. In the morning, I told my folks. At breakfast, my mother asked the woman about it. She turned pale and changed the subject. When my dad was paying the bill, he asked her husband. Dad was a lawyer. He knew how to ask things. The story was, a few winters back, in a snowstorm, a woman's car stalled on the road. She got out and blundered through the woods and came on this cabin and knocked and knocked — they could tell because her knuckles were raw and bloody when they found her — but the cabin was unoccupied, and she froze to death at the door. They didn't like renting that cabin because this kept happening."

Cutler sees his father and the young blond woman in the car with the cloth roof that wouldn't keep the cold out. Sitting there in their ski outfits, angled in some ditch in the dark and driving snow, freezing to death in each others' arms. He has made up the picture. He never even read a word about how it actually was. But the picture is real to him. He can't figure why, since he never gave a damn about the man, much less about the woman. How he wanted to cash that cashier's check and run away. From his mother. Whom he also cared nothing about. But he wasn't smart enough to know how. And he feared that even if he was, she was smarter, and would catch him and do awful things to him. He slid the check back into its envelope and laid it where his father had laid it on the coffee table.

On the night-time yacht, a young woman is saying: "Oh, it looked like a haunted house, all right. Big old frame place with hardly any paint left, big yard all grown up with weeds and bushes and untrimmed trees. Porches with steps caving in, broken windows. We drove up from L.A., and we didn't get there till sunset, and you expected bats to come flying out of the towers. No, it did—it had towers. Rusty iron fence, creaky gate. Just the way Annette told us it would be."

"So you were going to be scientific," Baron says.

"Right. Psychic research. College freshmen. Were we scared? Maybe they weren't. I was. But no one acted scared."

"You really did it?" a young voice marvels.

"Right. Took sleeping bags, flashlights, a thermos of coffee, sandwiches, and brownies—no lie, brownies." She giggles and coughs. "We bedded down on the living room floor, okay? And it was laughs, wasn't it? I mean, spooky—but we didn't really think anything would happen."

"A dark, stormy night?" a voice says. "Clouds scudding across the face of the moon? A dog howling?"

"Just a dull, small-town night." A match scratches. The little flame lights the storyteller's face for a second. Cutler noticed her earlier—wiry red hair, the trim body of an Olympic swimmer. The match goes out. The smell of tobacco smoke is sweet in the night air. "Only, of course, we were out on the far edge of town. We flipped a coin for who would take the first watch, and blew out the candles. Annette woke us. Something was running around upstairs. Slamming doors. We got the flashlights and climbed the stairs." The giggle again. "Hanging onto each other. Annette kept calling, 'Who's there?' Her voice was shaking. I didn't even *have* a voice. At the top of the stairs we shined our lights all around, but there was nothing to see but dust and broken plaster and cobwebs."

"Probably vagrants," Quinn says. "Any wine bottles?"

"No," the young woman says. "Nothing like that. And do you want to know why?" She waits for an answer, but only long enough to draw smoke from her cigarette. The tip of it glows in the dark. "We didn't see them that night, but we went back up in the morning. All over, up and down the hallway, and in and out of the bedrooms, we found tracks."

"Like the man said," Baron says. "Tramps, squatters."

"Not human tracks." The young woman gets up off the deck and dim in the near dark moves to the rail where Cutler stands and leans there beside him. "They were the tracks of some huge bird."

"What was an ostrich doing in Mill Creek?" Cutler says.

"The ghost of an ostrich," someone says.

"It wasn't a ghost," Quinn says, "it was a demon. Look at the paintings of Heironymus Bosch. Demons have feet like that—big, scaly bird feet, with long claws."

"My producer," the black actor says from the dark.

While everyone laughs, Cutler goes below. The

134

rear cabin is sinister in its shadowy lamplight with no one in it. He hurries. There is no hurrying operations in the head, however. A long iron handle sticks up beside the toilet fixture. To get the toilet to flush, this handle has to be pumped. And pumped. And pumped. If Baron can afford a yacht, can't he afford to fix up the head? Making aft again, along a narrow varnished plank passage, he hears whispers and soft laughter through a closed cabin door. He isn't the only one who doesn't care about ghost stories. He climbs to the deck.

Baron is talking now. "I was sure it was Irv. It couldn't be. He was dead. But there he sat. The street was narrow, everybody in it took his time, cars, bicycles, burros. The jitney crawled. I yelled out the window. 'Irv! Irv Liebowitz!' The aisle was full of luggage. I couldn't get to the driver. I yelled at him to stop, but not in Spanish. I couldn't remember a word. And he didn't stop. When I looked back at the cantina, Irv wasn't there anymore. And I told myself he never had been.

"It was terribly hot, and by the time I got dropped at my pension, I'd forgotten him. I wanted a long, cold drink and a shower. But after dinner, when I tried to go to sleep—sleep was what I'd come for, right, two weeks of complete rest, no telephones, no typewriters?—I remembered Irv sitting at that table in that cantina. I dressed and went out to find him. I couldn't locate the street we'd come down, couldn't remember the name of the bar. Nothing looked familiar. Only the skinny little brown boys tugging at me—'Hey, mister, you want my sister?' That never changes."

"Racist bullshit," the black actor says.

"Sorry about that," Baron says. "I found a dozen wrong places, and then there it was, La Paloma Blanca, seven small tables, six square feet of dance floor, a black and white TV on a high shelf back of the bar, a band on a corner platform, guitar, concertina, trumpet, a bartender with a two-day beard and a clean white shirt, collar buttoned, no tie. He was busy. I had to ask my questions in installments. The name didn't register. The description, old tweed jacket, leather elbow patches, Dodger baseball cap, gray hair straggling over his collar? A gringo. Can a sixty-year-old Jewish boy from Brooklyn be a gringo? It didn't matter. The bartender kept shaking his head. *Lo siento mucho, señor.* He was sorry."

"Irv had more than just one jacket like that," Quinn says, "that he wouldn't get rid of. It drove the teenage bitch crazy. And he hated barbershops. And loved the Dodgers."

"I went back to La Paloma Blanca the next day, the day after—afternoon, night, early, late. He was never there. How could he be? I'd made him up, hadn't I? You grow old, and your world starts to empty out. People die on you. It's natural, but who says you have to like it? I wanted Irv to be alive, didn't I? Why was I here? Nervous exhaustion. I began wondering what 'nervous exhaustion' might really mean. Was I losing my mind? I couldn't afford that. I stopped going back to La Paloma Blanca. I had to forget Irv Liebowitz.

"And I almost did. Then, one hot night when I couldn't sleep, I was standing at my window, and I saw him in the next street. He stood under a streetlamp. They weren't bright there—too many trees. But his face was turned up. He was looking right at me. And it was Irv. I was positive. I pulled on pants and ran downstairs, across my patio, out into my street, and back through a passageway to the street where I'd seen him — if it was him. Nobody. Nothing. Silence, emptiness. It was three in the morning. Sometimes, when you're there, you think the life in the streets never stops, but it does — the laughter, the fights, the music. It stops. And when it does, the silence is eerie. I went back to my room, looking over my shoulder all the way."

"That's it?" someone says.

"I'm a better storyteller than that," Baron says. "I saw him one last time. I mean — I thought I saw him. The morning of the day I was scheduled to fly home to Tinsel Town. I had things to buy to bring back to friends. And I saw him in the *mercado*. Buying pigsfeet. My heart started racing. But this time I didn't shout. I figured I'd scared him when I called his name from the jitney. He'd gone into hiding. This time, I went up quietly, stood next to him at the butcher's cart, and laid a hand on his sleeve. 'Irv,' I said, 'what are you doing here? What's going on?'

"And he turned and stared at me. It wasn't Irv. Of course not. Pigsfeet? Talk about nervous exhaustion! He wore the baseball cap and the old tweed jacket with the elbow patches. He was short and skinny like Irv, he was Irv's age. But he was Mexican. He gave a little smile and said he didn't understand *ingles*. I apologized in *español*. And" — Baron pushes to his feet with a sheepish laugh — "it isn't much of a ghost story, but it looks as if it got us home."

The young crewmen have begun to hurry on their soft soles up and down the deck. The yacht slides through water like black glass. The lights around the harbor waver yellow in the water. The guests stir, stretch, yawn, sigh, their feet begin to thump and rumble in the companionways. Baron comes and leans beside Cutler on the bow rail.

"See?" he says. "No need for the lifeboat."

Cutler straightens, turns, peers. "Have you seen Chick?"

"Right here." Pelletier steps smiling out of the dark. Veronica clings to his arm. He says, "Thanks, Mr. Baron."

"Tony," Baron says. "Glad you enjoyed it."

13

A yellow truck stands on the shoulder of the road above the house. Trucks develop mechanicals and stall. The sight is not uncommon, but he wishes this truck weren't where he ordinarily parks. He stops with the Celica's front almost nosing the truck's bumper, switches off the engine, and gets out frowning. The rear doors of the truck stand open. And on the ground behind the truck are stacked cartons, storage files, bundles of papers. Papers begin to blow across the highway. A man jumps heavily down from the truck's back, turns, hauls out another stack of cartons.

"Hey," Cutler says, "what is this?"

The man is squat, middle-aged, and wears anonymous coveralls. He eyes Cutler from under thick black brows. "You're Darryl Cutler. That's your house down below, ain't it?"

"I didn't order this." Cutler eyes the stuff. It looks familiar. A twist of wind wraps a loose page around his ankle. He bends for it. He designed the letterhead—STEWART MOODY SCRIPT SERVICE. He blinks at the dark man. "You're Ernie Fargo. What do you mean, bringing this here?"

Ernie shrugs, grunts, sets down another stack of storage files. Dust puffs out of them. "My sister's orders. Business records. Important. You were the owner. The Japs that bought the property—they wasn't about to save it. Just leave it in the storeroom, the attic, the garage. Let the wreckers bulldoze it away." He climbs up into the rear of the truck again. "She says you got to keep business records for five years, seven, something like that." He nudges cargo grittily across the steel truckbed with a foot, then jumps down to the road shoulder again. "She was sure you'd want to do the responsible thing."

"She was sure I'd hate this." Cutler kicks a box.

"She hates being turned out after all these years with no job," Ernie Fargo says. He pauses, a twine-tied bundle of scripts in his arms, and looks into Cutler's eyes. "She's smart in some ways, but awful dumb in others. I warned her it would happen. When pretty boy turned up and"—Ernie sets the bundle down with a grunt—"just like that, old man Moody kicked off, I seen the handwriting on the wall. She says, 'Darryl needs me to run the business.' I says, 'Won't be no business, Sis. He'll sell the place. All he wanted from Moody was money. And there's more money in the land under it than the business could earn in a lifetime.'"

"Old man Moody's time was up," Cutler says. "He was due to die, and he died. That's how emphysema works."

Ernie Fargo laughs and slams the truck doors. "If somebody gives it a little help, yeah." He drops the long bolts into place that hold the doors, and starts for the truck cab.

"Wait just a damn minute," Cutler says. "You're not driving off and leaving this stuff. Look. It's littering the highway. Put it back, Ernie. Take it away with you."

"It's got nothing to do with me." Ernie says it indifferently. With hairy fingers, he pries Cutler's grip off his arm. "It's yours. Anybody can see that."

"Whose drivers license did you use when you rented this truck? The court took yours away, I seem to remember." Cutler turns for the white wooden staircase that zigzags down the cliff to his backdoor. "I'm telephoning the sheriff, Ernie." Cutler starts down the stairs. And sees Veronica Quinn in sandals, jeans, a windblown blouse, trudging away from the house up the sand, making for Cormorant Cove. What is that case she carries? Cutler feels the stairs tremble and looks down. Below, Pelletier's hair shines in the sunlight. He is mounting the stairs. He turns up his face in dark glasses. "What's going on? I thought I heard your voice."

Behind Cutler, the cab door of the rental truck slams. He turns to scramble back up the stairs. "No. Ernie. Wait." But the engine of the truck clatters to life. "Damn it, wait!" Cutler shouts. He runs for the truck, but the highway is free of traffic and Ernie swings the truck onto the road and it roars off, clashing gears, poisoning the air with blue exhaust. Cutler coughs. Behind him Pelletier reaches the cliff top.

"What's all the junk?" He walks to it and circles it, slowly, frowning, cocking his head this way, that way. He lifts his head and gazes through his dark lenses at Cutler. "It's from Moody's. How come?"

"Moody's is no more. What was Veronica doing here?"

"Teaching me backgammon. She's lonesome. She misses Quinn. And every skill an actor learns—"

" '—is money in the bank'," Cutler says bleakly.

Pelletier pushes the sunglasses up on his hair and frowns. "What do you mean, 'Moody's is no more'?"

"Why did she take off when I arrived?" Cutler says.

"She feels guilty. She dragged me into a bunk on Tony Baron's yacht that night when you were telling ghost stories up on deck. Now she's got the hots for me."

Cutler picks up a storage file. "Did you sleep with Saluto, too?" The file sags. Its cardboard has lost stiffness. He turns with it in his arms, starts down the stairs.

"What for?" Pelletier says. "You going to keep this?"

"Can't leave it out here. It will be days before the trash truck comes. It's already blowing all over."

"So?" Pelletier repositions the glasses on his nose. "Who gives a fuck? Your mother?"

"Yours," Cutler says. "To any man who asks, right?"

Pelletier's laugh is short. He follows Cutler down. "Did I collapse Moody's?" He sounds a little awed by this notion, but not displeased. "What are you going to do for money, now? You promised me a boat, remember?"

"The details from the brochure are imprinted on my brain." At the stair landing, Cutler rests the file on the white rail. "Length, forty-one feet nine inches, beam, twelve feet ten, displacement twenty-five thousand five hundred pounds, sail area eight hundred thirty seven square feet, fifty horsepower diesel engine, handfinished teak interior. Made in Taiwan. Price, one hundred twenty-five thousand." He rests the file against his hip, reaches out, takes off Pelletier's glasses, looks into his eyes. "Did I ever break a promise to you yet?"

"You better not." Pelletier kisses him lightly, and takes the glasses back. "Phil's getting old. Veronica keeps talking about divorcing him and marrying me." He puts the glasses on, picks up the file, and goes down the stairs with it. His voice drifts back up on the sunwarmed breeze. "I could live very high on the kind of alimony she'd get."

Now it is loose, calf-length white cotton trousers, and a kicky little white cotton kimono cinched with a sash. Pelletier takes stiff, stylized poses among the wicker and sailcloth of the long sea-lit room, utters harsh cries, and lunges at imaginary enemies, toppling attackers like a comic-book hero. It is all right with Cutler. Anything is all right with Cutler. He likes the cotton costume, likes taking it off Pelletier. They buy a blue mat and lay it on the bedroom floor. Pelletier stands there poised scowling against the high wide rectangle of smiling sky and sea and sunny beach—stands one foot, one shoulder forward, knees slightly bent, elbows pressed to ribs, hands cocked, two fingers raised, two fingers curled, thumbs up. And Cutler attacks. A shout copied from a karate movie yelps from Pelletier. He catches Cutler's arm, flings him into the air. Cutler slams on his back on the mat, breath thumping out of his lungs with a grunt. He grins, catches Pelletier's ankle, upsets him onto the mat, and wrestles the white pajamas off him. The rest is not like a karate movie. It is like some of the video cassettes Pelletier has brought home, but more sincere.

*   *   *

"I'm looking for Chick Pelletier." A frail figure steps from the red-orange glare of the sea and sky at sunset off the deck into Cutler's workroom. The workroom has become a storage room. The brown brindle files from Moody's, the old office-supply cartons, the bundles of scripts and printing samples crowd the place. There is scarcely room at the table that holds the word processor for Cutler to wheel out the chair so he can seat himself. He still does seat himself here sometimes when Pelletier is absent, and smokes a lot of cigarettes, and fails to write. His head aches from the effort, and the frail man's interruption is welcome. Cutler edges from between desk and chair, shakes the man's cool hand, ushers him out to the deck again, and up the stairs. The man is old and tiny. He must weigh no more than a hundred pounds. His summer weight clothes in pale pastel colors are impossibly clean. His cufflinks are gold nuggets that look too heavy for him. In the shadowy living room, when Cutler touches a switch and lamps go on, he stares at the emptiness, turns, blinks mild surprise at Cutler. "He isn't here?"

"He's studying karate," Cutler says, "five nights a week. The studio is on Pico. One of those addresses with five digits."

"I know where it is," Hoffy says. "He isn't there. That's why I came here."

Cutler feels bleak. "Sit down. Have a drink."

"Perrier," Hoffy says, and pinches the neat creases of his trousers when he sits. "With a slice of lime?"

Cutler goes up the room to the kitchen. "Maybe he'll be here soon." He winces in the glare from inside the refrigerator, reaching for one of the little green labeled bottles. He finds loose ice cubes in the freezer compartment, puts a fistful into a tall glass, pries open the bottle, fills the glass. He takes a lime from a basket on the breakfast bar and cuts a slice from it and fixes it to the edge of the glass. He opens the freezer compartment again and drops more ice cubes into a stubby glass, which he fills with scotch. He carries the drinks back. "If not, I can give him your message — right?" He puts the tall glass into the tiny man's hand, on which big showy rings twinkle with diamonds. "Anyway, it's good to meet you." He smiles, pushes glossy video cassette boxes aside, sits on the couch. "He talks about you a lot. He has faith in you."

"This script" — it lies neatly on his neat knees — "has a great part in it for him. He wants to be in theatrical releases. This will be a theatrical release. Of course, he kills his mother, father, sister. The handsome, intelligent, very nice child of handsome, intelligent, very nice, successful parents. President of his high school class. Scholarships to college. The whole middle-class dream, see? Only he murders his whole family one night at dinner."

"There's no future for an actor in that," Cutler says.

Hoffy sips the bubbling water, sets the glass down, gets to his feet, holds the script out to Cutler. "There's solid money behind it. Good director. Good co-star. He should do it."

"I'll tell him," Cutler says.

"You don't know where he could be?"

Cutler shakes his head. "I'm sorry you had a long drive for nothing. Why didn't you telephone?"

"I'm on my way to a party in Zuma," Hoffy says. He glances at his watch and walks out of the circles of soft lamplight to stand in the open space left by a sliding glass panel. It is dark outside now. Sunsets never last long. He stands gazing at distant lights along the shore. His pale colors make him ghostly. He says, "That's the trouble with you gays." He lifts a hand without turning around. "Don't stop me. I know. I had a brother that was that way. Couples can't maintain a relationship when you don't know where one of you is all the time. You have to tell each other everything. I was married forty-two years. Total honesty with each other. Trust. Faithfulness. It's the only way."

"To a woman," Cutler says, "forty-two years."

"It's all the same." Hoffy steps out into the dark. His expensive heels tap lightly on the deck, on the stairs — like the hoofs of deer. Cutler could have shown him out the kitchen door. He'd have had less climbing to do that way. Cutler doesn't get up off the couch. He takes slow swallows from his glass. From the sand below, Hoffy calls, "Goodnight."

Cutler begins to tear up the script.

Streetlights shine along the streets that form curved shelves down to the shore in Cormorant Cove. The windows of the sprawling houses shine. Driving slowly down, he can see into backyards. Swimming-pools glow blue. Tangy smoke from barbecues gives an extra edge to the salt air. People move among tropical plantings in backyards, holding drinks, holding plates, smiling. In one pool youngsters swim, sleek heads bob, hands flail. A beachball curves and splashes, drops sparkling like glass beads.

All is quiet and dark at the Phil Quinn place. But Pelletier is here. The Porsche waits with the little red Alfa and the stodgy BMW by the mailbox. Cutler lets the Celica roll past and parks it in the shadow of a big oleander. He gets out of it, and closes the door quietly. Canvas shoes let him go down the steps to the front deck quietly too. A weak lightbulb glows there, inside a rough stone Chinese lantern that stands on the planks near the French doors. As on his first time here, he looks through the panes and down the long room to the French doors at the other end, and makes out dimly the night ocean and the stand of sharp black rocks out in the surf. No one moves in the room, or on the deck beyond.

How is the house built, exactly? He doesn't know. He was never shown all of it. But maybe, like his, on two levels. He follows a narrow deck along the side. Stairs down don't materialize. He reaches the front deck, where he talked that day with Quinn about writing, where he remembered the night-bicycling boy, where he drank those big martinis, where Veronica looked at him with contempt and gave up on her crossword puzzle. No steps go down here, either. The steps must be inside, then. Because there are rooms below. He can see light reflecting off windowpanes down there.

He kneels and peers between the planks to be sure. He holds his breath and listens for their voices. There's only the sigh of the surf and laughter from a party up the street. He leans over the rail of the deck and peers down through the darkness. He can't judge the depth of the drop. And if he gets down there without breaking his neck, what will he do — beat a fist on the window and shout? What will that accomplish? Pelletier won't be embarrassed. Pelletier will only laugh at him. He swings away, barks a shin on the redwood chaise, swears. What did he come here for? He limps away along the narrow side deck, back to the street and his car.

14

He is shaking so that he can hardly manage the stairs down from the road to his dark house. He hangs onto the rail. The key scrapes around the slot in the kitchen door before it fits in and he can turn it. He bats at the lightswitch, and winces in the glare. He yanks open cupboard doors, snatches a glass. The glass spins out of his hand, flies across the kitchen, smashes against the bronze surfer figurine on the breakfast bar. The thick neck of the big green J&B bottle chatters on the rim of a glass he manages not to drop. Half the ice cubes meant for the drink skitter winking along the counter. The glass rattles against his teeth when he tries to drink. Whisky runs over his hand, runs down his chin.

The first swallow weakens his legs, and he sits on the floor that glares in the hard light. His back is against a cupboard door. Sweat pours off him. Is he going to throw up? He tries to gulp more whisky. It goes down the wrong way, and he coughs and chokes. He can hear his own voice echo in the emptiness of the house. "Bitch, bitch, bitch," it shouts, it sobs. "Bitch, bitch, bitch." Tears run, his nose runs. He wipes them on his arm. When the whisky is gone, he has stopped shaking, stopped crying. He drags himself to his feet, fills the glass again, carries it out to the deck.

The sea wind cuts through his sweatsoaked clothes and makes him shiver. He sets the drink on the rail and pokes fingers into a shirt pocket for a cigarette. The pack is damp, limp, and the cigarettes are bent, but he lights one anyway, cupping the flame of a cheap plastic lighter — no platinum for Darryl — to shield it from the wind. The wind snatches the smoke from his mouth. He drops the lighter into a pocket and picks up the glass again. He drinks steadily, scowling out into the darkness. He wants to hurt Pelletier. But if he tries, Pelletier will leave him.

And good riddance, his mother says inside his head.

Cutler ignores her. What about Veronica? Like most cheap pretty things, she is fragile. He could disjoint her like a dinnertime chicken. His hands open and close. He would enjoy that. But would it help? Does Pelletier really give a damn about her, or is he only tangling naked with her to torment Cutler? Cutler's mouth twists. He grunts sourly. Probably. Probably Pelletier would stare at the scattered wings and legs and thighs, shrug and walk away. Bleakly, Cutler finishes off the whisky. Then he remembers Quinn. Quinn does give a damn about Veronica. And one of these days, Quinn will return from Turkey.

Cutler laughs aloud and flings his empty glass into the night. He holds both fists up to the stars. That is the answer. There's no need for him to do a thing to Pelletier. He will tell Quinn what's been going on in his absence, and Quinn will beat hell out of Pelletier. While Cutler watches — Cutler will be sure not to miss it. Grinning, he showers and goes to bed. He wants to be asleep when Pelletier gets home. From Veronica's, but having timed it so Cutler will think he's coming from his karate lesson. But it is early to try to sleep. When he closes his eyes, he sees Pelletier naked with naked Veronica, golden, clean-limbed, both of them. Clinging, thrusting. He hears their gasps and moans, sees them tense and shudder, hears Pelletier's shout, Veronica's cry. Sees them slump, panting, sleek with sweat, roll away from each other on crumpled sheets, smiling, spent.

He sits up sharply in the dark, gropes for a robe, climbs to the kitchen for another drink. He drops onto the couch, switches on the television, stares without seeing at the shifting, colored images. He is kidding himself. He will never tell Quinn—he hasn't the nerve. Anyway, Quinn isn't some character in a soap opera. Quinn would never use his fists on Pelletier. Quinn would hire a lawyer. And even if Cutler's fantasies were likely, a beating would be no answer. By sleeping with Veronica, Pelletier is telling Cutler that he wants something from him. And when Pelletier wants something, he will not accept substitutes.

Not the boat. Pelletier knows the boat is on its way. No—Pelletier wants to be a star, doesn't he? He wants to be in *People* magazine. And now, tonight, here came Hoffy with that rotten script. Cutler has kept believing that he had time. Now time has run out. In a few days at most Hoffy will be on the phone to Pelletier about that script. Cutler has to give him something to take the place of that script. Which means another script, his script. He groans, wags his head, switches off the television. Nothing else has made writing the script possible. Will pressure do it? He gulps his drink, sets the glass down with a bang under the lamp, gets to his feet, and thumps downstairs.

The planks of the stairs and decks are sandy. He brushes sand off his bare feet, crosses the carpet, switches on the desk lamp and the computer, and sits himself down. His hand gropes the cool white surface of the desk for cigarettes. The pack is empty. He goes through the dark hall and into the bedroom for another pack. The robe is wrong to work in. He pulls on a turtleneck and jeans. Smoke swirling around his head, he taps out in capital letters on the quiet keys LOSERS WEEPERS. He snorts derision. FINDERS KEEPERS. FINDERS WEEPERS. What? He needs a title.

The story is clear in his mind, has been for weeks—beginning, middle, end. A young woman, a talented artist, is crazy in love with a surfer who only wants to surf. Along comes a young fellow who cares deeply for the girl, but she only wants the surfer she can't have. A, B, C. Nothing to it. His fingers trouble the keys again. THE SURF, MY LOVER? That isn't bad. The hell with it. He can get the title anytime. What he has to do now is write—write, write, write. He writes a lonely stretch of beach in the early morning, fog, dune grass, a girl walking the beach alone, sketch pad under her arm. Sometimes the surf licks her bare feet. He sets her on a dune. She watches gulls circle in the chilly gray air, sandpipers run on their fragile legs along the damp sand. The sun comes over the hills behind her. She begins to draw. And. And?

He starts again. A young man is asleep in a motel room. We see the room, the battered air conditioner, the kitchenette with empty tin cans, pizza pans, unwashed dishes in the sink. The boy lies asleep naked in a rumpled bed. Surfboards lean against the wall of the room, a brightly colored sail for windsurfing, a picture of a surfer riding a giant wave cut from a magazine, taped to the wall. A clock radio switches on, the boy wakens groggily, turns it off, rolls over in bed to sleep some more, then instead gets up. We see the beach motel from outside, see the door of his unit open. He comes out, carrying a surfboard. He heads for the surf. And. And?

Cutler frowns, lights a tenth cigarette. He touches a button on the computer. The printer that stands beside it grinds, grinds. Paper comes up out of the printer with the words on it that he has seen greenly on the readout screen. The printer stops. Cutler tears off the paper. The typed result amounts to pitifully little. Five pages. A script runs a hundred twenty, a hundred fifty. This is going to take forever. And he hasn't got forever. He rakes fingers through his hair. His hand comes away wet with sweat.

Panicky, he pushes the chair back on its wheels. It jolts a stack of Moody's junk, and a box drops on his shoulders. The edge of the box is sharp. The weight of it hinges him forward and his brow bangs the computer. He struggles to free himself from the chair and bruises his thighs on the underside of the desktop. In a rage, he grabs up the carton and hurls it down the room. It lands in the open doorway, bursts, and its contents sluice out across the deck — file folders, computer printouts, manila envelopes. Right away, the wind begins to sort them.

He doesn't know whether to laugh or cry. He compromises with a moan, and hobbles down the room and outside, to chase after the papers and snatch them up. When he has an armful, he rights the carton with a foot, and dumps what he has rescued into the carton. Tidiness can wait. He chases down more papers. At last, everything is back in the box. Whatever blew onto the beach will blow back, and he can retrieve it tomorrow. For now, he repacks the carton, goes to a cabinet for brown tape, and closes the split corners of the carton. He is about to close the top flaps and tape these down when a name catches his eye.

The name is printed by hand with a felt tip pen in the upper left corner of a scruffly manila envelope. Stamps are glued crookedly in the upper right corner—a number of them dollar stamps. Cutler picks the envelope up. It is thick and heavy. FIRST CLASS has been rubber-stamped all over it. It is addressed to Stewart Moody Script Service, in the same felt tip pen printing, which looks shaky. The postmark is blurred, but the town name appears to be Perez. The date is two years old. He reads the return address beneath the sender's name. *Golden Poppy Motel, #9, Perez, CA.* The sender's name is Irv Liebowitz. Was. Cutler turns the envelope over. It is sealed. He sits on the floor and rips open the flap.

A letter, very roughly typed, lies on top of a thick sheaf of pages. He scarcely glances at the letter. He is interested in the pages under it. He shuffles them. They are the pages of a shooting script, again roughly typed, and much scrawled over with ballpoint corrections. A GOLD FOR LIVING. *By Irving Liebowitz.* Out of more than curiosity, Cutler begins to read. In his day, Irv Liebowitz won Academy awards. But he turned into a drunk at the last, didn't he—before he drove off into the desert to die in a ditch and be eaten by buzzards? Perez was in the desert. He'd holed up there to hide from his ex-wife's attorneys. He was a man at the end of his rope. So what kind of script would this be?

It is good. Cutler reads with growing involvement and excitement. His muscles cramp, and he switches position, lies belly down on the floor, like a little kid, and reads and turns the pages faster and faster. After the final page, he is so moved and shaken that his eyes are wet. He sniffles, sits up, gropes around for the letter. His vision is blurred. He wipes his eyes with his fingers, and reads the letter.

Dear Stewart — I know this is even messier than my usual typing job, and it has more corrections than anyone ought to be asked to deal with, but I beg you to bear with me. You were always tops in making impeccable copy out of my lousy typing and indecipherable handwriting, and I'm asking you to come to my rescue yet again. I know you will. You have never let me down. I haven't succeeded in finding a Xerox machine out here among the Joshua trees, so this is my only copy. Don't let anything happen to it. Make me twenty beautiful copies, register one for me with the Guild, and mail the rest to me at the return address on the envelope, okay? I'm in a state of advanced paranoia, so keep the address secret, all right? Don't mind the Victorville check. The bank is sound. If the amount isn't enough, let me know, and I'll send more. Thanks, old pal — Irv.

Cutler smiles crookedly. Moody would have preened at the phrase "old pal." How very butch. Cutler up-ends the envelope, and out flutters the check. He lets it lie, yellow on the blue carpet, and stares at it. He frowns, blinks, his tongue moistens his dry lips, his heart thuds. He has figured the damps of time resealed the envelope. Not so. If Moody had opened it, the check would have gone to the bank with the rest of the day's receipts. Moody still did the banking back then. So Moody never opened the envelope. Why? There could be only one answer—before it arrived, the news had reached Moody that Irv Liebowitz was dead. Moody hadn't known what to do with the package, and in the end had done nothing. Cutler laughs. Moody is still doing him favors.

The Porsche rattles onto the roadside gravel above the house, and Cutler stands sweating in the headlight beams, panting beside heaps of Moody's trash he has hauled up for the truck tomorrow morning. Pelletier switches off the headlights and steps out of the Porsche in his karate outfit. There is no light but starlight, but Cutler can see him. Pelletier says, "I thought you never would."

"Had to make room down there," Cutler says. "Tomorrow I start on the shooting script for your movie."

"Yeah?" Pelletier locks the car. "What's it about?"

"An Olympic gymnast who gets cancer and goes on to win anyway. The Olympics are next summer. It will break everybody's heart. They'll love you forever."

Pelletier tilts his head. "You never mentioned it." He sounds skeptical.

"I didn't have the story worked out." Cutler steps to him, puts hands on his shoulders, kisses him. "I wanted to be sure." Pelletier should smell of the shower at the karate place. He smells of Veronica. Cutler takes his hand and leads him to the stairs. "I didn't want to build you up and then have to disappoint you."

"I'm not a gymnast." Pelletier starts down the stairs ahead of him. His clothes glow ghostly in the dark. The ocean rustles out there in the dark. Its breath is chilly. "Why did you do that to me?"

"Because you're gymnast size, and the Olympics don't have surfing or karate." He grins. "Look at it this way—every skill an actor learns is money in the bank."

Pelletier grunts. "I'll have to find a coach. How long have I got? How long is it going to take you to write this shooting script?"

"It's just a matter of typing, really," Cutler says.

"They'll have to hire a double for me," Pelletier says.

"Kathy Rigby," Cutler says.

15

Heat shimmers off the sandy earth and makes the spiny Joshua trees and the straight strip of blacktop waver ahead of him. He should have started earlier. But he didn't want questions from Pelletier. The sun was high before the blond kid ambled off up the beach in little yellow swimtrunks. On his way to play with Veronica. Not backgammon. Cutler ought to have started before sunup, while the kid was still asleep. This heat is not to be believed.

The Celica has no air conditioning—when he bought it, he was trying to save money. Sweat pours off him. The fake red leather bucket seat beside him is strewn with wadded tissues. But no matter how often he wipes his face and neck, the sweat comes right back. The windows and the sunroof all are open, and he drives fast to keep air blowing, but the air is like the air from an oven. Once he stopped and took off his shirt. His skin stuck to the seatback, and he stopped again soon and put the shirt back on.

He grabs the rumpled map off the dashboard and scowls at it for the twentieth time. There is the ink dot he made before he set out. It marks Perez. Or it would, if the mapmaker had been sober that day. No wonder Irv Liebowitz died out here. Like Cutler, he probably thought deserts were only in the movies. You could get a big, quenching, ice-filled drink just by leaving your seat and walking up the aisle to the lobby. Cutler's mouth, throat, lungs feel sandblasted. He slaps the map back on the dashboard. And stares. How they can live out here he doesn't know, but he knows how they can die out here. Wasps, grasshoppers, moths. They commit suicide against windshields. But through their splatters now he thinks he sees, far down the road, a sprawl of buildings shivering in the heat. Unless it's a mirage, Perez is where it is supposed to be.

First comes a rusty metal filling station, with a small frame house out back, the roof of the house in three different colors and patterns of asbestos shingle. A black dog sleeps by the softdrink and cigarette machines beside the filling station doorway, where a girl in soiled white short-shorts and an empty halter leans watching the road. The buildings of Perez also watch the road and each other. All have battered air conditioning units hanging from their windows. The buildings lean a little off plumb, weary from the dry relentless push of the wind.

The buildings are mostly frame. One is a general store. LEVI'S a sign says. The diner doesn't bother with a name — it is simply EATERY. Here are the scaly stucco boxes of the ROAD RUNNER MOTEL. Cutler frowns. It's not the one. A gaunt false-front tavern, like something off a John Wayne movie set, is LUCKY'S STRIKE. A painting of a bearded gold prospector and his burro fades on its wooden side. *Coors* in red neon tubing hangs in a flyspecked window. Cutler is thirsty, but he doesn't like the look of the heavy motorcycles and decal-plastered dune buggies parked outside. Anyway, here is the GOLDEN POPPY MOTEL.

A narrow, picket-fenced grass patch in front of the yellow shiplap cabins bristles with little wooden whirligigs. When Cutler parks and gets out of the Celica, he hears the whispery flutter of the small carved propeller blades that turn them. The whirligigs are wooden cutouts, handworked. Bright paint shines on them. Each features figures, a horse that wind power makes run, a man shoveling, a dog jumping at a cat in a tree. Bigger examples of these toys spin, jitter, and jump on the roof of the cabin marked OFFICE.

Inside, the office is chilly and panelled in woodgrain plastic. Planters hold plastic California poppies. Signs in neatly incised brown plastic are everywhere, from NO SMOKING to HAVE A NICE DAY, from SORRY, NO CHECKS to TAKE TIME TO SMELL THE FLOWERS. And, of course, UNITS MUST BE VACATED BY 11:00 A.M. The air conditioner drones. The air smells faintly of sawdust and lacquer. And emptiness.

Cutler taps a bell on the counter. A voice calls something, and pretty soon a big man opens a woodgrain plastic door from the rear. Before the door closes, Cutler gets a glimpse of a workbench and bandsaw. The man looks sixty. Sweat gleams on his bald head. The faded red T-shirt that stretches over his massive belly is mapped with sweat. He offers a smile marred by missing teeth, but his eyes twinkle. They are the eyes of a small boy. "Howdy." He pushes a registration card at Cutler wrong way to. A ballpoint pen clicks down beside it. "Didn't hear you drive in."

"I parked out front." Cutler pushes card and pen away. "I won't be staying."

The man's face falls a little, but only for a moment. "Well, I'm not buying anything," he says. "Nobody steals my towels. Nobody steals my ashtrays."

Mischief tugs the corners of his mouth. "You want to know why?"

"Because nobody rents your rooms," Cutler says. "I'm not selling anything. Can you spare me a few minutes?"

"Between hustling around making beds and cleaning bathrooms?" The man chuckles ruefully. "Afraid I can."

"I'm writing a book about a man who stayed here a couple of years ago. Irving Liebowitz."

The blue eyes cloud. "I identified the body. Awful."

"It's not about that." Cutler gets out a cigarette.

"Hold it." The man points at a sign. Not the one that says NO SMOKING. The one that says ICE CUBES. Cutler puts the cigarette away. He says, "He was an important writer."

"Hard worker," the man admits. "Hard drinker, too. Oh, he run that typewriter to beat the band, but he'd have got farther faster if he didn't hit the bottle the way he done. I'm not telling you anything I didn't tell him to his face. I says, 'It'll kill you.' And it did. Fifth of whisky a day? Whew! Little skinny fella, too, you know. Man built like me can drink that way, but not a little skinny fella. Doctors tell you that on the radio."

"What was he writing so hard at?" Cutler asks. "When you went to do up his room, did you ever look at any of it?"

An expression Cutler puzzles about comes and goes in those childish eyes. The bald head shakes denial. "Just tidied up the papers if they was strewed all around, is all." He frowns at Cutler speculatively. "You know what I'd have said you was, if you hadn't told me you was writing a book? I'd have said you was a movie star."

Cutler laughs. "You're trying to sell me a whirligig."

"Aw." The big man blushes. "No such a thing, now. I only spoke what anybody could see, the minute they laid eyes on you. You got them movie star looks."

"I'm writing a book," Cutler says. "And I'd very much like to know what Irv Liebowitz was writing when he died."

"Screenplay." The man's sausage fingers pull tissues from a box. He mops his scalp, face, fat neck. "That's all he told me. Oh, now, that's not true. He told me it was the best he ever wrote. Says that's what suffering done for you. Made you a better writer."

"But he never showed you the script," Cutler says.

The odd, dodgy look comes and goes in the man's eyes again. "We didn't talk a lot. He kept to himself mostly. Just passed the time of day for a minute now and then."

"He ever mention plans to go to Mexico?" Cutler asks.

"Don't think so. Israel—he'd been there. Jew, you know." Headshake. "Not Mexico, no." The tissues are soaked but he dabs at his sweaty face with them again. "Say, you want a beer? I want a beer." He goes out through the woodworking shop. A refrigerator door clicks open and thuds shut, and he comes back with sweaty golden cans. He sets one in front of Cutler and pops the top of the other, which is almost hidden by his big hand. He guzzles beer, belches, wipes his mouth with the back of a hand.

"This heat dehydrates you. Dangerous. Doctors tell you that on the radio."

"Did he finish the script?" Cutler opens his can.

"Night he disappeared, he says it was finished, and he was going to mail it in the morning. I found it laying by his typewriter when I went down to tidy up the unit. He hadn't slept in the bed. I didn't know where he'd gone, but he'd do that, you know—just take off, drunk, sometimes. Never gone more than a day or two or three at most."

"Except this time." Cutler drinks some beer.

"A week went by," the big man says, "and I figured I better mail it. Package was all sealed and the address was on it. I walked across"—he jerks his chin toward the highway—"to the general store, there. They got a post office branch. And I shipped it off to him."

"Where to?" Cutler drinks. It is lousy beer.

"Oh, hell." The bullish shoulders lift and fall. "I don't know. I just poked it through the window, and Helen, she weighed it, and I paid her for the stamps. Hollywood, I guess. That's where they make movies."

"You didn't read the address?" Cutler says.

"None of my business," the man says.

"You waited a week. When did they find his body, then?"

"Maybe it was more than a week," the man admits uncomfortably. "Could have been ten days. His body? Oh, not long after that. Day or two at most."

"You didn't mail it till he was dead, did you?"

The man bows his head. "Well, truthfully, no. Shamed of myself. I always was a putter-offer. Used to drive Wilma crazy, God rest her. I had it back on my bench. Turned out he was dead, I felt awful. Run out and mailed it right away."

Cutler sets down his beer can and goes to the door. He pulls it open. Heat rushes in. He turns back. "The reason you don't know where that envelope was addressed to is that you can't read—isn't that right?"

The man winces. "Don't tell the whole world."

"Don't worry," Cutler says.

Pelletier turns cartwheels on the sand. He wears white cotton drawstring pants and that is all. Cutler counts the number of cartwheels. Six, seven, eight. Pelletier lets himself sprawl on the sand, and lies there on his back for a minute, panting. Then he scrambles up, and begins to turn flips on the sand. Leaning on the rail of the deck, Cutler counts again. Five, six, seven. Pelletier rests. He sits, this time, head resting on his knees. He breathes hard. The rise and fall of his shoulders tells Cutler that. Cutler calls out to him, and goes down the steps to the sand, and down the sand toward him. Pelletier has not looked up. Cutler stands in front of him.

"You found a coach," he says. "You're practicing."

Pelletier's head comes up slowly. He eyes Cutler in the late afternoon light as if he had never seen him before. He wipes sweat off his forehead with a palm. He pushes his hair back. "Stand down there," he says, and points.

Cutler blinks, shrugs, walks toward the surf. And Pelletier lands hard on his back, bearing him down. Pelletier is giving karate yells. The sides of his hands, his wrists, his elbows pummel Cutler. He digs a heel hard into Cutler's crotch and the pain is blinding and sickening. "Stop," Cutler gasps, and scrambles in the soft sand to get away. "What are you doing? Are you crazy?" Pelletier jumps on him and holds him flat on the sand under him, face down. He grabs Cutler's hair and yanks his head back. He says:

"Hoffy called me today. He left a script for me to read. Left it here with you, nights ago. You never said anything, you son of a bitch."

"Let go," Cutler gasps. "I can explain."

Pelletier does not let go. He pushes Cutler's face into the sand, rubs it in the sand. Cutler can't breathe. Pelletier says, "So explain. It better be good."

Cutler wrenches his head to the side. "Let me up."

And suddenly Pelletier gets off him. As if he had lost interest, he turns his back, bends, brushes sand off the cotton trousers. Aching, bruised, spitting sand, Cutler sits up. "I was trying to protect your career. It's a bad part, Chick. A kid who murders his whole family. You'd never get any other kind of role again. Pathological killers — all your life." Cutler paws sand off his face, rises. "I've got a beautiful script for you. Sympathetic. Chick, you want the public to love you, not cross the street when they see you coming."

"Fantasy," Pelletier says in a bored voice, and starts off up the sand toward the house. Shakily, Cutler follows. "How the hell long do you expect me to go on believing in that script? It's strictly smoke, Darryl, and you know it. You been blowing smoke up my ass so long, I need a chimney sweep." He mounts the deck, walks into the work room, and gazes around him. "Where is that script Hoffy brought?"

"I tore it up," Cutler says. "If you didn't want that to happen, you could have been here when Hoffy came." Cutler wants to stop his own mouth, but it keeps working. "Where were you that night, Chick?" His heart thuds, his breath comes hard. Pelletier turns slowly to look at him. Cutler tenses. To dodge, run, fight. But Pelletier doesn't attack. He smiles. The smile is unpleasant, but that is no surprise.

Pelletier says, "You know where I was. At Quinn's. We saw you from inside. From the bed. Stumbling around out there in the dark. You're pathetic sometimes, Darryl, you know that? What did you think you were going to do to us? I mean, I'm touched that you're acting like a stage mother about my career. But I'm no kid, Darryl. I never was. And what I do with Veronica is strictly my business, right?"

"I didn't bother you," Cutler says numbly.

"No. Instead, you came back here and tore up that script. So guess who the kid is. It's somebody in this room, and it isn't me."

"No. Mature people jump on other people's backs, and sit on them and rub their face in the sand."

Pelletier shrugs. "Act like a child, get treated like a child." He steps to the desk, picks up a red folder. "Is this the one you wrote? 'A Gold for Living'?"

"Isn't that what it says?" Cutler asks. " 'By Darryl Cutler'?" Pelletier grunts, flips over pages. Cutler says, "I was going to ask you to read it tonight. But, of course, you'll be spending the evening with Veronica."

"Not tonight." Pelletier tucks the script under his arm. "Old Phil is back. Just for a few days. Something about editing. The editor in Ankara screwed up. Istanbul? Turkey. He's a butcher. It's about a third of the picture. It's got to be cut all over again from scratch."

"And they want a kosher butcher," Cutler says. But the joke is automatic. He is stunned by his persistent good luck. "I'll run copies over to him tonight. He promised to read it."

"Approach with caution," Pelletier says. "I get Veronica a little crazy with my body and the way I fuck. She talks pretty wild sometimes. She could just lose control and tell Phil about her and me. And I'm your fault. And without him to plug it, what good is your script?"

"It's your script too," Cutler says.

Pelletier heads for the deck. "Hoffy's got a script for me. And it's already sold. I'm all right." His bare feet thump the stairs. "Do I get any supper tonight?" His voice fades upward in the fading light. "Do I ever get a drink?"

"Right now." Cutler hurries after him.

16

He lies on a bunk, sunlight from a porthole slanting above him. This boat is only half the size of Tony Baron's. The Dakota barn bleakness is missing here. The woodwork is handsome, the hull is tight. There is no creaking to remind him of barns creaking in prairie wind, to remind him of the loneliest time of his life. This boat skims the ocean, light and sleek and easy. It smiles at the power of the sea. This does not mean that Cutler smiles. He is bored and bitter. He remained on deck with Pelletier and Veronica while land was in sight. Drinking champagne. This is Pelletier's first time out in charge of the boat himself. A voyage to celebrate. But Cutler panics out of sight of land. So he is below and alone. He can hear them laughing in the cramped cockpit. He wishes Souza were up there. Even drunk.

For two weeks Souza was always up there, in a greasy yachting cap, a perpetual three-day growth of beard stubble, filthy dungarees, tank top. Souza sneered and snarled at Cutler because Cutler refused to be taught how to handle the boat, tiller, sails, ropes, anything. It was Pelletier's toy, and Pelletier could kill himself scrambling its tilting deck and climbing its swaying mast if he liked. Cutler wanted none of it. The only thing he likes about it are the high slim rails around the deck. They ease his fear of falling overboard. If he fell overboard, Pelletier might not think it was important to save him. Not that this boat rolls like Tony Baron's. It doesn't. This is because it has a shallow deadrise. Pelletier made a drawing of a cross section of the hull to show Cutler what deadrise means. But Cutler knows what it means. Something very different. And he doesn't want to think about it.

He turns his thoughts sharply from this boat, this morning. He wants to be happy. He returns to another morning weeks ago. Cold, foggy, early. He woke with a start to the shouting of his name. He knew the voice. It was Quinn's. Quinn's fist was beating on the kitchen door above. Jesus. Had Veronica lost her head and told the man she was sleeping with Pelletier? Cutler half fell out of the bed and groped in the half dark for his jeans on the floor. He tried to call out but not much sound came. He kicked into the pants.

"Coming, Phil." That was better.

"Move it," Quinn bellowed. "I've got a plane to catch."

Pelletier mumbled from the bed, "I'm not going to forget this, Darryl."

Cutler stumbled down the room, slid the door, tottered across the planks and staggered up the stairs, still half asleep and hung over from too much late brandy. Pelletier was drinking hard because he couldn't sleep with Veronica, and Cutler was keeping him company, hoping he might realize Veronica wasn't the only sex along this beach. Against hope. He lurched up the dim living room, dodging furniture, fumbled with locks, pulled open the door. "Sorry," he panted. "Something wrong?"

"Congratulations." Quinn rattled the screen. It was locked. Cutler's shaky fingers clicked the latch.

Quinn yanked the door wide, grabbed Cutler, and gave him a bear hug. "You sold your script, kid. Network, yet. How about that? You got yourself a winner."

"What?" Cutler couldn't take it in. "What?"

"Your script. I didn't have time to read it. Forgive me. Crazy trip. No time for anything. So I just handed it to Eddie Axelrod. My agent. How long has he had it? Four days? The deal is all lined up. Must be some script. He never worked that fast for me." Quinn squinted at his watch in the poor light. "Have to run. Look, you phone Eddie. He'll fill you in." Grinning, Quinn grabbed Cutler's dazed hand and pumped it. "Way to go, Darryl. Shows how wrong I can be. I didn't think you had it in you." And Quinn was out the door and jogging heavily for the cliff stairway and the white BMW waiting up there by the road, Veronica at the wheel. The man had almost reached the top of the stairs before Cutler came to his senses enough to shout thanks.

This is the moment when he wants to fall asleep on the sunny bunk, smiling. His eyes are closed, but sleep is not going to come. He is going to remember all of it, now that he has started. Not just the happy part, but also the part he hates to face. He ran downstairs and into the dim, sea-chilly bedroom. He threw himself on the bed with a whoop, and gathered Pelletier's warm sleepiness into his arms. Pelletier struggled.

"Hey, it's not even daylight yet. What the fuck is going on?" Cutler was chuckling, humming, plastering the kid's mouth, eyes, hair with kisses. "Will you cut that out? No sex, okay? I've got a bitch of a hangover, Darryl."

"It wasn't smoke," Cutler said. "It wasn't smoke, Chick."

Pelletier stopped moving. He peered sullenly into Cutler's face. "What are you talking about—the script?"

"The script. Exactly. That was Quinn at the door."

"I know who the son of a bitch was. I'll bet they heard him in Samoa." Pelletier moaned, pulled free, rolled away on the rumpled bedclothes. He hung his legs over the edge of the bed and slowly pushed himself to a sitting position, bent forward, elbows on knees, hands covering his face. He moaned again. "Christ, do I feel awful. You know what brandy does to me. Why do you let me drink brandy?"

"Never again, I promise." As if he or anyone could stop Pelletier from drinking gasoline if he wanted to. Cutler thumbed open the brass waist button of his jeans, ran down the zipper, peeled the jeans off, and kicked them away. On his knees on the bed, he pressed against Pelletier's back, put arms around him from behind, nuzzled the nape of his neck. His hands caressed Pelletier's chest and strayed down his flat belly. "The script is sold, Chick. Four days was all it took."

"No shit." Pelletier spoke as if it meant nothing.

"You wanted to be a star." Cutler's hand found Pelletier's genitals and gently squeezed. "You wanted to be in *People* magazine." Pelletier's cock stirred. "I promised to make it happen, didn't I? And I kept my promise."

"Yeah. Thanks." Pelletier lifted his head and found Cutler's mouth with his mouth. There was nothing indifferent about the kiss. For weeks, now, yes. But not this time. The kiss went deep, searching and urgent. Pelletier broke it with a small breathless laugh. He slipped out of Cutler's arms and lay back across the bed. "You want to make something else happen?"

"I thought you'd never ask," Cutler said.

Eddie Axelrod said, "I hate like hell to disappoint you." He was a bony man whose eyes swam like bewildered fish behind thick lenses. His office was two stories high, at the top of a tall building west of Beverly Hills. Trees grew in the office. Plants. Vines trailed from hanging pots. The two-story high window was like the window of a greenhouse, and the air was moist and smelled of earth like a greenhouse. "But no way can they use your friend."

Cutler was staring at the check Axelrod has just handed him in an envelope. The envelope had drifted to the floor. Cutler sat in a deep leather chair that faced Axelrod's desk. He held the check between thumb and forefinger of each hand and read the sum printed on it. Forty-five thouand dollars. It was nowhere near as big a check as the one the Japanese developers had given him for the land on which Moody's house stood. That was damned near a quarter million dollars. But this meant more. It meant fame. People would envy him and love him. For a minute, he didn't register what Axelrod had said. Then he looked up from the check and frowned.

Axelrod grimaced apology. "It's nothing personal." He held out hands that seemed to be all knuckles and were very, very clean. "They want a star. They can't go without a star. So it's going to be Nicky Wyatt, isn't it? What can I tell you? It's the picture business."

"He's dark," Cutler said. "He's too tall."

"He's signed." Axelrod held out across the desk the envelope that contained Pelletier's photographs. On top of the envelope lay the video cassette of Pelletier in those commercials. "I hated like hell to give in." Since Cutler made no move to take the envelope, the agent laid it down again. "I told them he was supposed to be small and fair, Kurt Thomas, Bart Connors—those little blond doll-boys. The public would know who the character was supposed to be. There's a high identification ratio working there." Axelrod paused for a second, liking the phrase he had made. He sighed, gave his head a shake. "They weren't buying. I can get your kid a part in the picture, but—"

"He has to be the star," Cutler said. "They promised."

"A handshake." Axelrod shrugged. "We can't prove it."

"That stinks," Cutler said. "Take it away from them."

"It's too late. If it isn't ready for the Olympics, who needs it? We sold them the property, Darryl. You signed the contract. Their lawyers would kill us. And if they didn't, we couldn't start over. It would be way too late."

"Shit," Cutler said. "Oh, shit."

The sun from the porthole shines hot into his face. He opens his eyes, flinches at the glare, gets off the bunk. He reads his watch. Time for lunch. In the neat little refrigerator in the neat little galley wait imported cheeses, pate, smoked pheasant. Cutler brings them out and with a knee shuts the refrigerator door. Up in the cockpit, Pelletier laughs. Clutching the cold food in his arms, Cutler stands, eyes shut, swaying slightly with the slight roll of the boat. The laughter stops. Cutler sets the food down, finds a knife in an elegantly beveled teakwood drawer, and begins to slice the pheasant.

It is too cold to eat out on the deck of the house, but they are eating there because that is where Pelletier wants to eat. The sky hangs heavy and dark with morning clouds, the sea is gray. Cold wind ruffles the feathers of the beach-running birds. There are no gulls. They know the first storm of the season is coming, and they have flown inland. Pelletier wears a bulky white sweater, a blue windbreaker, and he shivers as he shovels down fried potatoes, eggs, bacon, before they can get cold. He slurps coffee. Cutler watches him desolately. He can't eat. He is cold to the bone under his heavy woollen shirt and corduroy trousers. But it is dread of what is bound to happen today, tomorrow, soon that chills him more than the weather.

Up on the road shoulder a horn beeps, and Cutler's stomach tightens like a fist. The horn belongs to the mail jeep. The mailman is letting them know he has left something in the box. It is quiet enough so that the clash of the jeep's gears can be heard. Mouth crammed with food, Pelletier looks at Cutler. He mumbles, "Well, that's the mail. Are you going, or not?" He sucks up more coffee.

"I'm going." Numbly, Cutler rises and passes through the house, and out the kitchen door to climb the cliff stairs, pull down the door of the box, and find there a big gray envelope with the logo of the network in the corner. There is no other mail. Only this. He pulls it out and closes the mailbox and stands staring at the envelope. Behind him, cars whizz along the coast road. When trucks pass, the earth under his feet trembles. The wind blows harder, and his face and hands sting with the chill of it, and his eyes run. And then he realizes that this is not the wind's fault. He is crying. But he does nothing about it. He simply stands with the envelope in his hands and his eyes run and his nose runs. He knows this is the end of the world.

It's not the end of the world, his mother taunts inside his head. *The world will go right on turning, no matter what happens to one little boy.*

He wipes his face with a handkerchief, pushes the handkerchief back into a hip pocket, and starts down the stairs. Rain blows against him. He unbuttons the shirt and pushes the envelope inside and buttoning the shirt again hurries down and across sand already puddling with rainwater, and ducks into the house and slams the door. Pelletier comes to meet him, carrying the breakfast plates. He sets them on the counter and frowns.

"It didn't come?" he says. "It didn't come *yet?*"

Cutler could lie, couldn't he? The script is out of sight. He can take it someplace and hide it. But that is panic speaking. In another day or half day or hour the telephone will ring. Or Hoffy will come here, or Eddie Axelrod, or the producer, or the network people, anybody. Cutler mutely opens his shirt and slides the gray envelope out, and Pelletier snatches it from him. He rips it open, yanks the script out, reads the writing on the cover, and his smile dies. He stares at Cutler.

"What the hell does this mean? *Mr. Chick Pelletier.* Quote. *Danny.* Unquote. Darryl, I'm not dumb Danny, for Christ sake." His hands are trembling. Cutler has never seen him so pale. "I'm Hoyt. I'm the star of this picture, Darryl. I'm the star. You promised me."

"Yeah, well," Cutler mumbles, "they had to have a big name. Nicky Wyatt. Nicky Wyatt is going to play Hoyt, Chick. I'm sorry."

"No!" Pelletier shouts. "You promised me, Darryl." Now his face is red. "You said you'd never break a promise to me. You said you told them it had to be me, and they agreed. You lied, you rotten son of a bitch."

"They lied." Cutler turns away, goes to the burner deck, fills a mug with coffee from the glass maker there. "They shook my hand and they said, fine, you could be Hoyt. But now they've signed Wyatt, and Eddie says we can't do a damned thing about it."

Pelletier howls, "You didn't get it in writing?"

"They wouldn't have put it in writing," Cutler says. "They knew all along they had to have a big name actor."

"Bullshit." Pelletier throws the script. It misses Cutler, strikes a cupboard door, splays open face down on the shiny floor. "You didn't give a fuck about me. All you wanted was to sell your stupid script. What difference did it make if I got the part or not?"

"Wrong." Cutler picks up the script, lays it on a counter top. "I love you, I'd do anything for you, you know that. I trusted Eddie Axelrod. I figured he knew what he was doing. I shook their hands and signed the contract. I thought they'd keep their word."

"You're an asshole," Pelletier says.

"Danny's a good part, Chick," Cutler says.

"Fuck you," Pelletier says, and runs away down the room, out onto the rain-glazed deck, and down the stairs. Through the floor, from below, Cutler hears drawers slam, the rumble of a closet door. The rain patters on the skylight overhead. Cutler gathers up the breakfast plates and washes them at the sink. They steam. He dries them, puts them away. Pelletier carries cartons past, filled with his clothes. He sets the cartons beside the door, and looks at Cutler. "You better pray Hoffy still has that psycho boy part for me." He yanks open the door, picks up the cartons. "You better pray for that, Darryl." He kicks open the screen and carries the cartons out into the rain.

17

It was finding the dead hog in the ditch that started him praying. In far corners of fields where corn grew high and rustled in the hot, dry Dakota wind. In the creaking emptiness of the barn, where twine-laced seedcorn ears hung drying from the rafters like blue, gold, crimson banners, and field machinery stood rusting in the shadows. Among the silly chickens when they came running on their yellow legs to meet him with the pan of feed he brought them after breakfast. His prayers went up to God while they squawked and squabbled around his feet. And in his slope-ceilinged bedroom with the faded paper, where the summer heat came to stay when darkness crowded it indoors at night. He prayed to go home to Portland and the gentle rains.

The hog was bigger than a man. His uncle owned such hogs. Cutler was wandering alone toward the river. Not to fish or swim. But he imagined that the river went to Oregon. All rivers flowed to the sea— they had taught him that in school. This was the middle of the country. The river flowed west. So it had to be the Pacific ocean this one emptied into, didn't it? So he went and sat on a rock and watched the river flow. Sometimes he tossed into the current dry live-oak leaves or bits of bark, and watched the river take them, and wished it would take him too. But he was afraid of it. It would drown him. Still, he went there often.

And on his way, one morning he saw the great hog lying in the ditch. Hogs were lazy, that he knew. And the male ones bad tempered and dangerous, and the female ones too, when they had litters of little pigs. But lazy. So he thought this hog was asleep. He was alarmed, and crossed quickly to the far side of the road. Hogs were supposed to be penned. Cows could wander wide meadows. He brought the cows back to the barn from such a meadow every night, and took them out there every morning. There was nothing to driving cows. He used a cottonwood branch to touch them with if they started off in a wrong direction. But pigs? What was a hog doing way out here?

It disturbed him that it lay so motionless. He stood and watched it, frowning. He shrugged and walked on. Then he came back. He called to it. "Hey, wake up." It didn't stir. He took a step or two closer and shouted louder. No movement. Flies buzzed around the hog's snout and its closed eyes with their long lashes. He found a stone beside the road, backed off a good distance, and threw the stone at the hog. If it reared up and scrambled after him, he wanted a good head start. The stone struck the hog and bounced off. It made a drum sound. The hog lay still, and the stillness filled Cutler with misgiving.

He looked up and down the flat, straight road, hoping to see a pickup truck coming. Alfalfa stretched to the horizon. Wheat fields rippled. At the far edge of a field, a stand of cottonwoods winked silver in the wind. The sky was flawless blue. Somewhere far off a rooster crowed. A barnyard dog barked and was silent. Cutler was alone. He found a small branch in the weeds, crooked, and gray, and dry. He picked it up and, swallowing hard, forced himself step by step to cross the road. He poked the hog. Nothing. He poked it harder. Its bloated hide split, and horrible, stinking liquid gushed out. Cutler screamed, dropped the branch, and ran up the road, stumbling, gagging, sick with horror. And it was after this that he began to pray.

He had never prayed before. He had seen it done only once. At a funeral to which his mother, smelling strongly of perfume, and wearing a new black dress, had dragged him. He doesn't remember why, if he ever knew. It was the one and only time he was ever in a church. He remembers it as cavernous, cold, and damp, with surfaces of hard, varnished wood. The day was rainy—what day was not?—and the light inside the church was murky. The stained glass windows showed muddy colors. Candlelight shone feebly on an altar draped in white satin with gold embroidery. A gold crucifix on the altar caught the candle light and glinted. A priest in white and gold robes stood over a gunmetal coffin blanketed with flowers, and read from a white prayerbook. In the pews, hinged benches rattled down, and the dozen mourners in their rain-damp coats, knelt and prayed aloud.

But death was not white robes and flowers and candles on an altar and beautiful words from a prayerbook. Death was the carcass of a huge hog swollen with putrescence in a ditch by a deserted country road and swarming with flies. This came as a shock to Cutler. He was frightened. He never walked that road again. He found another route across fields to the river, and as often as possible through farm yards, where he could hear human voices.

But he was not safe. He found a coyote bitch, breasts swollen with milk, hanged with all her pups to a barbwire fence. Once he saw a dead crow nailed to the door of an abandoned shed, white bones showing through the feathers. He saw his aunt twist the heads off chickens when company was coming on a weekend. A mare dropped a dead foal in a field. He stumbled on jackrabbits stiff in death, long legs caught in traps.

His uncle was away from the farm one day, and when he came home talked all through supper about the slaughtering of lambs he had helped with at a neighboring farm. Death was all around Cutler here. It did no good to write to his mother that he wanted to come home. She had troubles of her own and his had never been real to her, anyway. *Stop whining,* she said. *Nobody likes a whiner.* He could die in a ditch like the hog, and she wouldn't care. She wouldn't even poke him with a stick to try to wake him up. He didn't know where to write to his father. If he complained to his aunt and uncle, they would tell his mother, and she would punish him. So he prayed. But it did no good. Not till summer reached its frostbitten end did money come for a bus ticket to take him home, away from that place of death. And by then he had given up praying.

You better pray, Darryl. The admonition, coming from Pelletier, surprised hell out of Cutler. He is walking the beach in cold and fog now, hands in pockets, shoulders hunched, nothing to do, nowhere to go, no one to talk to. And he keeps hearing

Pelletier warning him to pray, and wondering about it. It is probably folksay, picked up when Pelletier was a kid. If he is anything, he is Catholic. On top of the highest hill in Montreal, Pelletier has told Cutler, stands a church with a gold dome. Penitents crawl on their knees up three hundred fifty steps to get there. Pelletier sneered. Maybe his frizzy, gin-soaked whore of a mother sneered too, but Cutler bets she used the phrase. Mothers stock our mouths. The kid was angry. Her phrase jumped out. *You better pray, Darryl.*

Pelletier has been gone for weeks. But not far. He is living with Veronica at Quinn's. The third or fourth day after he left, Cutler wondered if he was wrong. He had to know. It was reckless, but if they saw him and jeered, so what? He drove past Quinn's. Sure enough, the Porsche stood by the mailbox in the rain, alongside Veronica's Alfa under a blue plastic cover, and Phil's white BMW under no kind of cover at all. Cutler drove home. The rain wept monotonously on the roof. The weight of breakers shook the house. He didn't know what to do with himself. He watched television, read, walked the beach in rain gear. He waited.

It's no use waiting, his mother said inside his head. *He'll never be back.* For a while, Cutler had missed his handsome, smiling father, and moped. Sometimes he sat out on the cracked steps that went down from the yard to the public sidewalk, and for hours gazed along the street, waiting for his father to come hurrying up the hill from the bus stop. Or if it rained, he leaned his elbows on the windowsill and stared out, breath fogging the glass, waiting for his father to climb the walk to the porch. *Find something to do,* his mother said. *He's not coming back. He doesn't care about you. Why should you care about him?* Cutler pretended as best he could that he didn't care, but in his small bed at night, he cried.

In his large bed at night here in the empty house on the beach, he didn't cry. He didn't sleep, either. Not easily, not soon. Usually not till daybreak. In the dark, even when he could forget Pelletier, he feared to close his eyes. Moody would come back. How next? Last time he'd been a small boy in dandelion yellow rompers, seated weeping on the floor under an old black castiron sewing machine, the shadowy figure of his long dead mother looming over him. Whimpering, shivering, Cutler switched on the lamp. Nothing. No one. Or the boy from Portland would come back, walking down the room toward him, the big helmet shadowing his face, and moans coming from him too deep for any human child to give.

Cutler waited for gray, rainy dawn. Then, one morning, sky and sea were blue. The storm had traveled on. He showered and shaved and drove the curved shelves of white street above the Quinn house, peering down, hungry for a glimpse of Pelletier. And he got it. His heart nearly stopped. The kid lay naked on the redwood chaise of Quinn's deck. He wore sunglasses. A tumbler of orange juice was in his hand. He was watching Veronica fuss with a jug of green fluid over planters and flowerpots. She wore a man's shirt. Its tails hung to her knees, but it was open, and she was naked under it.

Cutler braked the Celica and looked around. Were they crazy? Windbreaking panels cut off view of the deck from the beach. But anyone else could see them.

Except that there was no one. The neighborhood was empty, quiet. Eucalyptus trees threw lacy shadows on roofs, decks, pools. His car was the only car here. Gulls circled slowly. He was the only watcher. He looked down again. Veronica sat astride Pelletier's narrow hips, upright, head thrown back, eyes closed, mouth open. Her teeth gleamed. Cutler imagined he could hear her laughing. A gust of wind spread the shirt like a sail. Her neat breasts stood out. How trim her little belly was. Pelletier's cock was inside her. He stretched lazily and grinned. She began to move gently up and down. The glass of orange juice stood on the deck. Her foot nudged it. It overturned and rolled. A stain spread on the planks. Sick and blind, Cutler fumbled with the gear shift, and drove noisily away.

He walked the sunstruck beach and tried to forget. He read, he stared at television, and tried to forget. He drank to forget, and when the drink finally stunned him, he went to bed. But oblivion never lasted more than three or four hours. Then he groped out in the dark for Pelletier beside him in the bed and didn't find him. The sheets were cold. When this happened one night too many, he groaned, pounded the bed with his fists, and wept. He wept hard and for a long time. It left his ribs and belly muscles sore. Next morning, when he glowered at himself in the bathroom mirror, his eyes were swollen almost shut. Beard-stubbly, in a grubby T-shirt he'd worn for days and nights, he looked like a dying wino. He stank. This was stupid.

He cranked the shower handles and stepped into steam and stinging spray. He stayed a long time, lathering, rinsing the filth away, lathering again, rinsing again. He washed his hair. He shaved with a new razor. He scrubbed his teeth hard. In fresh clothes, he climbed the sunny deck stairs. His legs were shaky. His stomach was queasy, but in the dusty kitchen he cooked an omelet. When had he last eaten? He peered at empty chili cans. Dear God. He forced a few bites of omelet down with strong, hot coffee, but he couldn't finish it. If he tried, he would vomit.

He threw the cans away. Dirty dishes were stacked in the sink. He washed these, sponged off counter and stove tops. Soiled clothes strewed the bedroom. He stuffed them into a hamper. He changed the sweaty sheets and blankets on the bed. He ran the vacuum, downstairs and upstairs. He stacked magazines and books and tape boxes where they belonged, wiped table tops and brushed dust from lampshades. The three big panes of plateglass at the room's end were foggy with blown sea spray, but he was tiring, and that was a big job. What the hell—he was only bringing home some trick from the Sea Shanty. How critical was he going to be? And who cared if he was? A haircut was more important. Cutler found his keys, shrugged into a jacket, locked the house, and climbed to the highway.

There was the mailbox. When had he last checked it? He couldn't remember. He checked it now. Envelopes crammed it, magazines, advertising folders. Shuffling through the stack, he frowned. Three letters were directed to Pelletier. That was new. When he was still checking the box, he'd never found anything for Pelletier. He squinted in the sunlight to read the postmarks. Yesterday. Day before. What did it mean? It had to mean Pelletier used to come over here every day and pick up what was his. Cutler felt a pang. He could have climbed up here and seen him. They could have talked. Cutler could have said—what? He frowned again. Why had the kid suddenly stopped coming?

At the Quinn place, the Alfa and the BMW were parked beside the mailbox, but where was the Porsche? Cutler went down to the small front deck of the Quinn place with its stone lantern. Jazz music reached him through the open French doors. He pressed a bell button and stepped inside. Veronica came from somewhere in a long, striped terrycloth robe, a towel around her hair, and stood far down the room, staring at him.

"What do you want?" Her voice was cold.

Cutler lifted the letters. "Chick's mail. Where is he?"

She made an impatient face, went away again. The music stopped. She reappeared. "He's working. They started shooting three days ago. Location stuff, where the boy runs away, and they track him down in the mountains, or something."

"How far away? Does he come home nights?"

"What do you care? When he does come home, it won't be to you. I wish you wouldn't come here, Darryl. If you want to leave his mail, leave it. But don't hang around."

Cutler felt his face grow hot. He laid down the envelopes and turned away. And turned back. "I just thought if he was only here nights, it would be safer for you both. I mean, fucking out there on the deck in broad daylight—the neighbors are going to see you, sooner or later."

"You really are a charmer." From a coffee table

with a square of mirror on it smeared with white powder she picked up cigarettes and lighter. "Creeping around, spying. Do you have any redeeming social value, Darryl?"

"Why won't the neighbors tell Phil?" Cutler said.

"Because the neighbors mind their own business." The cigarette smoked now, and she laid down pack and lighter. "The neighbor on the north, Mr. Bianchi, brokers narcotics. The neighbor in back has a fleet of Cessnas to fly money down for laundering in the Caribbean. The neighbor on the south pirates video cassettes." She came toward Cutler now. It was always a shock how young she was. Yet she seemed ages older than he. "Did you think honest, hard-working, God-fearing people could afford to live in a neighborhood like this? Chick is right about you— you're stupid."

Cutler said stiffly, "Why won't I tell Phil?"

"Because Chick wouldn't forgive you." She brushed past him, stepped out on the deck, where the light had changed. He went to the door and peered upward. Dark clouds were riding in, covering the sun. The wind grew chilly. Veronica crouched by a planter where a fern showed dead fronds. She snipped them off one by one with her nails, cigarette held in a corner of her child-pretty mouth. "It wouldn't get you Chick back."

"He doesn't give a damn for you," Cutler said. "He just wants to live off your alimony when you split with Phil."

"I'm not going to split with Phil," she said.

"You will if I tell him. He'll kick you out."

"It won't be the gas chamber," she said. She didn't look up at him. She laid the brittle brown fronds tidily beside her on the deck. He couldn't catch his breath. He gaped at her, at the curls of damp blond hair at the nape of her neck beneath the edge of the towel. His voice came out a croak. "What did you say?"

She gathered up the dead fronds. "You murdered that sick old man you lived with. Stewart Moody. You pushed a pillow down on his face and suffocated him. Chick told me." She got to her feet. "He saw you." Her smile was serene. "So you're not going to say anything to anybody about anything, are you?" She brushed past him again, and walked purposively down the long, sea-lit room to disappear once more. Water splashed in a sink or basin. She came back without the cigarette, rubbing her hands down the robe to dry them. She raised her lovely brows. "You still here?"

"Chick is lying to you," Cutler said. "I never killed anybody in my life."

"You don't have screaming nightmares? About a little boy on a bicycle? You didn't kill him with your car? Is Chick making that up too?"

"It's how he treats people who love him," Cutler said. "Lies about them. You'd better watch out for him."

"I guess we'd all better watch out for each other," she said, "hadn't we?"

He only stared at her. She was small and fragile. They were alone here. It would be easy to kill her. And he would like to do that. He hadn't wanted to kill the bicycling boy. He hadn't wanted to kill Moody. But he would love to snap her neck, to stop her smirk forever. Pelletier would come back to him, if she were dead. What was the matter? Her smile faded. She was watching him distrustfully. She took a step backward. Had he spoken? He didn't think he had spoken. His thoughts must be showing in his face. He turned and left. He wanted to run — she wasn't the only one afraid of Darryl Cutler right now. He didn't run. He walked across the little deck that had begun to spot with raindrops, and slowly climbed the stairs to the street. He was going to get his hair cut.

18

Rain lashes the glass door of the laundromat. He stands inside the door, smoking a cigarette, the fat, warm weight of a green plastic trash bag of clean wash leaning against his leg. It will soon be midnight. He is alone here, except for the owner, a muscular, middle-aged Japanese in a jumpsuit, who is tinkering with the soap vending machine. When he gets it fixed and puts his tools away in a back room, he will want to lock up. Midnight is closing time. Cutler is hoping for a break in the rain by then.

He waited for a break in the rain all day, the bag slumping ready beside the kitchen door. No break came. He waited until half past ten at night. The rain still fell. The storm has stalled on this stretch of coast—so say the weather reports. But he had no clean underwear, no clean sheets. He brings home a new bed partner nearly every night now. They let him forget Pelletier, they keep the ghosts away. So he has to have clean stuff. So he drove here at last through the pouring rain. And now the owner replaces the enamel and glass front of the vending machine, and Cutler must drive home through the pouring rain.

He pulls the door open. Rain rushes in on a cold wind. He shivers, drops his cigarette and steps on it, picks up the bag, and lunges, head down, into the night. The empty parking lot reflects colored lights from shopping center signs. There are wide puddles, which the rain pockmarks. Cutler splashes through the puddles at a clumsy run, the bulky bag bumping his leg. Water soaks into his shoes, soaks the legs of his corduroys, and makes them heavy and clammy. He swears at the awkwardness of his fingers with the car keys. At last he gets the hatchback open, and heaves the bag inside. He slams down the hatchback, and fights with the key in the driver's door. He ducks inside, yanks the door shut, and shivers again. He is drenched. He wants a hot shower.

From the deserted coast road littered with rocks washed down from bluffs, he glances through the streaming side window of the car at the modest red neon sign of the Sea Shanty, tucked back in its fold of hills, and nearly obscured by the shaggy eucalyptus trees. Yearning tugs him, but he does not turn off. Tonight, in such bad weather, the place won't have customers enough to matter. One of them might be beautiful. That can happen any time. But Cutler is not going to chance it. Tonight, after his shower, he is going to fix himself a tall glass of hot whiskey, honey, and lemon. Then he is going to turn up the electric blanket, and sleep. Alone.

If anything, the wind is stronger, the rain heavier when he reaches the road shoulder where he parks above his house. Before he leaves the car, he rummages a flashlight out of the glove box. But its batteries are almost dead. It shines only feebly on the white paint of the stairs down which he hauls the bag of clothes. It flickers and threatens to quit before he reaches the sand. But it still has life enough to shine on a huddled figure at the back door, before he stumbles over it. The figure feebly unfolds and stands. It is Pelletier.

"Where the fuck have you been?" he says. The wind whipping the rain against the roof and sides of the house is loud, and Pelletier's voice is hoarse, scarcely a whisper. He coughs. It is a horrible sound, like the ripping of canvas. "I'm dying out here."

"You sound like it." Cutler nudges him out of the way so he can unlock the door. He pushes the door, and puts an arm around Pelletier, and guides him inside. He switches on the lights. "What happened to your keys?" He drops the green bag, and closes the door, closes out the storm. Pelletier hunches on a stool at the breakfast bar, clutching himself and shuddering.

"I forgot them," he wheezes, and coughs again, holding both hands to his mouth. "And I was down here before I discovered that. And she was gone. She brought me."

"I wondered where your car was. Why?"

"I couldn't drive. I'm too sick." A puddle has formed around the feet of Pelletier's stool. In his wet clothes, he gets off the stool and staggers into the kitchen area. "I need a drink. Darryl, this is very bad."

"I can see that." Cutler pours whiskey into a glass and pushes it at him. He fills a kettle at the tap, and sets the kettle on the stove. He switches on the burner. "Get those wet clothes off, will you?"

Pelletier gulps the whiskey. He nods, sets the glass down, and begins struggling with his jacket. He lets his arms fall, and looks bleakly at Cutler. He shakes his head. "I can't. I'm too weak." And he drops to his knees, falls forward, face down on the floor. Cutler kneels. He helps him sit up, propped against cupboards. His clothes are cold to the touch, but he is not cold. Heat pours from him. "I'm sick, Darryl. Jesus, I'm so sick."

Cutler wants to cry. He is frightened, but he is also happy. Pelletier is back. He works at peeling the jacket off him, the shirt, the T-shirt under it. All are soaked. He scrubs Pelletier's wet hair with the T-shirt. "You mean you were already sick, and that bitch came and dumped you here in the rain?"

Pelletier's eyes are closed. He shakes his head and mumbles. "Why should she get out of the car and get soaked too? She didn't know you weren't home."

"Cunt," Cutler says. "Can you lift your ass? Let's get those pants off, get you into a hot shower."

"Can't stand up for it," Pelletier whispers.

"Hot tub, then." Cutler unfastens Pelletier's belt and drags his pants down, his little red shorts. They won't go over the hightop shoes. The laces are wet and the knots hard to undo. He curses, gets a knife from a drawer, and cuts the laces, pulls the shoes off, the socks, the pants and shorts. He kicks the sodden clothes aside, fetches a raincoat, wraps it around the shuddering Pelletier, and picks him up the way he used to pick up Moody. He carries him down the room. The kid has lost a lot of weight.

"Not out in the rain again." Pelletier's head lies on Cutler shoulder. His mouth is close to Cutler's ear or Cutler wouldn't hear him, he speaks so weakly. "No more rain, damn it."

"It will only take a minute." Cutler slides open the glass panel. The wind-driven rain slaps them, and Cutler catches his breath, it is so cold. He rolls the panel shut and makes for the stairs, hair streaming in his eyes. He has to take the stairs carefully. He hasn't put on lights out here. No light shines from below. He feels his way with his feet in their soggy shoes. He carries the whimpering kid straight to the bathroom. The ceiling holds a radiant heat element. The walls hold hot air blowers. He sets the kid on the closed toilet, takes the drenched raincoat off him, wraps him in big, thick towels, switches on the radiant heat, the blowers. Pelletier clutches himself, huddling over, moaning. With that fever, why doesn't he sweat? His breathing rasps. Cutler says, "How could she let this happen?"

"Not her fault," Pelletier mumbles. "My idea. Bad cold. Just wanted to be left alone."

"Wonderful." Cutler opens the medicine cabinet. A thermometer should be here somewhere. He often had to check Moody's temperature. He wipes the thermometer with a square of cotton soaked in rubbing alcohol. The old motions return mechanically. He stands over Pelletier. "Look up. We have to take your temperature."

"And it got worse and worse," Pelletier wheezes, "and she wanted to take me to a hospital. She'd pay. And I said"—the coughs come again, wracking him—"how was she going to explain the check to Quinn? 'Forget the hospital,' I said. 'I'll be okay. Just let me rest a few more days'." His breathing is labored. It reminds Cutler of Moody's near the end. The kid can't seem to get enough air. "Only I wasn't okay, was I? And tonight she got really frantic."

"She was afraid you'd die on her," Cutler says.

"No, no. She went to the phone to call an ambulance. I wouldn't let her. Quinn would find out. I said to bring me here. You'd know what to do. You knew how to look after sick people." Pelletier coughs again, clutching his chest. "Where's my whiskey?"

The racket of his coughing ricochets off the shiny surfaces of the bathroom. The bathroom is hot now. But the boy doesn't sweat. Cutler can't figure why this is, and it scares him.

"Temperature first." He sets the thermometer in Pelletier's mouth, and reads his watch. "I'll fix the whiskey and be right back. Don't touch that, okay?"

Dismally, Pelletier nods. He coughs softly, with the thermometer in place. It is still in place when Cutler, wet and cold again, returns with a tall glass where whiskey swims thickly with honey, lemon juice, hot water. An old remedy from his mother. Supposed to make you sweat. Cutler sets the glass beside the wash basin, takes the thermometer, holds it to the light to read it. He moans inside. A hundred four, nearly a hundred five. He pushes Pelletier's hair back, lays a hand on his forehead. Dry and hot. He puts the glass in Pelletier's hand. "Drink that. There's no heater in my car. I'll call an ambulance."

"I'm scared of hospitals," Pelletier whispers.

"I don't want you to die," Cutler says. "I love you."

"Yeah," Pelletier says dully. "Okay."

"Drink that," Cutler says, and goes to phone.

Pelletier is unconscious when the ambulance arrives in the dark and the rain. He stays that way for thirty-six hours in intensive care at a hospital in Santa Monica. The storm keeps on. Cutler spends his days at the hospital, and through a big window at the end of a corridor watches the storm, the rain-glazed traffic, the blowing, dripping trees, the people in raincoats, hurrying along glassy sidewalks, trying to hang

195

onto gaudy umbrellas. He stays as late as the rules permit, then drives home through the wind and the rain.

The telephone rings, but he doesn't answer it. It will be Veronica for Pelletier. Why doesn't she come over? Is she that frightened of him? He hopes so. But maybe it is only the weather that keeps her indoors. It kept her from helping Pelletier down the stairs in back here on the night she dropped him. She wouldn't get out of her car. Cutler smiles at the ringing of the telephone in the cold dark, turns over in the warm bed, and goes back to sleep.

On the third day, Pelletier is out of intensive care, in a room of his own. He seems tired, but Cutler is allowed in for five minutes to smile at him under his clear plastic oxygen tent. "You're going to be all right," he says.

"Where's Veronica?" Pelletier's voice is still weak.

Cutler pretends surprise. "Hasn't she been here?"

Pelletier's eyes fall shut, flutter open. "You didn't tell her, did you? She doesn't even know I'm here."

"She doesn't care, Chick. She never even phoned."

Pelletier seems to drift off to sleep. Cutler waits and watches him. He is terribly pale, and the bones stand out in his face. His eyes seem to have sunk in their sockets. He could be dead. This thought shocks Cutler. His fingers fumble at the stiff plastic of the tent. Then Pelletier looks at him again. "But you did tell her?"

"I went to the house in the rain and I told her. She made faces. She doesn't like hearing about illness. Sick people disgust her, Chick." Cutler has stolen this from a character in Irv Liebowitz's script.

"And, baby, she isn't going to divorce Quinn. Never. She told me."

Pelletier's eyes close again. "You're a liar."

On the fifth day, the storm moves on. Tatters of cloud cross the sun now and then, but as the hours pass, the sky clears. The sky is gloriously blue. The same blue is now in Pelletier's eyes, the same clarity. The oxygen tent is gone. He more or less sits up, propped on pillows in the hospital bed. He still looks frail, but when they bring him food, he eats. Hungrily. All of it, while Cutler watches and smiles. The waddling black woman in starchy green uniform who comes to collect the lunch tray with its empty dishes chuckles:

"Can't keep a good man down."

"You have to keep trying," Pelletier says.

She doesn't understand what he means by that, but she laughs happily as she waddles out to dump the tray into her cart and wheel it rattling on down the hall. Pelletier's face, which has a little color in it today, stiffens. He tilts his head at the stand beside the bed. A moss green telephone sits there.

"All the conveniences," Cutler says.

"I phoned Veronica this morning," Pelletier says. "Why do you always lie to me, Darryl? It's stupid, you know? You never went there, you never told her I was here. She rang your phone day and night, and you never answered."

"I was here day and night," Cutler says. "Ask anyone."

"She left a note on your door."

"In the wind, in the rain? Be serious. She had your key. Why didn't she leave the note inside? She's the one who's lying, Chick. Wake up." He gestures at the room. "Where are the flowers, the fruit, the latest bestseller? Where is she? If she cares so much about you, when you phoned, why didn't she come running?"

"Quinn gets home today," Pelletier says.

The Porsche is parked in its old place on the road shoulder above his house. It has stood out in bad weather and shows it. Cutler tries the doors. Locked. He finds the cartons of Pelletier's clothes — most of them in need of a wash — standing on the breakfast bar by the surfer figurine. A manila envelope lies on top of one of the cartons. It holds Pelletier's wallet, bank book, keys. Good. He wants to take the Porsche tomorrow morning to bring Pelletier home from the hospital. Home. Here. Quinn's timing has been perfect once again.

Smiling at his luck, Cutler carries the cartons downstairs. He stuffs the dirty underwear and socks into the hamper, lays the few clean ones in the drawers Pelletier emptied weeks ago, hangs jackets and jeans in the closet on the hangers Pelletier stripped them off of weeks ago. He drives the Porsche to be washed and waxed. In the time this takes, he hikes along the highway to the shopping center, and rolls a glittering cart down the shiny supermarket aisles, filling the cart with the makings of great meals for Pelletier. It is forbidden to take the carts away from the parking lot but he doesn't care. He wheels it jittering along the gravel road shoulder to the car-wash and the Porsche.

The next morning, when he drives into the hospital parking lot, he glimpses Hoffy pushing out the doors of the building with two other men. The fresh morning sunlight gleams off Hoffy's silver hair. He wears a pale sports jacket and pale slacks. The wind flutters these on his tiny frame. One of the men with him wears a dark business suit and carries an attache case. The other wears cowboy boots, cowboy hat, Levis, sheepskin vest, dark glasses. Cutler loses sight of them while he drives up and down, trying to find a parking slot. He locates one at last, gets the clothes he has brought for Pelletier out of the back, and heads for the hospital doors, but Hoffy and friends have vanished.

They have left behind flowers—a shopful. The air of Pelletier's room is damp with their sweetness. Cutler's smile drops when he steps inside. Pelletier's bed is not cranked up. It is flat. He lies with his back to the door, blanket pulled up over his head. Cutler's heart gives a thump. What's wrong? Is the kid sick again? Cutler drops the clothes on a chair and gently shakes Pelletier's shoulder. It is even more wasted than when the kid came here. It will be a while before he is himself again. A week's more bed rest, the doctors have said, and two weeks of very restricted activity. A little at a time.

"Hey," Cutler says, "I've come to take you home."

"The sons of bitches." Pelletier doesn't move.

"They brought you a lot of flowers," Cutler says.

"It won't help them. I'm going to sue their ass." Pelletier turns over. It is a sudden move. He glares up at Cutler. "You know what they did? Kicked me off the picture. They say it's in the fine print. It's automatic. You don't show up, you're canned."

"But you got sick. Illness or accident. That has to be in there too."

"Yeah, well, I was sick too long, wasn't I?" Pelletier struggles to sit up. It is hard for him. "They shot around me for a week. Then they hired another actor."

"But it wasn't your fault," Cutler says.

"It was their fault," Pelletier says. "They made me sick, running me up and down that lousy creek in that godforsaken canyon, up to my ass in water, falling down half the time. Three days of that, Darryl. And it was cold up there. I mean cold. Then do I get to dry off? Oh, no. I have to hide in my stupid soaking wet clothes in a God damn cave. It will be about twenty seconds of film, all right? You know how long it takes that fucking phony cowboy to shoot twenty seconds of film? They made me sick, Darryl. And I'm going to sue their ass."

"It was a bad picture. You're better off out of it."

"Whose side are you on?" Pelletier says.

"I've brought your clothes." Cutler picks them up. "Come on. I'll help you dress. Let's get you out of here. You'll feel better when you're home."

19

The crate is too big to get down the staircase from the road where three strong men have unloaded it from a big gold delivery van. They shift the crate off the lift at the rear of the van, then walk to the cliff top to study the narrowness of the stairs. They dolly the crate to the stair head, balancing it cautiously on wheels that are too small. They stand it on the gravel. They could get it down by holding it high, but it is too heavy for that.

"How much of it is packing?" Cutler asks. "If you take it out of the crate, can you get it down?" It has to go down. Pelletier has asked for it. He is waiting below, lying on the couch, where he demands to be during the hours when he isn't sleeping — and even during some when he is. "Maybe the set itself isn't so bulky."

"We suppose to unpack it in the house." The doubter is a tall, heavy-set black man with gray in his hair. He looks around at the beach, the road, the empty hills. "Not suppose to unpack it outdoors."

A young Mexican with smooth terracotta skin and long, dark eyelashes kicks the crate gently with a workshoe. All three men wear gold coveralls with GIANT TV appliqued in blue and white across the backs. "I think it is mostly packing." He grins, playing. "I think the set is about this wide." He holds his hands a foot apart. The third man is the largest and youngest, but paunchy, his blond hair thinning.

It blows in the breeze. "What the hell," he says. "If it's the only way to get it down, what the hell?"

They shift the crate off the dolly and apply crowbars to it. The top shrieks up. Nails squeal. A side falls away. Styrofoam packing looks like tamped snow inside. They loosen cleats and packing, and pull these out. They slide the set out, unwind its clear plastic swaddling, and stand sizing it up in the morning sunlight. Its glossy wood finish glows. It stands chest high and a yard wide. The brown kid grins at Cutler again, showing big, handsome, even teeth. He is flirting.

"What did I say? Thirteen inch. Black and white."

The others toss the crowbars into the truck and come back and stand beside the set, arms hanging. Their expressions do not reassure Cutler. The black one steps to the top of the staircase and looks down. "Seem like two of us got to handle it," he says. "Ain't room for three on these here stairs." He nods at the big youngster. "You get down halfway, and take over for me when I get there. I'll go on down then, and take over at the bottom, get it in the house." He looks at the brown kid. "You take the top."

And that is how it is done. Cutler watches from above, hand to mouth, afraid they will drop it. Pelletier makes matters worse. He comes out in his bathrobe and pajamas, shuffles close to the stairs, and stands gawking up. If they drop it, it will fall on him. He is slow on his feet these days. He won't be able to dodge. Cutler wants to order him back out of the way, but the kid is so eager. He hasn't smiled once since he came home from the hospital, and now he is smiling, and Cutler won't spoil that. There is no need. They get the machine down safely, dolly it into the house, and install it where the other television set stood, which Cutler earlier shoved, heaved, and skidded down to the bedroom. The new one has a forty inch screen.

"You won't like it," Cutler said. "It'll be blurry."

"Get one that isn't blurry," Pelletier said. "Darryl, you've got a quarter of a million dollars. What good is it, if you can't even buy a television set that isn't blurry?"

The boat took half that quarter million. Taxes bit deep into the balance. Horses. Cards. Roulette wheels. Pelletier's hospital bills were horrendous. But Cutler doesn't say this. He wants the kid to go on believing he is rich. The picture is blurry, but luckily Pelletier doesn't care. It is big, therefore it must be good. He hugs himself in glee. "Hey," he laughs, "this is more like it. Didn't I tell you it wouldn't be blurry?"

"I have to go to the market," Cutler says, folding a list he has pencilled on a slip of paper, and sliding it into a pocket. "Will you be all right? What about the bathroom? I don't know how soon I can get back. I have to go to the bank too. And the dry cleaners."

"That's okay," Pelletier says. He can't manage the stairs. Down, yes. Back up, no. Not yet. Only partway. So, as with Moody, Cutler carries him. *Do you like carrying people? Not people. You.* Pelletier says, "If I have to, I can pee in the sink."

"Sorry I won't be here to watch," Cutler says, and goes out and climbs the stairs to the road, and finds that the truckers have left the crate behind.

Another storm comes, harder and colder than the

first two. The moon is full, and the tides are high. This makes for big waves and they pile up and come crashing down much farther up the beach than common. Cutler worries, and in several thicknesses of sweaters and a raincoat and a canvas hat, stands out on the deck watching the waves making for his house, and breaking and falling back only meters away. Pelletier is oblivious. He lies and stares rapt at his new toy. When there are no pictures scheduled he wants to see, or only those he has already seen, he has cassettes. And when he has exhausted these, he sends Cutler through the rain for more. Cutler worries that while he is rummaging for titles in the shops, the sea will take the house, and Pelletier with it. Pelletier is so young. The notion that he could die only lately struck Cutler, and it haunts him.

The weather clears, and slow walks along the beach begin. The careful way Pelletier steps over the driftwood left on the sand by the storm makes it hard to credit that he was turning cartwheels and backflips out here only a couple of months ago, all sweat-gleaming muscle. Half naked. Now Cutler bundles him in bulky clothes. He must not catch cold, and the wind off the ocean has a raw edge to it. They walk only a short way at first, using a stand of sharp rocks out in the water as a marker. Still, Pelletier breathes hard by the time they reach the house again, and climbing the steps to the deck is not easy. He is even willing to remain below, lying on the bed for a while. Ordinarily, he refuses to use the bed until night. He is pale, his eyes closed. Cutler lays a blanket over him.

Pelletier says, "Let's skip the walk tomorrow."

This alarms Cutler and he broods about it. But the next morning, Pelletier wants to walk, and is noticably better at it. By the end of the week, they are walking twice as far, and Pelletier can climb the steps to the upper deck with only a little boost from Cutler. On Sunday, he rattles open the padlock on the locker under the stairs and brings out the volleyball. They toss it back and forth between them four or five times before Pelletier shakes his head and turns away. The ball bounces down the steps onto the sand.

"No more." Pelletier leans back against the deck rail, panting, head hanging. "Tomorrow. Maybe. Shit."

But doggedly, the next morning, after their walk, he gets the ball out again, and this time there is a little force to his tosses. And soon he is able to put enough strength behind them so the ball stings Cutler's hands when he catches it. Pelletier likes that, and grins. He likes to see Cutler wince.

Cutler likes to see him eat. He fixes massive breakfasts of three or four eggs, fried potatoes, steak, sausage, bacon, pancakes, biscuits, cornbread. No combination and no quantity daunts Pelletier. He eats what is set before him and asks for more. All of his meals are big, and slowly he gains weight.

One morning, Cutler wakes to slapping sounds he can't identify. The room shakes. Is it an earthquake? He sits up in bed, squinting. Pelletier, in a yellow sweat suit, is skipping rope at the glassed end of the bedroom.

"Where did you get that?" Cutler says.

"From a little girl, who else?" Pelletier puffs. "Alone

on the beach. Said if she didn't hand it over, I'd strangle her with it. Buy me a Nautilus, okay?"

He does not mean a mollusk or a submarine. He means exercise equipment, weights, pulleys, everything Nautilus makes. Cutler orders it. Before it arrives, the morning walks become morning jogs. This may be good for Cutler, who has been eating to keep Pelletier company, and who does not need to put on weight. But it winds him and gives him leg cramps, and soon he leaves Pelletier to it.

And one morning Pelletier is late getting back. In the kitchen, where bacon splutters and baking rolls smell yeasty, Cutler reads his watch and frowns. Can the kid have started jogging too soon? Has he collapsed somewhere along the beach? Cutler sheds his apron, grabs a jacket, and starts off to find him. He goes only a few yards. Pelletier waves and comes toward him. Cutler stands and waits.

"Are you all right?" he asks.

Pelletier jogs in place. His cheeks are red. He breathes hard but healthily. He nods. "Just ran into"—he pants, swallows—"the Quinns, is all."

Cutler scowls along the sunny beach. "Both of them?"

Pelletier gives him a disgusted look, and jogs off up the slope toward the house. Cutler follows, limping. At the breakfast bar, pushing half a hot roll into his mouth, butter leaking dandelion yellow down his chin, Pelletier says, "Quinn sent you a message. He's been busy, but he'll read your script as soon as he can."

It is December. Darkness has come early. Under the

glare of the kitchen fluorescents, Cutler washes the supper dishes. Below, the Nautilus clanks and jars. It gets a lot of Pelletier's attention these days. Almost as much as the television set. Far more than the boat. When Cutler worried about it in the storm, Pelletier said, "It's insured, isn't it? If it gets smashed, we get another one, right?" His weights and pulleys obsess him. The day they arrived, he ripped the shiny parts out of their cartons and, muttering and frowning over instruction sheets and tools, assembled them himself. In Cutler's workroom.

They take up a lot of space. A whole baseball team could use them. Cutler's white desk with its glossy word processor is now jammed into a corner. If Cutler wants to use it, he will face not the ocean and the sky, but a blank white wall. He doesn't want to use it, but he doesn't tell Pelletier this. It would spoil Pelletier's pleasure at having ruined something for Cutler. The kid would sulk, and knock Cutler's hand away when Cutler reached for him in bed. So now and then Cutler pretends to try to work at the desk and, after slamming drawers and grumbling, leaves the room, conspicuously annoyed.

He smiles thinly to himself now, dries his hands, fills a mug with coffee, pours three fingers of brandy into a little snifter, switches off the kitchen lights. He takes brandy and coffee to the couch, where he stretches out and watches the news. Larger than life. He would like it smaller. This is like having Mount Rushmore in the living room. He will go down to the bedroom and watch on the old set. He gropes around in the dim lamplight to switch off this set, but the picture arrests him.

The sports segment has begun. A gymnastic competition has taken place somewhere. And here is one of those blond doll boys in skivvy shirt and tight white pants, turning, balancing, kicking on a pommel horse. Cutler smiles and swallows some brandy. It is an omen. The whole world loves looking at this. His picture will be a hit. Filming has already started. Summer Olympic pre-publicity is running strong. Eddie Axelrod says the network may run the picture before instead of after. The image changes. A boy flings himself somersaulting in dark air high above a steel bar, catches the bar again, spins around it, and flies off it again in somersaults and twists, to land on the mat below and stretch his arms high to catch the applause. Cutler laughs aloud with pleasure. It is all in his script.

The kitchen screen rattles. The sound is an angry sound. Someone pounds hard on the doorframe. Someone shouts, but the television is too loud for Cutler to make out the words. He finds the control unit and switches off the set. He swings up from the couch and stands gaping at the door. "Darryl, I know you're in there." It is Quinn who is shouting. "Come on, open up." Cutler feels cold. Quinn is plainly mad as hell. About what? What has Cutler done to Quinn? If it's about Veronica, then Chick's name is the one Quinn should be roaring. Cutler looks around in panic for a place to hide. There is no place. He heads for the glass doors, the deck, the dark beach. But a sound stops him. A squeal of twisting metal. Has Quinn torn the screendoor loose? Something bangs the wooden door—no fist, a foot. Quinn is trying to kick it in. He shouts, "Open this God damned door, Darryl. I swear to God, I'll—"

"All right, stop!" Cutler shouts. He forces himself

to move out of the lamplight and into the shadowy kitchen area and to turn the deadbolt and the spring lock and the knob. He pulls the door open. "You must be drunk," he says.

"And you must be crazy." Quinn storms in. The script is in his hand. Not his hand, his fist. He flaps the script in Cutler's face. His own face is twisted in outrage. His color is pasty. "To think you could get away with this."

"Calm down," Cutler says. He is staring at the screen door. Quinn has bent it back, cattycorner. Was that easy for him? He says mechanically, "Get away with what?"

"This. You didn't write this script." Quinn laughs disgust at himself. "I should have known. The way Eddie sold it so fast. And to a network. They don't buy shooting scripts. They develop their own properties. That kind of script could never have come from an amateur."

"Who's an amateur?" Pelletier comes toward them in the little white shorts in which he romances the Nautilus. "Darryl wrote ten books, Phil." A blue sweatshirt hangs from the kid's hand. "He wrote that script for me." Pelletier pulls the sweatshirt on over his head. "Only I didn't get the part." He shakes out his hair. The light is behind him and makes a halo of his hair. "Your fucking agent screwed me out of it."

Quinn acts as if Pelletier weren't there. He keeps his hard gaze on Cutler's face. Cutler figures his face must be white as paper. Quinn says steadily, "That script was written by Irv Liebowitz."

"What?" Cutler hears himself. Exaggerated. Unconvincing. "Irv Liebowitz is dead. Two years dead."

"He wrote it just before he died," Quinn says. "In

that motel in the desert where he went to hide."

Cutler's knees give. He takes hold of the back of a stool to prop himself up. "You went there? You saw him? He showed you the script?"

"Shut up, Darryl," Pelletier says. "So this Liebowitz wrote about the Olympics, and Darryl wrote about the Olympics. So what? Probably a hundred writers have."

Quinn still doesn't look at him. He keeps his eyes on Cutler. "No, I never went down there. I didn't know where he was. But we had a last lunch together before he left. And he told me the idea. He was excited about it."

"Told you?" Pelletier says. He leans elbows on the bar, runs idle hands over the bronze surfer figurine. "Can you prove it? Who else had lunch with you that day?"

"No one. It doesn't matter." Quinn lays the script down, and digs envelopes from inside his jacket. "He wrote to me about it. No one to talk to down there. Just thinking aloud, developing the story, nailing down the details. He didn't want comments from me. If he had, he'd have given me an address to write to." Quinn slides a letter from one of the envelopes. "Listen." He fumbles in his jacket for reading glasses and puts them on. "The kid is named Hoyt. His father is a veterinarian. Stivers. His wife is called Ellen, the kid's mother. His girlfriend is Chrissie, right? His sidekick is Danny?" Quinn jams letter and envelopes back into his pocket. "When you copied the script, you didn't even change the names. The plot, the sequence of events, the locations — everything is the way he planned it."

"This is insane." Cutler tries to laugh. "Where

would I get Irv Liebowitz's script? If he ever wrote such a script."

"He wrote it, all right," Quinn says. The bows of the reading glasses click as he folds them. He tucks them away. "I'd recognize his stuff anywhere." He slaps the script on the counter. "No one wrote dialog like Irv. Where did you get it? From Moody's—that's obvious, isn't it? Irv sent it there to be copied and multigraphed. He always did. And when he died, you ripped it off."

"Where is it, then?" Cutler waves an arm. "You want to search for it? Be my guest."

"Oh, you destroyed it, once you'd copied it and put your name on it." Quinn snorts. "I tried to like you, tried to be fair. But none of this surprises me. Deep down, I never trusted you. The whole relationship with Stewart—love, devotion? Somebody else, maybe. You? It didn't add up. You were in it for his money. At first I wondered if you didn't kill him. But no—you haven't got the guts. You got the money, though, didn't you—fancy house, fancy car, fancy boy? And to frost the cake, you became a big-time writer. The easy way. Stole a stript you thought no one else knew about—a script by the top man in the business."

"You can have half what they paid me," Cutler says. "You can have all of it. Just give me those letters."

Quinn picks up the script and turns away. "Excuse me. I have phone calls to make. I can't reach the Guild till tomorrow, but I can get Eddie now. He'll be at home. He never misses 'Hill Street Blues.' I'm going to destroy you, Darryl." He stops in the open doorway. Fog has come in. It hangs dense and white and silent outside. Quinn turns back. "I should never have doubted my instincts. I knew from the start exactly what you were."

"There's a phone right there." Pelletier points. In the dark kitchen, the phone is a pale blur, a wall phone fixed to the side of a cupboard. "Help yourself."

Quinn frowns, glances at the phone, at Pelletier, at Cutler, who is gaping at the kid in horror. Quinn tucks the script under his arm. "All right, why not? The sooner the better." He rattles the receiver down. Back turned, he punches little lighted buttons.

Pelletier lifts the surfer figurine off the breakfast bar and pushes it into Cutler's hands. It is heavy. Cutler stares at it blankly, stares blankly at Pelletier, who jerks his head toward Quinn. "You better stop him."

Cutler tries to pass the figurine back. "I can't."

"Don't give me that shit." Pelletier grabs Cutler's shoulders, pulls him off the stool. "You have to. You heard him. He'll destroy you. Do it, Darryl, before Eddie can answer that phone."

Cutler feels sick. He can't move. Pelletier pushes him. He staggers forward. Two steps, four. Despair fills him. He lifts the figurine high over his head, and brings it crashing down on the back of Quinn's skull.

20

It is the end of February, late at night, and Cutler is alone. He feels he has been alone for a long time, but in fact Pelletier has been gone only a couple of weeks. He is with Veronica again. At Quinn's house. Except, of course, it is no longer Quinn's. Nothing is. Rain falls, the surf thunders on the beach and shakes the house, the wind takes breaths, blows hoarsely, breathes again. Rain spatters the glass that faces the beach with a sound of flung sand. There is another sound. Quinn is shouting, out on the beach, shouting Cutler's name.

Quinn is missing. The police can't locate him. Friends, business associates have not seen him, have not heard from him. Since he didn't take his car, the police at first thought he was kidnapped. Then his clothes were found on a deserted beach, and they decided he had taken a long walk, gone for a swim, and drowned. But his body has not been washed up along the coast. His wife has been no help. She went to sleep without knowing he had left the house. He did sometimes swim at night—alone, because night swimming frightened her. But he hadn't told her he meant to do this. He hadn't told her he meant to leave the house for any reason. Next morning, she telephoned around. No luck. Then, when she went for the mail, and saw his car parked in its usual place, she ran back down the stairs, into the house, and telephoned the police.

Quinn shouts out there in the storm. Cutler moans, gropes around in the dark, pulls a pillow over his head to shut out the sound. It shuts out wind and rain and crashing surf, all right, but not Quinn shouting for him. Cutler has Veronica's story by heart. She told it on television newscasts, told it to a reporter from the *Times,* a writer for *People* magazine. Her picture was shown and printed often. She is beautiful, and Quinn was rich and famous. Sometimes they photographed her at home. The house looked handsome and expensive, the sea glittering blue and glamorous beyond the deck. She wore dark glasses to conceal eyelids swollen from weeping. But before long, she could take them off. The press lost interest in Quinn's disappearance and in his grieving widow. And Pelletier could move in with Veronica. Cutler gaped and said:

"What do you mean? I thought that was over."

Pelletier said, "What do you think I got you to kill him for? So you could see your name on a TV screen for a couple seconds? Wake up, Darryl. You said yourself she'd never divorce him. Didn't you say she told you that?"

Cutler lurched to the bathroom, fell to his knees, threw up. He rested his forehead on the cold whiteness of the toilet bowl, eyes closed, hearing Pelletier rattle coat hangers in the bedroom closet. He breathed slowly, shakily, in and out, until the nausea passed. He pushed to his feet, flushed the toilet and, at the basin, rinsed out his mouth and splashed his face with cold water. Drying his face with a towel, he stood in the bedroom doorway and watched Pelletier lay clothes in cartons on the bed. Again. Cutler couldn't help grinning. Pelletier glanced at him.

"You look like an idiot," he said.

"Where's the caviar going to come from, over there? The champagne? Thousand K losses at poker, the races, Las Vegas? What's she going to buy you Porsches with, boats, platinum lighters? How's she going to pay for trips to Acapulco, meals at Ma Maison? You going to spend *your* money?"

"Why don't you shut up?" Pelletier yanks open a drawer.

"You outsmarted yourself, Chick. Phil has to be declared dead before she gets his money. And that won't happen for years. It's the law. Unless they find his body. And they won't find it, will they? You saw to that."

Out on the beach in the cold, the wind, the rain, Quinn shouts for Cutler. His voice is louder, now. He has come closer to the house. Cutler groans, throws off sheet and electric blanket, sits on the bed edge and gropes in the darkness for clothes. He does not switch on the light. He pulls on a heavy sweater, heavy socks, and kicks into thick corduroy trousers. Old Moody, naked, skeletal, howling at him from a black and toothless mouth, vanishes when Cutler puts on the light. The little boy, pawing at him with helpless bloody hands and whimpering, is less than nothing when the light goes on. They are creatures of darkness. He wants Quinn to show himself. Then he will turn on the light.

He ties the laces of lowtop boots and stands. He can't figure out why Quinn, so strong in life, is no more than angry shouting in the dark. He shouts for Cutler to come out every night. Unless Cutler has a boy in bed with him. Tonight, Cutler couldn't face driving to West Hollywood to buy a boy. And he has left his raincoat and canvas hat where he can find them in the dark. He shrugs into the coat now, and pulls the hat down hard on his head. A new, strong flashlight weighs heavy in one pocket of the coat. Not to probe the dark for Quinn. Quinn would only vanish in its beam. If there is a Quinn. No, the flashlight is just to keep Cutler from missing his footing. He slides open the panel, flinches in the lash of rain, steps out and slides the glass closed behind him.

Quinn shouts Cutler's name, but already the shout is fainter. Doggedly, Cutler crosses the deck and goes down the steps to the sand. This is a ritual of which he is so weary that he scarcely feels afraid anymore. The first time Quinn shouted to him in the night, he was terrified. That was a calm and starry night, the first after Pelletier went back to Veronica. Cutler had not then reasoned out the logic of the light. He had shone its beam across the deck, up the stairs. Heart hammering, hands shaking, he had tottered down the beach after the voice, raking the sand with the beam of light. He was sure as death that Quinn had risen from his watery grave to kill his murderer — at the exact spot where he had waded ashore on that bright morning shortly after Cutler bought the beach house.

This is a dangerous place to swim, Cutler said.

So they tell me, Quinn said. *I forget. The urge comes on, I'm in the water. No matter where, no matter when.*

But on that starry night, no Quinn was there. The shouting had been in Cutler's mind, hadn't it? There was no one out on the beach to shout. He'd had a nightmare. He trudged back to the house, but not to bed. He climbed above for a drink because he was still shaking. But with whiskey and ice in his hand, he kept studying the floor of the bright kitchen, the cabinets. The floor where Quinn had slumped and bled, the cabinets spattered with his blood and brains. Cutler set the glass down and ran a hand on the cabinets. He got to his knees and searched the shiny vinyl with his eyes. He rummaged detergent, sponges, a plastic pail from a cupboard, and washed floor and cabinets again. Thoroughly. The whiskey was warm when he got back to it.

He shines the light at his feet and walks miserably after the retreating voice. His shoulders are hunched, his head bowed. Rain leaks off the brim of the canvas hat and drips cold down the back of his neck. The wet sand sucks at his boots. How many times has he washed and rinsed and waxed that corner of the kitchen? He has lost count. He wishes he could stop. Quinn's shouting is getting lost in the voices of the storm. Cutler begins to run, the spot of light wobbling ahead of him, and only stops when it shows him the reaching mouth of the murky surf. "Quinn!" he shouts into the wind. "I'm here." Here meaning the exact place where Quinn came twice out of the sea, once alive, and once as dead as the hog in the ditch.

"What the hell are you doing?" Cutler said.

"Getting his clothes off him." Pelletier was on the bloody floor beside Quinn, struggling with Quinn's bulk, Quinn's weight. "Help me."

"What for?" Cutler's mind swam. "What for, Chick?"

Face red from exertion, Pelletier stopped tugging at Quinn's jacket to give Cutler a look of disbelief. "He went swimming, stupid. He went swimming out there. In the undertow. And it took him, and smashed his head against a rock, didn't it? And he drowned. All right? Now, are you going to help me, here, or not?"

Stunned and speechless, Cutler knelt to help. Quinn was heavy. Pelletier wrapped a towel around his head, and they carried him down the living room and out onto the deck into the fog. The fog seemed luminous. The white of the towel and of Quinn's undershorts picked up that luminosity. The weight of him winded them. They had to stop, lay him down, and pick him up again, before they reached the surf.

"Tide's going out." Panting, Pelletier stripped. "That will help. Come on, Darryl. Don't just stand there."

"I can't swim." Cutler looked at the black water.

"You don't have to swim. All you have to do is wade. Take off your clothes. Will you wake up, please? Some asshole could walk along here anytime."

"Too foggy," Cutler said, but he shed his clothes. It was cold, and he shivered. The black water looked strong to him, and terrible, the way it swirled and churned. Naked Pelletier, a pallid silhouette against the darkness and the deep, bent to grip Quinn's thick and hairy body under the arms. Lifting, he grunted. Bleakly, Cutler bent and took Quinn's legs. Under the knees. A leg on each side of him. They lugged him into the cold water. Pelletier moved backward quickly, almost at a run. The water rose to Cutler's thighs, to his waist. Panic surged up in him. A strong wave came, and water splashed into his mouth. He cried out, and almost dropped Quinn's legs.

But he was afraid of Pelletier's contempt. He hung

on, and lunged after the kid, hopelessly sure he was going to drown. And then, the water buoyed Quinn's weight. "Okay, go back," Pelletier gasped. And Cutler let go of Quinn, turned and, fighting the tug of the outgoing tide, stumbled ashore. There was only the bloody towel from Quinn's head to dry himself with. He didn't touch it. Teeth chattering, he flapped into his clothes, and stood shivering and hugging himself, trying to see through the fog. He was frightened. Why wouldn't the undertow take Pelletier when it took Quinn?

"Are you all right?" he shouted.

"Shut up," Pelletier called. His voice sounded watery but strangely near. Fog could do that. Or had he given up? Was he coming back? Cutler stood still, holding his breath, listening. The surf sucked and sighed. He couldn't hear any splash of swimming. He waited, enfolded in fog. But Pelletier didn't come wading up to him. He must be going to try it. But it was crazy. Quinn was heavy. Pelletier wasn't strong enough. It would exhaust him. He would drown before he could swim back.

Now, Cutler stands as he stood on that foggy night, but it is the ghost of Quinn he shouts to out at sea in the darkness. And no answer comes. And he isn't about to wait here longer in the wind-whipped rain. He waited that awful December night till time lost meaning. At first, he stood in place, head thrust out, trying to see, trying to hear. At last, the cold got his attention. He had to move, rub some warmth into his arms, get his circulation going. He jogged along the sand. How loud the crunch of his shoes was. Another trick of the fog. He didn't want to hear it. He wanted to hear Pelletier swimming in. He held still again, listened again. Nothing. He jogged and halted and listened. How many times he doesn't remember. But he had given up hope, when he heard splashing in the surf, and Pelletier, gasping, choking, came staggering to him out of the fog. He started to fall, and Cutler caught him. He was icy cold. He clung to Cutler, panting, limp, spent.

"The son of a bitch is gone," he coughed.

"Come on." Cutler picked him up. "Have to get you warm."

"You should have felt that riptide grab him," Pelletier said. "Like a shark. Shit—he'll never be back."

Cutler smiles grimly to himself now, wind pushing him, hiking up the slope toward the black, sharp-cornered shape of the lightless house. He switches on the flashlight to show him the steps. The yellow beam reflects off the streaming glass as he crosses the deck. Inside, he switches on lamps. He hangs coat and hat to drip in the shower, sets his boots in the tub, and goes to the workroom. Bottles and glasses glitter on the white desk. Weather like this makes having a bar down here common sense. He has even installed a little refrigerator. It felt good, spending money on himself, for a change. He pours a drink and stands staring without seeing at the Nautilus equipment. It has begun to gather dust. Pelletier was wrong about Quinn.

The kid was pale, his lips blue, and he shuddered uncontrollably. Cutler filled the tub with steaming water and lowered him into it. When he went back half an hour later to check on him, he was asleep, chin on chest. Cutler hoisted him out of the tub, dried him off, got him into a sweatsuit and into bed.

He didn't wake up enough even to mumble. Cutler envied him, wished he could have worn himself out like that. But he hadn't, and he wasn't going to sleep. He was going to live the murder, and what followed the murder, over and over again, all night.

He dropped into one of the wicker barrel chairs in the dim bedroom, and stared at the glass panels and the thick fog beyond. He smoked cigarette after cigarette until the pack was empty. He didn't even glance at his watch. He knew he had sat there a long time by how stiff he felt when he got up to go fetch a drink. When he switched on the kitchen fluorescents, the shock almost felled him. Quinn's blood and brains were still there. Gulping hard to keep from throwing up, Cutler feverishly washed them away. He set the surfer figurine in the sink and washed that, and set it back in its place. By then, the floor was dry, and he coated it with liquid wax.

Quinn's clothes were strewn around. Cutler snatched them up into a rough bundle. He put on a jacket, dropped his keys into a pocket, and with the bundle under his arm pulled open the kitchen door. The hinges of the screen door screamed. He stood for a second, staring at the twisted thing, then gave himself a shake and hurried off up the cliff stairs. He would attend to the door later. He wasn't sure it mattered. The clothes did matter. If Quinn had gone swimming, Cutler didn't want it to be from the beach in front of his house. He threw the clothes into the hatchback, and drove off up the coast road, fog swirling in the headlight beams.

He remembered a lonely beach where Saluto had taken them once. He clambered down difficult rocks there, slipping in the dark, scraping his hands. The tide was coming in. He left Quinn's shirt, sweater, trousers, socks and shoes where the tide would reach them. What was that on the back of the jacket? A black blotch. Damp. Blood. He couldn't leave the jacket. Baffled, turning it over in his hands, he felt Irv Liebowitz's letters in the pocket. He had almost forgotten them. He was in awful shape. He burned the letters in a big pot on the kitchen stove. The fan in the hood above the stove took the smoke. He scrubbed away the soot and ashes from the pot, and hung it back in place.

The jacket lay over a stool. While he made himself a drink and tasted it, he frowned at the jacket. He could take scissors to it, couldn't he, and burn the scraps one by one? He wasn't sure. He would ask Pelletier what to do when he woke up. Pelletier would think of something. Then Cutler thought of something. Pelletier's shorts and sweatshirt. And the bloody towel. They lay out there on the sand, didn't they? He'd better fetch them. He set the drink down, put his jacket back on, found the flashlight, and went out into the darkness, the cold, the fog. He had put fresh batteries into the flashlight, but it wasn't powerful. He must remember to get a bigger one.

The tide had come up. The sound of the surf told him this before the flashlight's sickly yellow beam found its foaming edge. The white shorts floated in the water. So did the towel. Something else dark washed up and back with the motion of the waves. The blue sweatshirt. He shone the light around, looking for a driftwood branch to snag them with. And he saw Quinn. He lay naked and dead, like the hog in the ditch. The surf washed over his big head and thick chest and washed back. It looked as if it longed to claim him. But then why had it shoved him back up here where no one wanted him? Cutler turned away so quickly he stumbled and fell. Scrambling up, he ran for the house. Pelletier had been wrong.

Pale gray dawn had come by the time they sailed out the long straight channel from the marina to the sea. The crate that had held the new television set hulked up on the deck. Nailed shut as if it had never been opened. The fog lay cottony on the still, dark water of the channel. The only sound was the steady pulsing of the diesel below. In sweaters, mackinaws, knitted watch caps, they sat close side by side in the cockpit. Cutler said nothing. Pelletier said nothing. When Cutler glanced at him, his face was stony. His hands in leather, fleece-lined driving gloves were tight on the little wheel. This was the first time Cutler had ever seen him frightened.

He had jerked, and nearly let go his corner of the crate when they were struggling to get it on board. From someplace, Souza had appeared, squinting, scratching his stubble. He was night watchman here. Till something better turned up. What was in the crate? Why at five o'clock in the morning? Where were they taking a TV in the fog? Where had they been all these months? Did Pelletier want Souza to sail the boat for him? It was dangerous in fog. Shouldn't Souza check the running lights? He helped them heave the crate aboard. The sea was calm this morning, but wind could rise when the sun broke through. He brought rope, and lashed the crate to the deck. He stood staring after them, until the fog shut him from view.

"He was drunk," Cutler said. "He won't remember."

"I don't want to talk about it," Pelletier said.

Two hours at sea, Pelletier grunted, switched off the diesel, and climbed out of the cockpit. Cutler followed. Pelletier went forward in the fog. Cutler heard the splash of the sea anchor. The boat rocked. Waves lapped the hull. Wordlessly, they unlashed the crate and pried it open. Quinn tumbled onto the deck. He was stiff as stone, locked in a crooked crouch. The jacket was on him. Pelletier's idea. They had loaded the pockets with rocks. Cutler had sewed the pockets and the front of the jacket shut with string and the curved needle meant for basting turkeys. They dragged Quinn to the starboard railings. But when they tried to heave him over, he was too heavy, the railings too high. He was too bulky to wedge under. Pelletier said:

"Climb up. You lift. I'll push from below."

Cutler obeyed. Feet on the lower rail, he clung with a hand to the top railing, bent, and gripped a rigid arm. He hoisted. Pelletier, in a crouch, worked his shoulders under contorted Quinn and strained to lift him, making tight sounds in his throat with the effort. Cutler grimaced and hauled again. Pelletier heaved upward. Quinn overbalanced Cutler. His fingers lost their grip on the rail, and he fell backward into the sea. Quinn's weight was on him, and the weight of the stones, and Cutler sank under it. He fought the dead man off him, who dropped away, somersaulting ponderously down into the murk. The air in Cutler's lungs bore him up, and he broke the surface.

What he saw first was the pale disk of the sun through the fog. Next he saw Pelletier on the tilting deck, struggling to untangle one of those rope and wood ladders. "Help," Cutler said, his mouth filled with water, and he sank again. He flailed with his arms. He kicked. *That's it,* said the young man of long ago. *Now, see? Nothing to it. You're swimming.* But Cutler wasn't swimming. Not then, and not now. His mother said, *You'll never learn.* He was sinking. No, rising. His head popped out into the air and light again.

But where was the boat? Waves splashed into his eyes. Gulping air, he looked wildly around. Had Pelletier gone off and left him? No, there was the boat. On the deck, Pelletier was flinging off his clothes. "Help," Cutler said, and sank again. For the third time. That meant the end—wasn't that what they said? He sank. How heavy his clothes were, dragging him down into darkness. Where Quinn was. Waiting. Horror filled him. Frantically he pumped with his arms. His lungs felt as if they would explode. Then he shot up through the surface one more time.

And Pelletier was beside him. Cutler clutched at him. Pelletier fought him off. "Don't do that. You'll drown us both. Relax. Let me hold you. Relax, damn it." He was behind Cutler now. His hand cupped Cutler's chin and tilted his face back up out of the water. "Relax. Lie on me. That's it. Go limp, okay? No, don't struggle, Darryl. I won't let you sink. Lie back. Relax. That's the way."

Waves still splashed his face. Relax was easy to say. He shut his eyes. That was better. Pelletier was warm under him. He felt the busy kick of the kid's legs, the backstroke of his free arm, his labored breathing. Then Pelletier shifted his grip, grabbed him around the chest, turned him, and slapped one of his hands at the bristly ladder. It swung dizzily away, swung back and rapped Cutler in the face. "Grab hold." But Cutler's hands were numb. "I can't." Pelletier bent the stiff fingers around a wooden rung. "There, now, damn it. Climb. You're heavy. I'm tired. Darryl—make a fucking effort." He ducked under the water and sank his teeth into Cutler's butt. Cutler climbed the ladder. He toppled over the rail and lay on the deck, gagging seawater. Pelletier scrambled up after him, and landed light on his feet, naked, panting, water streaming from his hair and skin. Cutler blinked up at him. He was very beautiful.

Cutler said, "I thought you'd let me drown."

"No way." Pelletier gathered up his clothes from the deck. "You don't have any rocks in your pockets." He headed for the little teak shutter doors to the cabins below. "Be serious. Am I the one who murders people?"

21

Giant TV is a white stucco hangar in a sun-bleak warehouse district by Ballona creek in Culver City. The streets are wide white concrete, like the creekbed, but the creekbed leads somewhere, the streets do not. At this early hour on a morning in mid-April, he drives them alone, and twice, after failing to reach the loading docks of Giant TV, has wound up instead on La Cienega boulevard, where it climbs into green, oil-welled hills and makes for the airport. He gives up, parks in front of the place, and goes inside.

Half an acre of tough gold carpeting lies underfoot. White fluorescent tubes hang in white enamel reflectors from steel girders high overhead. At the far back of the place, glass-walled offices are suspended at mezzanine level. On the sales floor, blankfaced television sets form aisles and squares. On carpeted shelves against steel plate walls, the sets are alight, all tuned to the same channel. A gardening show is on, flowers in close-up, the colors savage.

No shoppers are here yet. Salesmen cluster far away, in cheap summerweight suits. They drink coffee from paper cups, and munch doughnuts held in paper napkins. Their voices reach him, faint but real between the unreally boomy words from the TV loudspeakers. The salesmen argue goodnaturedly. About some sports event? A losing bet? Cutler hikes toward them. It is a long hike, and when he reaches them, the man he wants is not there. These men eye him.

"Gordon?" Cutler looks around. "Hy Gordon?"

"He's no longer with us," says a red-faced man in a red tie. "Something I can help you with? We're moving out some top-of-the-line sets this week. I can get you twenty-five percent off. Maybe a third. We're prepared to deal. Any reasonable offer." The other men stray away. The red-faced man lays a chapped-looking hand on a sleek cabinet. "This one normally goes for a thousand ninety-five. Cable ready. Stereo. Remote. Four hundred line image."

Cutler shakes his head. "I got a better one from Hy last fall. I just want to ask him a question."

"My name's Pat." The raw, red hand comes at Cutler, who ignores it. "Pat Mackey. And you're—?"

"Do you know where Hy Gordon went?"

"If it's a service problem," Mackey says, "we've got a full service department." He jerks his head toward the back. "Did you buy our service contract? Worth it. Covers labor for two years, parts for four, except picture tube of course."

"It's not a service problem. Where is Gordon?"

"He passed away," Mackey says. "I'm sorry."

Cutler is not surprised. The man's clothes hung on him loosely. He wore a wig. Cheap, but a full wig, not just a hairpiece. There was a sick glitter to his eyes. His skin had a waxy look. "Cancer," Cutler guesses.

"Doctors shouldn't be allowed to do it to you," Mackey says. "Take every dime, house, car. Put you through all that chemotherapy stuff. Torture, Hy said, plain torture. And then you die anyway. You know what the average doctor in this country makes a year? Ninety-nine thousand dollars, that's what. There ought to be a law."

Cutler walks away. "Loading docks back here?"

"You can't get through that way. What do you want?"

"A trucker left his gloves at my house," Cutler lies, "when he delivered my set last fall. I've been meaning to return them. I just don't get up this way often. I live at the beach."

"You have to go back out the front doors. There's stairs up the side of the building. To the office." Mackey jerks a thumb. "Go through the office. There's inside stairs down to storage and shipping. Which trucker?"

"Eduardo." Cutler is tired of hustlers. He wants Eduardo now. He keeps remembering that smooth brown skin, those soft, laughing black eyes, the big, white, even teeth. "Mexican kid. Twenties. About five nine."

Mackey shrugs. "They all look alike to me."

Cutler hikes back to the glass doors, pushes out into the white sunglare of the empty street, the silence. The staircase up the outside of the building is steel, painted white, the paint turning yellow, beginning to scab. At the top, a metal door has a pane of wired glass lettered OFFICE. He turns a steel knob from which fingers have worn the paint, and steps inside. The stiff lacework of the girders is lower here, closer to the heads that move beneath it, and the fluorescents seem brighter. Typewriters chatter. Telephones ring. File drawers rattle open, slam shut. The screens of computers flicker. Their printers snore, and spew folds of greenish paper.

A very young woman with hair that looks as if

a disturbed child had taken dull scissors to it, raises her head where she sits at a steel desk, is plainly struck by Cutler's looks, eyes him with instant hunger, smiles with her tongue between her teeth as if her next move will be to unzip his fly—and then, pouting, points him out the door he asks for. The steel plate walls of the narrow inside staircase bear long deep biased scratches. The steel door at the foot of the stairs opens into a vast gloomy space stacked high with crates and cartons, where the air is cold. Forklifts hum past in silhouette against wide freight door openings where daylight dazzles and, beyond a black shelf of loading dock piled with cargo, the rear ends of big, gold delivery trucks gape open. Men in gold coveralls with GIANT TV stitched to the backs in white and blue are loading the trucks.

Cutler's heart lifts and begins to beat faster. He moves toward the light, smiling. A horn beeps behind him. He jumps aside. A forklift stacked with cartons passes, driven by a black in goggles and a hardhat. A hand is lifted, a finger touches the hat. Cutler reaches the doorway and leans there, eyes narrowed because of the brightness of the sunlight, and searches with his eyes along the loading dock, trying to pick out Eduardo. His heart, which has lifted, drops. The kid isn't here. A dozen truckers are, but not the kid. Then his smile returns.

Across the tarmac of the loading yard comes Eduardo in his coveralls and workshoes. He carries stacked pasteboard take-out boxes from a doughnut shop. At its far end, cement steps climb to the loading dock. He comes up these and sets the boxes on an empty crate. The men quit loading the trucks and head for the crate. The warehousemen climb down from their forklifts and head for the crate. Cutler takes three steps out of the shadow of the doorway onto the loading dock and stands watching Eduardo, who passes out change and bills to the men, who then take doughnuts in paper napkins, and coffee in paper cups, and sit on the edge of the dock in a row. Cigarette smoke spices the still air.

Cutler lights a cigarette, and Eduardo notices him. He stands still, paper cup half raised to his mouth, and stares, head tilted. Then he smiles, almost smiles, picks up a second cup and brings it along the dock and holds it out to Cutler, who takes it and says, "Thank you." Steam curls on the surface of the coffee. He tastes it and smiles at Eduardo, who watches him, eyes puzzled, and still not quite smiling. "Good morning," Cutler says.

"I remember you," Eduardo says.

"I remember you too," Cutler says. "Cigarette?" He digs the pack from a breast pocket and holds it out.

Eduardo takes a cigarette. "The house at the beach." He sets the cigarette in his mouth and Cutler clicks the plastic lighter to get it going. "All those stairs." The men lined up along the steel edge of the loading dock laugh at something. Eduardo looks back at them. He looks into the gloom of the warehouse, runs his gaze along the line-up of waiting trucks, eyes the bleak white buildings and the green hills beyond their roofs. "What are you doing here?"

Cutler puts the cigarettes away. "I came to see you." He raises his cup and smiles over it. "I thought if I came to see you, you might come to see me."

"It is a long way," Eduardo says. "My car is old."

"Six o'clock," Cutler says. "Drinks and dinner. You remember how to get there?"

"I remember." Eduardo tastes his coffee. He breathes in smoke deeply, lets the hand with the cigarette drop to his side, and flicks ashes from the cigarette, looking down, watching the ashes scatter. Smoke comes out of his mouth with the words, "Do you still have that big TV?"

"Yes. Is that what you want to do? Watch TV?"

Eduardo looks at the sky. It is wonderfully blue, but there is nothing to see there. He says, "I guess your friend will be watching it. You did not buy it for yourself. You bought it for your friend. He was sick. Is he better, now?"

"He went to live with a woman," Cutler says.

"Six o'clock is too early," Eduardo says. "We are supposed to be off at five, but sometimes we do not get back on time. And I have to go home and clean up. And sometimes others are using the shower."

"You can shower at my house," Cutler says.

Eduardo shakes his head. "Seven," he says.

"Seven it is," Cutler says. "Smile for me."

"What?" Eduardo glances back in alarm at the truckers in their overalls, the warehousemen in their hard hats. They have begun to get up and push their empty paper cups and crumpled napkins into trash cans whose tops flap and clatter. Eduardo scowls at Cutler. He keeps his voice low. "Smile for you? Do you take me for a woman?"

"I just like to see you smile," Cutler says.

Eduardo turns away. "I have to work," he says.

*　　*　　*

Cutler skids the Celica to a halt above the beach house, the little tires scattering gravel. His luck has run out. This proves it. He flings out of the car and slams the door behind him. He has hurt Eduardo's feelings. He will not come. Not at seven. Not ever. *You're pathetic sometimes — you know that, Darryl?* A sizeable rock has come to rest on one of the cliff steps. He sets a foot against it and sends it flying. It doesn't hit the sand. It lofts, lands on the roof of the house, and rolls clunking back down into the rain gutter.

The rain gutter snaps, squeals, and hinges slowly down, making a chute for the rock, which tumbles out on the kitchen doorstep. *If you kick things,* his mother says, *they'll kick you back. You'd better learn to control that temper of yours, little boy.* Cutler jolts down the rest of the stairway, swearing. He grabs the tin trough, works it side to side until the broken weld comes loose, and the section is free. He throws it down, shoves the rock aside with his foot, and barges indoors.

He rattles ice into a glass, measures two jiggers of gin over it, covers that with orange juice, and takes the drink down to the bedroom, where he switches on the television set, and lies staring at it while the gin finds its way to his brain. It is safe to sleep alone in the daytime. Moody won't come wailing, nor the bloody boy. Quinn will not wade in shouting from the sea. And what reason is there not to sleep? What point is there to waking? Beyond the glass wall of the bedroom, sea, sand, sky are empty. He is empty. Maybe he will go to the Sea Shanty tonight. It's been a long time — he began coming home alone too often. On west Santa Monica boulevard he could buy what he needed. But why won't someone be at the

Sea Shanty tonight with a smile like Eduardo's? With his luck? Who is he kidding?

The television shows an old Joel McCrae western, black and white. Cutler watches glumly, working on his drink. He lived, one long-ago rainy winter, with a pale, thin, stoopshouldered young man in an apartment filled with movie junk, old stills and lobby cards, old Kay Francis and Lloyd Nolan posters fading on the walls, stacks of ragged *Silver Screen* magazines underfoot. He told Cutler that in the thirties Joel McCrae and Nils Asther were lovers. A gossip columnist found out. The studio threw her Asther and kept McCrae.

Was it true? Cutler doubts it. Film freaks believe anything. This one—Gary, Jerry, Mary?—wanted to believe all male stars were queer. Pathetic. Still, it was the only time in his life Cutler ever heard of Nils Asther. Sleep is not coming. With a sigh, he gets up and draws the curtains. Darkness should help. It doesn't help. And he pads to the bathroom, where he swallows two of Moody seconols. And soon Joel McCrae's beauty blurs, and Cutler sleeps.

He wakens tense. Someone is in the room. He doesn't have to open his eyes to know it. Sounds say so, soft footfalls, the quiet slide of dresser drawers. He opens his eyes. The room is shadowy. From the way the sunlight falls on the pleats of the curtains, he judges it is late afternoon. His heart thuds. Slowly he raises his head. No one is in sight. He tries to ask who's there, but sound won't come from his throat. Pelletier steps in from the hall. Naked to the waist, in baggy camouflage pants, barefoot. The pants look scruffy. So does the blond hair.

"Darryl, for Christ sake, where's the checkbook?"

It has been two months since Cutler has seen him, but Pelletier acts as if not a day has passed.

"You mean"—Cutler's tongue is dry—"my checkbook."

"Our checkbook." Pelletier rolls open the closet, paws among the clothes that hang there. He is rough about it, heedless, in a hurry. A jacket falls, and he doesn't bother to pick it up. "I need money."

"I warned you, didn't I?" Cutler gets numbly out of bed, naked, sweaty. "You should have stayed with me, Chick. I always gave you everything you wanted."

"All I wanted was Veronica." Pelletier begins yanking clothes off their hangers, searching the pockets, hurling them behind him. "Where's the God damn check book, Darryl? I'm not kidding."

"I gave you Veronica too," Cutler says bleakly.

"Yeah, well, thanks a bunch." Pelletier rolls the closet door shut. Too hard. It jumps its tracks and a corner gouges the carpet. He stands among the strewn clothes and glares. "Veronica does dope, and she owes her friendly next door neighbor twenty thousand bucks, and he won't wait any longer. He wants it today."

"She doesn't even wash your clothes," Cutler says. "She doesn't feed you. You're thin." Pelletier comes away from the closet, around the bed. He doesn't look at Cutler, doesn't seem to hear him. The clothes Cutler shed when he lay down this morning lie on the floor. Pelletier drops to his knees, rummages in the pockets, finds the checkbook, holds it up. A sour smell comes off him, days of stale sweat. "You're doing dope too," Cutler says, "aren't you?"

"Write a check, Darryl." Pelletier fumbles the pen out of the folder. "Twenty thousand dollars."

"I don't keep that kind of money in the checking account," Cutler says. "And if I did, the bank still wouldn't honor a check that big. I'd have to go there and get a cashier's check. And it wouldn't be that simple. They'd ask questions. They'd want to know what it was for."

"Well, make up something." Pelletier paws around on the rug, finds Cutler's briefs, tosses them up to him. "Get dressed. Go, already."

Cutler catches the briefs, but he doesn't move to put them on. He glances at the slanting sunlight on the curtains again. He picks his watch up from the bedside table and peers at it. Four forty-eight. "The bank is closed, Chick."

"What?" Pelletier snatches the watch, reads it, throws it down the room. "Damn," he says, and slumps back on his heels, head hanging. But only for a few seconds. He looks up. "Write small checks, then — two-fifty, three hundred, like that." He scrambles to his feet, pushes Cutler so Cutler sits on the bed, lays the checkbook open on the bedside stand. "Till they total twenty thou. You can transfer enough to cover it into the checking account Monday morning. Write, Darryl." He grabs Cutler's hand and fits the pen in his fingers. "Payable to L. Bianchi."

Cutler says, "Only if you promise to come back to me."

"Darryl. I saw you murder Moody. I saw you murder Quinn. Which one do you want me to tell the cops about?"

Cutler feels cold and sick, but he says, "Why would they believe you? What proof have you got? Who's going to back up your stories?"

"I can show them where to find Quinn's body."

"And explain to them," Cutler mocks him, "how you know? You're the one that's living with Quinn's widow — not me. How will that look to them? It's your word against mine, baby. I've got a quarter million dollars in the bank, an expensive beach house, I'm a successful writer. You're trash, no job, not a dime to your name. You're not even a citizen. Now, who are they going to believe, Chick?"

"Trash?" Pelletier yelps. "You said you loved me."

"Look at yourself," Cutler says. "Filthy, scrawny, haven't shaved for days. That's what she's done to you, Chick. You were beautiful when I had you."

Pelletier begins to cry. This is something new. It must be the drugs. His head hangs, the tears run. Sobs hiccup out of him. He whimpers, snuffles, wipes his runny nose with his hand. He looks at Cutler pathetically, shaking his head. He stretches out the mucus-smeared hand and begs, "Please, Darryl?"

It is almost more than Cutler can bear not to get up and take the weeping kid in his arms and comfort him. But he does not. He watches without moving, without expression.

"Bianchi's going to hurt her," Pelletier wails.

"It's time somebody did," Cutler says.

"Aw, Darryl, don't." And Pelletier drops to his knees again. In front of Cutler, where Cutler sits on the bed. He parts Cutler's thighs and buries his face between them. Nuzzling. Hungrily. The surprise is breathtaking. And the joy. The kid's mouth finds him, and Cutler is helpless. For a whole minute. Then Pelletier looks up at him, and whines. "Little checks, Darryl. Please?"

And Cutler puts a hand on his chest and sends him sprawling backward on his butt. "Sell the Porsche." Cutler stands and pulls the briefs on. "It's yours. You've got the pink slip." He kicks into his jeans while Pelletier stares up at him, face greasy with tears. Cutler says, "It won't bring twenty thousand, but it will bring enough to quiet Mr. Bianchi down for a while."

"Don't make me sell the Porsche." Pelletier climbs pitifully to his feet. "Give me the money, Darryl. I'll come over and love you every chance I get. I promise."

Cutler flaps into a shirt. "Get lost," he says.

Pelletier's expression hardens. He stamps to the window wall and yanks the cord that opens the curtains. They jerk and swish. He rolls the glass panel aside, steps out, turns back. "You'll be sorry," he says. "I'll figure out a way to make you sorry. Just wait."

"Fuck off," Cutler says, and watches Pelletier cross the deck and drop down the steps, and thinks his heart will break. He runs to the opening. And stops. Not far up the beach, Veronica waits, in a bikini and a man's camouflage jacket. Her hair blows. When Pelletier reaches her, she listens for a second, then she slaps him. Cutler grins.

22

He becomes *Querido* instead of Darryl. *Querido* echoes through the sunny house on weekends. *Querido* this, to the whine of the blender in the kitchen, *Querido* that, above the cheerful racket of *salsa* on the stereo. *Querido* shouts from the surf, where Eduardo stands knee-deep, water gleaming off his sleek brown skin as he pushes back his hair. Questions — *Querido?* Answers — *Querido!* It means beloved, and Cutler can't help himself — he likes it. It fills him with happiness every time he hears it.

Eduardo said it first in a sleepy whisper in the dark, lying naked against Cutler in the wide bed, the panel at the room's end open to the warm night, the tide whispering out beyond the moonlit deck, the empty, moonlit beach. The word hummed from his strong mouth between slow, searching kisses. It gasped from him when Cutler caressed him and he trembled. It cried from him when he arched and jolted, clutching Cutler, shuddering in spasm after spasm. It sighed softly from him as he drifted into sleep, an arm and a leg limp across Cutler, who lay still, smiling up into the darkness, marveling.

Now Cutler even calls himself *Querido*. Wakening here alone on weekday mornings, he murmurs the word before he opens his eyes, murmurs it and smiles as he stretches. He gets out of bed feeling fine. He doesn't have to drink and drug himself to sleep anymore. And he does sleep. Moody has quit coming, so has the bleeding boy. If Quinn is still out there in the night, he has lost his voice. Cutler doesn't understand it, but does he need to? In the shower, he sings *Querido* to lame self-made tunes. "Good morning, *Querido*," he says to his reflection in the steamy bathroom mirror when he shaves — in Eduardo's accent, laughing.

Not only has he never been so happy in his life. He understands that until now he never knew what happiness was. What happens to the days he cannot say. They pass, which is all he cares about. Far off as it always seems when he stands on the road shoulder late Sundays to be sure Eduardo's fifteen-year-old, faded green Chevette will start, and watching its one good tail light disappear up the dark highway, Friday night does come again. He fills the time in lonely, loping runs far up the beach, in cleaning house when it doesn't need cleaning, in poring over a stack of Mexican cookbooks hunting up recipes to surprise and please Eduardo. He reads. He watches television. The days pass.

The first ones, the first week, were torture. All right, he was *Querido*. But had that been only for one Friday night, one Saturday, one Sunday? Would Eduardo come back? "I will borrow tools from my cousin," he had said. "Also solder and a soldering iron." To fix the rain gutter. Eduardo was holding it and looking worried when Cutler went that first night to find him at the door. At precisely seven o'clock. His first words were, "This will have to be put back."

"I thought you weren't coming," Cutler said.

Eduardo looked almost slight without the shapeless coveralls of Giant TV. He wore neat chinos and a shortsleeved cotton shirt, brown-checked. His workshoes had made his feet look big. But Cutler judged the size of his brown and tan imitation Nikes to be no more than seven. Eduardo squinted up at the roof edge. "The strips of metal—I don't know the word for them—they are bent." He leaned the tin trough carefully beside the door. "I will bring new ones, and put it back for you next time."

"I thought I'd offended you," Cutler said. "I didn't think you'd come."

Eduardo brushed sand from his hands, and held one out for Cutler to shake. "I gave my word," he said.

Cutler shook the hand. "Come in," he said. "I'm glad to see you, very glad." He felt himself smiling as if his whole being smiled. He watched Eduardo step inside and look around. Cutler wished the place were neater. He had meant to vacuum, dust, straighten it up, but when he thought Eduardo would not come, he had only slept, hadn't he? And had that fight with Pelletier. And spent the next two hours lying to himself that because Veronica had slapped him, Pelletier would leave her. When he heard the rapping at the kitchen door, he thought it was Pelletier he would find standing there, not Eduardo grieving over the rain gutter. Cutler said now, "You don't have to fix it. On Monday, I'll call a repairman."

"Be patient. There will be no rain. It is almost summer." Eduardo walked down the room, stepping softly as if afraid he would harm the carpet, and caressing everything with his eyes. "Do not throw money away. I will fix it for you." He turned and at last smiled. "I can do it."

"Fine, then. Thank you." Cutler looked at the life-less kitchen. "I promised you food, but I thought you were angry and weren't coming. So I didn't fix anything."

"This is a beautiful house." Eduardo stood gazing out at the beach and the ocean. The sun was dropping. It would be gone soon. "You were not going to eat?"

"Not without you," Cutler said.

"I was angry with you." Eduardo lit a brown Mexican cigarette. The breeze off the sea brought the smell of the smoke to Cutler, strong and sweet. "But you meant no harm. I am new here." Eduardo came back up the room. "I sometimes forget — your customs are not our customs."

"And you're not angry anymore?" Cutler said.

"I am pleased that you want to be my friend," Eduardo said. "I do not have any friends here. Only my cousins — the ones I live with. And they" — he shrugged — "care only about getting enough money to marry and have kids and grow old, you know? There is no one in my life like you." Through cigarette smoke, he gazed steadily at Cutler, eyes large, dark, and solemn. "No — I am not angry."

"Good." Cutler said it briskly with a brisk smile, and turned to switch on the kitchen lights. He wanted to take Eduardo in his arms and kiss and caress him. But he was afraid he might make him angry again. He said, "You've been working all day. You must be very hungry. I'll make you a drink, and fix something that doesn't take long." He touched bottles. "Margarita?"

Eduardo laughed. "Margaritas are for rich American tourists in highrise hotels in Mazatlan. I used to work there. In the kitchens." He opened the refrigerator and peered inside. "Ah — *cerveza,*" he said, and brought out a brown bottle. "That is what we *indigenas* drink." The refrigerator door swung shut, and he looked at Cutler doubtfully. "*Perdone me.* It is all right? I have your permission?"

"My house is your house," Cutler said.

"*Gracias.*" Eduardo twisted off the cap with a hard, brown fist, and drank from the bottle. Cutler studied refrigerator shelves, frowned into the freezer, opened cupboards and felt grim. This meal he ought to have spent a day on. Eduardo probably ate out of cans all the time. Or survived on fast-food burritos. Cutler remembered how that was, and the memory repelled and saddened him. But what could he put together now that would be halfway decent? Eduardo stepped up behind him, reached over his shoulder, and took a fat yellow bag of cornmeal down from a shelf. "You make your margarita," he said and, twisting out the brown cigarette, "I will cook for you."

Cutler gaped. In his mind, Eduardo scowled and muttered between clenched teeth, *Do you take me for a woman?* In his mind, his mother said sharply, *Cooking is not man's work. People will think you're not normal.* He couldn't stop himself — he grinned. Eduardo, crackling the skins off onions at the sink, glanced at him. "I made a joke?" he said. And Cutler said, "They taught you to cook in those highrise hotels?"

Eduardo shook his head, probed drawers for a knife with which to cut the onions. "I was the oldest child. My mother became sick — what you call multiple sclerosis, yes?" On a sleek butcherboard, he began to chop the onions. The knifeblade clacked on the board. The smell was sharp. "And my father had to work. Or search for work. I have five younger brothers. Someone had to cook, no?" He smiled briefly, stepped past Cutler, and took from the refrigerator a steak in a flat styrofoam tray wrapped in clear plastic. "And it was me."

Cutler found a glass, opened the freezer, dropped ice cubes into the glass, and poured scotch over them. "They have an apprentice system, don't they?" he said. "Chefs in those big kitchens? They pick and choose who they're going to teach."

"*Sí.*" Eduardo nicked the wrapper on the steak with the point of the knife, ripped the wrapper away, laid the steak on the cutting board. "Oh — one of them taught me." He began to slice the meat from the bone. Quickly, neatly. Cutler leaned back against the breakfast bar and watched. Eduardo glanced at him again. A smile twitched the corners of his mouth, and he winked. "But not to cook," he said.

Eduardo will cook every meal if Cutler lets him. If Cutler fixes breakfast above, below Eduardo makes the bed and, if he isn't watched, vacuums, or cleans the bathroom. The second Saturday, he climbed an aluminum ladder and, with tools and the strips of metal he promised to bring, put back the rain gutter, and soldered the break. With all the excitement that went on between them in the shower, he noticed that the spray head leaked, and the next week he installed a new one. It is all Cutler can manage to keep him from washing the plate glass of the sliding doors every weekend.

This is the only unsettling part of this season with

Eduardo. Every day the sun shines. Gulls wheel white against skies of perfect blue. The blue ocean glitters. The shore curves away in low brown hills. The breeze off the water cools the sun's steady summer heat, yet the nights are not cold. They can sleep naked as they want to sleep after they make love, wake naked and make love again. It is May, it is June, so the beach is often peopled on weekends, the only time Eduardo comes here. But now and then, far into the night, they have made love out on the beach under the stars, when they are the only ones. Eduardo is goodnatured and funny, and the hours pass without friction. So Cutler tries to dismiss his uneasiness.

He knows where it comes from. During the years with Moody and Pelletier, he was the chore boy. Because Moody had money, because Pelletier was beautiful. And mean. And Cutler can't get used to being waited on. At first he more than distrusts this, he dislikes it, it seems wrong to him. And on the third or fourth weekend, driven by feelings stronger than he has reckoned on, his tongue loosened by too many margaritas — yes, he coaxed grumpy Eduardo into trying one at last, who became an instant convert — he says aloud that he dislikes it and wishes Eduardo would quit it.

Eduardo frowns. "It is nothing. I am used to it. I did it at home. I do it for my cousins, now."

"And that's enough," Cutler says. "You work all week. I have nothing to do. I can clean my own house."

The television set is on. They are paying no attention to it. They are paying attention only to each other, close together on the sailcloth cushions of the couch, their eager, seeking movements making the wicker of the couch creak. The shifting colored light from the big screen is the only light in the long room. It plays on Eduardo's face, which he raises to Cutler's. He puts a kiss on Cutler's mouth. "You live in your mind," he says. "I live in my body. Your mind must always be busy with something, no? It is the same for my body." He smiles. "Besides, I cannot bring you gifts." Most of his pay at Giant TV he sends home to Mexico. "I can only do small, common things for you. It is little enough. You must allow me."

Cutler allows him. When it can't be helped.

With a squeegee and a green plastic bucket of suds, he is on the upper deck, barefoot in jeans, washing the sliding glass panels, when he feels the deck vibrate and turns. Pelletier climbs the stairs from the beach. He wears the baggy flower-print surfer trunks from last year. They look ragged. He has spilled something down his chest to which sand and dirt have stuck. His hair is almost to his shoulders and dingier than last time. He needs a shave again. His teeth are smoky, but he shows them in a grin of triumph, and waves a newspaper, a section of the *Times,* folded over on itself. Cutler says nothing. He simply stares. Seeing Pelletier stirs no feeling in him. It is the first time this has happened, and he doesn't know what to make of it. He ought to feel relieved. Or maybe sorry. Something. Pelletier was life to him, so short a time ago.

"You haven't seen it, have you?" Pelletier takes the long green handle of the squeegee out of Cutler's hand and puts the newspaper into it. "Read it, Darryl. Read it, and weep."

Coffee has splashed the paper. The brown stain is still damp. Cutler runs his eyes over the quarter page. The name Quinn stops him. This is the story. The broken skull of what was once a human being washed up on shore far down the coast one morning last week, where a dog belonging to a family living in a camper on the beach found it. The lower jaw was missing, but the teeth in the upper jaw made it possible to determine from dental records that the remains are those of the screenwriter, Phil Quinn, who disappeared mysteriously last December. He apparently drowned while swimming alone at night, and his body was swept out to sea by an undertow. The story is not very long. Cutler hands the paper back.

"Outsmarted myself?" Pelletier tosses back the squeegee. He still grins with those stained teeth. "Isn't that what you said?" He nods and jeers. "Yeah, well, we both know who I outsmarted, don't we, Darryl?"

Up on the cliff, a car door slams. It is early, but it's also a big holiday. Crowds will be swarming onto this stretch of sand as onto every stretch of sand from Crescent City to the Mexican border soon. But the sound of this car door is familiar, and Cutler feels a chill. "Me," he says, "every which way. Okay, Chick? You want to run along now?"

"Quinn had money that makes Moody look like a welfare case," Pelletier says. "I told you it would work out. I told you I'd live like a king off her."

"Why don't you just go, okay?" Cutler says.

Pelletier frowns, tilts his head. "What's wrong with you? You always wanted me to stay before. Aren't you going to beg me for some sex, as long as I'm here?" He giggles and pushes down the tattered trunks. "How about a little head, Darryl? To start the day off like old times?"

"What's the matter—Veronica not putting out?" Cutler says. "Pull those up." Footsteps echo off the cliff stairs. "Somebody's coming."

"She can't get enough. I like variety, that's all." But Pelletier pulls up the shorts. "Somebody?" He eyes Cutler sharply. "Who? Aren't you going to introduce me?"

"People." Cutler is frantic. He wants to shove Pelletier. Hard. Right off the deck. "It's the Fourth of July."

"And you won't let me shoot off my rocket." Pelletier slips a hand down inside the trunks and makes fast pumping motions with his fist. Cutler swings the squeegee at him. Pelletier ducks, laughs, dances backward out of range. And stops. His expression changes. He stares. At Eduardo who stands inside the glass where the soapsuds have dried in milky streaks. He looks out. He appears a little surprised. Cutler rolls the panel open.

"Eduardo Ortiz," he says, "Chick Pelletier."

Pelletier looks Eduardo up and down for a cold-eyed second. He glares at Cutler. This is startling. Surely, he can't be jealous. He mumbles, "Yeah, I remember you," turns, and drums his heels down the stairs. He is out of sight for a moment, then they can see him heading up the beach toward Cormorant Cove. Once he stops, turns, and looks back, shielding his eyes with the paper. Then he walks on, slapping the paper against his thigh.

"He was beautiful before," Eduardo says.

"Forget him. I have. I'm glad you're here. Only what about the picnic with your cousins?"

Eduardo makes a face. "They got a girl for me," he says. "I told them I had to work. They did not argue. They think I will be paid double time."

He wakens because Eduardo has taken away his hardness and his heat that lay tight against Cutler's back as the two of them slept. The bed shifts, the frame that holds the box spring rattling a little. Cutler mutters and turns over. He sees a flutter of white in the darkness. Eduardo is pulling on a T-shirt. He stands and tucks himself into white jockey shorts. There is a whisper of fabric as he kicks into his jeans. The zipper rasps softly. Cutler squints at the red numerals of the clock.

"It's three in the morning," he says. "Something wrong? What did I do?"

"I have a surprise for you," Eduardo says.

"I don't need surprises." Cutler props himself on an arm. "I like things with you just the way they are."

Eduardo laughs softly and moves away from the bed. He must be barefoot because Cutler doesn't hear him any more than he sees him, but he knows he has gone down the room. The next moment, the pulleys of the curtains squeak. And Eduardo is framed against the starlight of the night beyond the glass wall. "You will like this," he says. "There should always be surprises." He rolls the panel back. "Wait here. Do not move until I call you."

Cutler grins. "Anything you say, chief."

Eduardo steps out and crosses the deck. "It will not take me long." He drops from sight.

Cutler sits up, draws his knees up, hugs them, rests his chin on them. He laughs and feels like a child. Like the child he was before his father left. After that, the only surprises in his life were unpleasant ones. What is Eduardo up to? Cutler can't wait. He pulls on sweatpants, ties the cord, goes barefoot out on the deck and looks up and down the night beach.

Swimmers, wind-surfers with their orange, red, yellow sails, suntanners, babies, dogs, grandmas in floppy hats, kite flyers—all have gone. The wind tumbles ghostly picnic trash along the sand. Except for the surf, there is no other movement. Except for the surf, there is no sound, not even of late trucks up on the highway. This makes the slam of the trunk lid of Eduardo's old car up there loud.

Cutler runs down the steps to the sand, around the corner of the house, and up the steep slope to the rear. The whiteness of the cliff stairs reflects enough light to show him Eduardo coming down. A long, flat carton is in his arms. Whatever is inside the carton rattles with his steps. Cutler trudges through the loose, coarse sand to the foot of the stairs.

Eduardo stops. "You were supposed to wait."

"What's in the box?" Cutler says, and starts up to meet him. "Is that the surprise?" He reaches. "Let me see." Eduardo clutches the box, and takes two steps backwards. Cutler laughs. "Come on, Eduardo. Show me."

"You will spoil the surprise," Eduardo says. He sounds strict. "It will be nothing if I show you. Are you a child? Go back." He points down at the shadowy house. "Close the curtains and wait. When it is ready, I will call you."

Cutler doesn't want to make him angry. "Okay. Don't shoot." He turns away. "I'll go peacefully."

"Be patient, *Querido*," Eduardo says. "It will be beautiful. I promise you."

"It always is." Cutler goes down the half dozen steps he has climbed, crosses the dark sand. At the corner of the house, he stops and looks back. But Eduardo isn't following. He doesn't trust Cutler. He waits on the stairs. Cutler laughs, shrugs, and goes back down the slope beside the house. In the bedroom, he finds the cord and closes the curtains. He stands listening but hears nothing. Waiting in the dark, like a child at hide and seek, tightens his bladder. The tile and mirror glare of the bathroom makes him wince. He pisses, flushes the toilet, reads his watch, switches off the lights, returns to the bedroom. The glass panel is open. The curtains are heavy but the wind stirs them. Cutler shouts, "What's happening? Are you ready? I can't stand it much longer."

"Wait, wait," Eduardo yelps from out on the beach. "Not yet. *Momentito, por favor.*" He sounds out of breath and busy. "I will call you. Wait." Cutler smiles, shakes his head, goes to the table beside the dim white bed for a cigarette. His hands need something to do. He fumbles the lighter and laughs at himself. *Are you a child?* Yes, he is a child, and very excited. He gets the lighter right side up and thumbs it. There is a loud sputtering and sizzling. He drops the lighter with a jerk. But it was not the lighter that made the noise. Eduardo shouts, "All right, *Querido*. Now! Come out, come out."

Cutler runs down the room, paws the curtains aside, stumbles out onto the deck. Down along the beach near the water, fountains of fire spout sprays of sparks, red, golden, white, green, blue, spout them high into the air, hissing, fizzing, blinding bright against the blackness of sea and sky. In their hectic glow, Eduardo runs along in a crouch, a little torch in his hand, touching it to black cones spaced out in a long row. And more fire fountains erupt as the first ones falter and fail, their last sparks winking out on the wet sand. Eduardo straightens, turns, the colored fires shining on his face. He holds out his arms and laughs. "It is beautiful, no?"

"Beautiful." Cutler leaves the deck and jogs down to him. He gives him a hug. "It is also illegal. Don't you know that?"

Eduardo nips his ear. "Why do you think I waited until three o'clock in the morning? Even the law must sometimes sleep." The fires of the last fountains are gold and green. The gold one sputters, gasps, goes out. The green one in a moment does the same. They wait. The blackness is complete. So is the silence. "You see? No one is coming."

"It was a beautiful surprise," Cutler says.

"Ah, but it is not over." Eduardo pulls away from him. The brightness of the fountains is still in Cutler's eyes and he can't see. He can only hear Eduardo running away from him along the sand. "That was only half of it. Wait. You will see."

"Where did you get these?"

"My cousin bought them. For the picnic. But he got too many. He could not have used them all." The light of the little torch flickers. There is a hot spurt of fire on the dark sand yards away. A whoosh. High overhead a rocket bursts. The explosion is loud and echoes off the water and the rocks. Showers of scarlet stars burst in the sky, a flower of falling fire.

Another spurt of flame, another whoosh, and overhead another concussion, and a dazzling burst of blue sparks opens in a spreading globe and drifts down into the sea. Eduardo runs along with his torch, and rocket after rocket soars, explodes in glory, and is gone. At last there are no more. Eduardo comes back. He pokes the flame of the little torch into the sand and it is dark. "There. Did you like the second half?"

"I loved it," Cutler says, "but I don't know how they felt about it in Malibu."

"They will understand," Eduardo says. "They are Americans. It is the custom. This is the day to celebrate freedom."

"Just the same," Cutler says, and nudges one of the charred paper cones with his toe, "we'd better clean up here. We'd better hide the evidence."

When the sound of feet on the deck wakes him and he sees the shadow of a man on the curtains he is afraid his joke about Malibu may not have been a joke after all. The shadow man raps the doorframe. Cutler gropes for his sweat pants on the floor and groggily puts them on. Eduardo stirs but does not wake up. Cutler pulls the sheet over him and limps to open the curtains. The sun glares in his eyes. People have come back to the sand. A fancy kite darts and dodges against a hard blue sky. Boys surf. Cutler peers at the man standing in front of him. He is not dressed for the beach. He wears a three-piece suit, tan, lightweight, but no real concession to summer. His face is egg shaped, clean shaven, he has combed his hair across baldness and fixed it there with hair spray. He is about forty, and ten pounds overweight. From an inside jacket pocket he draws a leather folder. When it falls open, it shows Cutler a badge.

"Hughes," the man says. "United States Department of Immigration and Naturalization. You have an Eduardo Ortiz living here. I'd like to talk to him, please."

Cutler moves to roll the door shut. "He isn't here," he says.

But he is too slow. Too slow for the man, who takes hold of the edge of the door and puts his foot on the stainless steel grooves in which the door slides. And too slow for Eduardo, who bolts out of bed, mother naked, rushes at the door, head down, knocks Cutler aside, dumps the immigration man on his butt, streaks across the deck, and into the arms of two men in tan uniforms waiting on the deck stairs. He struggles, but they are bigger and stronger than he is. People on the beach stare. The immigration man gets to his feet, puts away his leather folder, brushes with his hands at the seat of his pants, and says to Cutler:

"Can I have his clothes, please?"

23

The sun rises blazing, and by nine in the morning the house is an oven. The wind doesn't come from the west, off the sea. It comes from jungles to the south, dense with wetness. Because he can't bear the heat of the house and its emptiness without Eduardo, he walks the beach for hours. And when a wave crawls up brown around his bare feet, it is warm. He wears only swimtrunks, but he sweats.

He wants to sleep by day, because at night Quinn is out there roaring on the beach, Moody claws and screeches, the boy in the crash helmet moans. But to sleep in the heat is impossible. He remembers the months with Pullen — how hot the Valley used to get. Only one thing made survival possible out there. Air conditioning.

In the workroom, he lifts a telephone directory from a white drawer. It is thick and heavy as a brick. He drops it on the white desk where the bottles jingle and the computer wears a sad, gray face. He thumbs pages. His sweat drips on the pages. Here are the air conditioners. He picks up the phone and taps buttons.

"You gotta be kidding." The voice is coarse as a file, the accent New York. "Buddy, we got a waiting list. Every unit I got on order is spoke for, right? And I'll be lucky to get half. You understand what we're talking — at the earliest? We're talking September."

Cutler hangs up and punches other numbers. When the numbers aren't busy, when he gets answers, they are always the same. He leaves the phone, the directory, the desk, strips and gets under a cold shower. He does this as often as he returns to the house. Standing in the spray, he tells himself the bastards will be sorry. The heat will break, and they'll be stuck. It has to break. In a hundred thirty years it's never held on like this. And this is the beach. What are they going to do with air conditioners for the next hundred thirty years—watch them turn to rust?

He dresses. Theatres are air conditioned, aren't they? He will go find a movie to stare at in a theatre. He is drenched in sweat by the time he has climbed to the edge of the coast road and the Celica. He cranks down all the windows, cranks up the sun roof. The way the heat blows in reminds him of his trip to the desert, the fat man who made whirligigs and couldn't read. It has been months since Cutler drove these broad, white, sunstruck boulevards. Banners stream from the thin silver lamp posts. Yellow, white, green, some plain, some printed with linked circles, others with streaking stars. Festive. The Olympics are about to start.

The sidewalk in front of the theatres—there are three of them side by side behind rows of dark glass doors—swarms with young people. They wear bright, matching sweat suits. Or have wrapped themselves in swaths of gaily printed cloth. Some wear turbans, some gaudily embroidered caps. Their skins are brown, black, yellow, blond. They are big and broad, small and fine. And lively. They laugh, and jabber in languages he has never heard. The

University is near. They must be barracked there. He grins with them. They make the Olympics seem real to him. At last.

They really will begin soon. Which means that they will end soon. And then his film will be shown on television. He has grown tired of waiting for it. Not while Eduardo was here—he scarcely thought of it then. Now, it obsesses him. He has frayed the script by reading it over and over again. He watches that looming screen in the living room late into the night for glimpses of gymnasts. He tosses aside the other sections of the morning *Times*. With his coffee, he wants only the sports section.

Not quite true. The entertainment section has printed pieces about the film, with photos of Nicky Wyatt in white shorts and bare chest and white ankle socks, doing back flips on a mat. Sexy. But the producer's name, the director's name, and the writer's name have been in the stories too, sometimes. So he looks at the entertainment section too. And waits each week for the arrival of *TV Guide* in the mailbox at the top of the white cliff stairs. There is going to be a feature soon on "A Gold for Living." A sulky young woman in faded jeans, a tanktop, and a rat's nest of black hair came a few weeks ago with a recorder, to tape his lies about how he wrote the script. A bearded fat boy with her stood, lay on the floor, climbed on the furniture, on the deck rails, taking Cutler's picture—fifty times in fifteen minutes. Then they were gone. It was like a dream. But these kids on this scorching noontime sidewalk are real. His time is coming.

*   *   *

The heat does not give up. It gets worse. Temperatures climb from the nineties into the hundreds. He makes it a pattern now, sitting the afternoons out in the dark, false cold of movie houses, finding hamburgers or pizzas or burritos for supper, then nodding in other movie houses afterward, until they turn up the lights, and he stumbles out among the popcorn boxes, paper cups, and candy wrappers into the humid night, to find the car and drive back to the beach, where Quinn and Moody and the boy await him. Not sleep. Not even out on the deck. He has tried that. Out there the air is stifling too.

But he can't get over the idea that out on the beach it will be cool, and now, when he reaches the foot of the cliff stairs, he bypasses the house. Locked up, it will have collected heat all day and will be holding it still. Anyway, he needs to stretch his legs. He has done nothing but sit for twelve hours. He goes down the steep slope in the shadow of the house, and walks out to the firm sand, where the surf curls, murmuring. He is stiff from all that sitting. He aches from it. And his head aches. He fills his lungs now to clear them with fresh salt air. A mistake. The heat is breeding and killing plankton in the water, microorganisms, billions of them. And they stink. He turns back, hikes toward the sharp-cornered shape of the house, climbs the steps to the lower deck and stops. At the place where the immigration officers stopped Eduardo.

Someone is sitting in a chair on the deck. He can't make out any features. It is too dark. Whoever is there is a shadow in shadow. It does not move. Warily, heart ticking, he steps softly up onto the deck, narrowing his eyes to try to see. The lumpy form remains motionless. What jumps into his mind is that Pelletier has come back again. Squarish shapes stand on the planks beside the chair. These would be the eternal cartons of his clothes, wouldn't they? And he has fallen asleep—drunk, or drugged, or both. Or simply because it's late. It is well past midnight.

"Chick?" Cutler takes two steps. "Are you all right?"

The lumpy form jerks. "Who is that? Darryl?" Something wooden clatters on the planks. Without getting up, the figure goes into agitated motion, bending, scrabbling. "It's no use robbing me. I don't have any money." An arm is raised. A stick waves. "Don't come any closer."

"It's me," he says. "What are you doing here?"

"Mercy, you frightened me." He hears quick breaths. There is a real tremble in her voice. "What do you mean, sneaking up that way in the dark?"

"It's my house." Digging keys from his pocket, he crosses the deck, unlocks the glass panel of the bedroom, slides it back. Hot air breathes out. He reaches inside and lifts light switches. A lamp glows by the bed. From boxy metal outdoor housings, light glares on the deck. "You don't sneak up on your own house."

"Where were you? I've been waiting here for hours."

"I wasn't expecting you." He looks at her. She has grown old. The scarf tied over her hair doesn't hide that her hair is white. She is fat. Unhealthily. Her ankles and wrists are puffy. He remembers her angular, sharp as her voice. If not for her voice, he wouldn't know her. "You should have written. You should have phoned."

She blinks in the harsh light. "I wanted to surprise you." She shifts an old soft leather shoulder bag from her lap to the planks, positions the cane, grips it with twisted fingers, pushes to her feet. She used to tower over him. How can she be so short? Her pants suit is of tough-looking fabric, an indifferent rose color, not new, not lately cleaned. A cheap cloth coat of the same color, also not new, lies across suitcases beside the chair. "You'll have to carry my bags," she says. "I have arthritis."

"I don't have a guest room," he says.

"That taxi driver didn't like it much, having to drag them down all those stairs and around out here where I could sit down. I gave him two dollars. You'd have thought I insulted him." Putting weight on the cane, she hobbles toward Cutler. "The fare was almost sixty dollars. I don't know why you live way out here, miles from civilization. You're successful now, you're rich. You could live anywhere you want to."

"You're going to have to stay at a motel," he says. "There's no room here."

"Oh, we'll work it out." She comes at him, and he steps aside. She looks around the bedroom, lifts the cane, points into the hallway. "There's another room over there. Isn't that a bedroom too?"

"Office," he says. And adds, "Gymnasium."

"Well, never mind," she says. "I can sleep on the living room couch."

"Living room's up above," he says. "I don't think you can climb the stairs." He goes out on the deck again. "No—tonight you'll sleep here." He hangs the limp old bag on his shoulder, lays the coat over his arm, picks up the suitcases. "Tomorrow, we'll get you into a motel." He steps back into the bedroom, and she is not there. He hears the bathroom door close. The bed needs changing. He sets her stuff down, strips the sweated sheets, stuffs them into the closet, brings out fresh ones, makes the bed. Down the hall, the toilet flushes, water runs, the bathroom door opens. Her cane thumps in the hall, but she doesn't come in here. She steps into the workroom, switches on the lights. He goes and stands in the door. The white office furniture gleams, the bottles, the metal tubing of the Nautilus.

"Why, there's a couch in here," she says. "Isn't it the kind that makes down into a bed?"

"The exercise equipment is in the way," he says.

"I'm surprised. You never cared for sports."

"People change." He switches off the lights and crosses the hall again. "We haven't seen each other for a long time." He frowns at her. "How did you know where to find me? Something in the papers, right?"

"About your movie. That journalism teacher at the high school said you had talent. I thought she'd just fallen for your looks." She makes her way to the chest of drawers. The top ones were Pelletier's. It is the top ones she opens. "I'll just put my things in here, shall I?"

"Lorraine," he says sharply, "I said you're going to a motel tomorrow. There isn't room here. This house isn't arranged for somebody who can't climb stairs."

"I'll manage." She sits on the bed and smiles at him sweetly. "You'll help me, won't you?" She doesn't wait for his answer. She hauls a suitcase up beside her on the bed and begins unbuckling its straps. "My, it's hot, isn't it? I hope it's not always like this."

"You'll soon be back in Portland," he says, "in the rain and the cold."

"Oh, no, Darryl." She looks up at him from above the open suitcase. Her eyes are round and childlike. "I've come to stay. Didn't I say that?" She lifts out a handfull of blouses folded flat, and holds them up for him to take. "Just lay those in the drawer for me, please?"

"No, you didn't say it," he says, "and I didn't say you could." He pushes the blouses back at her. "If you haven't got the money for a plane ticket, I'll give it to you. But you're not staying here, Lorraine. No way." He laughs. "I can't believe this. I really can't."

"Well, it's true," she says, and smooths the blouses on her knees. "Darryl, I am your mother. I am no longer able to work. I had government disability insurance, but the administration changed, didn't it, and my claim was disallowed. That pension fund I contributed to all those years at the department store pays me about a hundred dollars a month. It will be four years before I can collect my Social Security. I've sold all there was to sell, car, furniture, silverware. And now even my watch and my wedding ring—to pay for this trip. I've been living for three years in one unheated room with a bath down the hall six people share. By the last week of the month there's nothing to buy food with. I get one meal a day in a soup kitchen in a church basement with the bums and bag ladies. Darryl, I am old and sick. And you are my son. You have a lovely house and plenty of money. You are not going to fob me off with a plane ticket back to Portland. I looked after you when you were small and couldn't look after yourself. Now you are going to look after me."

"You're out of your mind," he says.

Her eyes harden in their fatty pouches. Her mouth turns down at the corners in the old way. "Darryl, don't make me get ugly with you."

"Are you threatening me?" He laughs again. "I don't believe this. In case you hadn't noticed, I'm no longer a little kid. You can't slap me around anymore."

Her puffy face looks genuinely shocked and hurt. "Slap you around? When did I ever slap you around? What a phrase. If I lost my temper sometimes, it was because I was worn out with work and worry. Do you think those times were easy for me, a woman, alone, trying to raise a child?"

"Don't get started on that," he says. "You never let me forget how hard you worked and how I made you suffer."

"Well, I don't remember ever slapping you," she says.

"I don't remember anything else," he says. "I need a drink. This is bizarre, you know that?" He barges across the hall to the workroom. The fluorescent lights there flicker and ping with startlement. He shouts to her, "And what do you mean—'plenty of money'?" He uncorks Jack Daniel's and tilts a tall glass half full. "I netted thirty thousand dollars for that screenplay." He ducks to the little refrigerator, paws out ice-cubes, splashes them into the glass. "How many sick old women is that supposed to support?" He slams the refrigerator door. "Most of it is gone now, anyway." He takes a long swallow of whiskey, shudders, and returns to the bedroom door. "I had doctors and hospitals to pay."

"You have a yacht." She is on her feet, has some-how managed to get the grip from the bed to the dresser, and is shifting clothes into the drawers. "It said so in the newspaper." She turns and blinks pity at him across the room. "I'm sorry you were ill. You should have sent for me. That's when a boy needs his mother."

"Jesus," he says, and takes another long gulp of the drink. "It's not a yacht, Lorraine. It's nothing but a sailboat, and after the storms we had last winter, it's probably smashed and lying on the bottom."

"Then there'll be insurance, won't there?" she says placidly, and goes back to her unpacking. "And that *will* help a sick, old lady."

"No sick, old lady I know," he says. "You're leav-ing here on the first flight to Portland tomorrow morning." He stalks across the room and flaps the soft, fake leather lid of the suitcase down on her reaching hand. "So stop unpacking and go to bed. Now. Because we are getting up very, very early. I can hardly wait."

She slaps him. Surprisingly hard. It brings tears to his eyes. She says, "Now you listen to me, Darryl, and listen well, because I am only going to say this once. I know why you left Portland. I know all about it. You ran over a little boy with your car. An eleven-year-old boy on a bicycle. With that new little red sports car I bought you for gradu-ation."

His face stings where she slapped him. "No," he says.

"Don't make it worse by lying," she says. "At a deserted street corner in the middle of the night. A woman who lived there heard it. She looked out and saw you."

"Not me," he says. "It was too dark."

"She saw the car. You killed that little boy, Darryl. But you knew that, didn't you? That's why you ran away and never came back."

"I ran away from you," he says. "All I'd been waiting for was the wheels."

"Rubbish. I fed you, clothed you, housed you, gave you pocket money. You'd never have left, if you could help it. Something frightened you. And when I read that woman's description of the car in the newspaper, I knew what it was."

"Then why didn't you go to the police?"

Her eyes shift. Her warped hand fiddles with the suitcase buckle. "You were my child," she says in a small, prim voice. "You'd done a terrible thing, but I had to protect you. I'd always protected you."

"You're a lousy liar," he says. "You always were. I was nothing but a pain to you. You told me over and over I was no good. And here was your chance to prove it. You're lying, Lorraine."

"All right," she flares. "You were no good — exactly like your father. But you were seventeen — a child. And who do you think the papers would have blamed — and the television? Me — that's who. They'd have said I was a bad mother. After all I sacrificed, all those years, to bring you up decently. I made a mistake — I bought you that car. But I was a good mother, Darryl. And they would have crucified me. I'd have lost my job, my friends, everything."

He stares. "My God, you mean it." He shakes his head, laughs disbelief, raises the glass to drink. She knocks it from his hand. It flies across the room, thuds on the carpet, strewing ice cubes, spreading a dark stain. Her face is red. He says, "You really are crazy, aren't you?"

"Maybe I was," she pants, "but not anymore. I don't care anymore. I don't care what people think. Poverty and sickness can do that to a person—take away their self-respect. Job, friends, a life? I don't have any of them anymore." Her laugh is bitter. "Nobody cares when you're down and out. So I have nothing to lose, Darryl. Nothing, understand me? And if you send me back to Portland, I will go to the police. And I'll tell them the truth."

He scoffs. "You don't know the truth."

"All right, then, I'll lie." Her mouth clamps shut in shock at what she has said. But she nods with ferocious conviction. "I'll tell them I was with you in the car. I was with you when it happened. I saw it all."

He turns away, sick. "Go back to Portland, Lorraine. I'll send you a thousand dollars a month."

"You won't," she says. "The only way I'll get any help from you is to stay right here."

"Go to bed." He crouches for the glass and the ice cubes. "We'll talk about it in the morning."

"Oh, no." Her voice is suddenly airy, almost gay. "We'll find pleasanter things to talk about."

24

When he believed Pelletier about the backgammon, he bought him an expensive inlaid table to play it on. He never used it. Now Cutler has pulled it from a closet and taken it down to the bedroom where his mother sleeps. He keeps hoping she will not wake up. But this morning is not that morning. She has struggled out of bed and sits in a basket chair in a nightgown with a torn lace collar and a faded floral print housecoat. Her flesh sags and bulges. Her face turns toward him, pouchy, dazed, mouth hanging open. She makes a try at a smile as he hinges out the little leaves and thin legs of the table and places it in front of her. But the smile doesn't work, and her eyes are dull.

"There." He walks off. "Breakfast is coming."

"Not with all those peppers again, I hope." Her voice has lost its edge. It has become a thin whine. "I keep telling you, I don't care for spicy food."

"You wanted to live in California," he calls back cheerily, and climbs the stairs. He loads her plate. She is a greedy old thing. Her eyes bulge as she shovels down her meals. The scrambled eggs he has laced with *jalapeñas*. The Mexican sausage is of the hottest sort. She will weep, but she will eat. The tray is Mexican, embossed tin over wood. He lays a napkin and utensils on it, sets a glass of orange juice there, a Mexican pottery mug of coffee, picks up the tray.

Halfway down the long room, he hears a rattle in the kitchen, and stops and looks back, frowning. He goes back to see. An amber plastic vial has fallen to the floor. Its lid has popped off, and red capsules strew the vinyl tiles. He makes a face, sets the tray on the breakfast bar, crouches and gathers up the capsules. When they are back in the vial, he snaps the lid on, and hides the thing at the rear of a high shelf. Heading with the tray for the hot sunlight of the deck again, he worries. Those were Moody's seconols. There were a lot of them, but now they're going fast, and where will he get more—if he needs more, and it looks as if he will. He sets the tray in front of her.

She picks up the fork in her gnarled fingers, and drops it. She makes a little impatient noise. He bends for the fork, hands it back to her. "Thank you. I don't know why I do that all the time. My hands feel numb." She unfolds the napkin, lays it in her lap, with dreamlike slowness. "I feel numb all over." She scoops up a forkful of eggs and crams her mouth and gulps. Tears run down the bread-dough whiteness of her cheeks. "And groggy, too." She hastily swallows half the orange juice. "All I seem to want to do is sleep."

"And eat," he says. "No wonder they took you off welfare. They're trying to balance the budget."

She stabs the sausage with her fork. Grease runs out, yellow with the juice of chilis. She slices away at the sausage with her knife, and stuffs a great chunk into her mouth. Chewing, weeping, she glares at him. "You have a nasty, mean tongue."

"I wonder where I got it?" he says. He wears a little interested smile. "That's not too hot for you again, is it?" And when she nods, gulping, and reaches for the remaining orange juice, "Aw, too bad. The package was marked 'mild.' How could they have made such a mistake—and after I told them how you hate hot food."

"You're doing it on purpose," she says. "You're making life hell for me."

He shrugs and briefly laughs. "Get used to it, dear mother. You asked for it. Coming here was your idea. And now you're stuck with it. And so am I, right? I can't let you go, can I?" He walks away, stands gazing out at the stunned ocean, the bleached sky for a minute. He turns back. "Look at it this way. You made life hell for me for eighteen years. Now is your chance to learn how it feels." He laughs sourly at himself. "Funny. I used to daydream this chance would come, and now—who needs it?"

"You're making it impossible for me to eat," she sobs, and pushes at the plate. "I'll starve to death."

"Suit yourself." He returns to pick up the tray. "You don't think I'll miss you, do you?"

"I want to go to a hospital," she whines. "I'm sick."

He snorts. "You were sick when you got here."

"This is different. I'm not myself." She gropes around on the carpet for her cane, grunting. "I've had a stroke or something. I can't even understand the television half the time." She gets the cane. "You don't have to drive me. I'll phone for a taxi." Gripping the cane in those swollen, twisted fingers, she heaves to her feet. "And I have my Medicare card. You won't need to waste any of your precious money on your dying mother."

"The police won't be interested in your Medicare card. And it's the police you'll go to, not a hospital."

He grips the tray with one arm, and snatches the cane from her. She gasps and drops into the chair again. It almost topples backward from her weight. She gapes at him. He tosses the cane on the bed, sets the tray rattling beside it, kneels and unplugs the telephone. The plug is a tiny clear plastic cube on the end of a clear plastic wire. He waves it in her face for a second, then sets the phone in the scrambled eggs on the tray. Across the hall, he unplugs the workroom phone and goes back, holding it high for her to see. He drops it jangling on the tray, hangs the cane over his arm, picks up the tray, and carries it past her toward the deck. Through the open wall section, air enters, sluggish and wet and hot. "Forget it," he says. "You're staying right here."

"You can't keep me prisoner. People walk along the beach. I'll scream for help."

He sighs, sets the tray on the deck rail, and goes back to stand in the opening. "In that case, I'll have to close this, won't I? And pull the curtains, so no one can see you? It's a hot summer, Lorraine. You said so yourself. When the sun shines full blast on all this glass, this room is an oven. You're going to hate that." He smiles, steps inside, and yanks the little rope that closes the curtains. "I'm so glad you reminded me of it. Talk about making life hell." He laughs, brushes the curtains aside, steps out, and rolls the panel shut. Through its thickness, and the muffling of the curtains, her voice reaches him, shrill, panicky:

"How will I get to the bathroom?"

"Crawl," he says.

*   *   *

She has stopped eating. On the road shoulder above the house, he raises the hatchback and lifts out sacks of groceries. Chicken is in them, noodles, butter, cream. For a day or two he will cook her food as bland as what she'd get in a hospital. He will cream the vegetables she likes — cauliflower, white asparagus, yellow beans. He will mash potatoes for her white as snow. Desserts will be custard, trifle, rice pudding.

He sets the bags one by one on the hot roof of the car and slams down the hatchback. He gathers the bags in his arms. In the mornings, he will soft-boil eggs, or poach them and lay them on white toast. He turns for the stairs and remembers the mail. It hadn't come when he left for the supermarket. At noon, he'll take her creamed soups or chicken broth. She'll soon be fed up with the pale and flavorless. Then he will start her again. Maybe with sirloin tips in a dark wine sauce. Veal parmigiana? She ought to welcome the change. She'd better.

Juggling the grocery sacks, he pulls the mailbox open. It is here — the *TV Guide*. Awkwardly, balancing on one leg, one knee up to support the sacks, he turns the magazine right side up. Sure enough. On the cover is a splashy Neilson painting of Nicky Wyatt in blue U.S. team skivvy shirt and white stretch pants, kicking a leg straight and high above a pommel horse. A GOLD FOR LIVING — TV MOVIE MIXES TEARS AND TRIUMPH. He elbows the mailbox closed, and hurries, grinning, for the stairs.

And sees her, out on the beach. In her rose-colored pants suit, bag over her shoulder. She plods along, bracing herself on a straw barrel chair from the bedroom, using it as a walker. Not easily. The legs poke into the sand. All the same, she is trying to hurry. Toward something. What? He squints against the glare of sun and sea. She stops, waves an arm, and her voice comes to him, far off but sharp as a gull's cry. And he sees them, up along the curve of sand by ragged rocks — a man and woman, young. They have been walking away, but when she cries to them, they stop and turn back. Yellow-orange Hawaiian shirts and shorts, sunglasses, straw hats, sandals, a camera on a strap around his neck. She squawks at them again and, hesitantly, they walk back toward her.

Cutler starts down the stairs. He wants to run, but the bulky sacks won't let him. He can't see his feet, can't hold the rail. At the landing, he sets them down. Hurriedly. One falls over and cans roll out, drop off the edge, plump in the sand below. He doesn't care. He hurls himself down the stairs, down the slope beside the house, out onto the beach. The sand is dry. Running in it is like trying to run in a nightmare. They have got to her. She is talking to them, waving that arm again, agitated. The woman helps her sit in the chair and crouches beside her to listen. The man stares at the house. Then he stares at Cutler running toward him, sweating, panting.

"It's all right," Cutler shouts, and waves open hands across one another, and shakes his head. "It's all right," he pants, and comes to a sand-spraying stop in front of them. "I'm her son. She'll be all right, now." He wipes sweat from his face with his hand and gives Lorraine a smile of tender reproof. "Mother, you know it's naughty to run away." He smiles at the couple, not so young as he thought.

Middle age will be along next week. They both have taken off their sunglasses and are regarding him doubtfully. "I had to go to the supermarket. I suppose I forgot to lock the door."

"You see," she cries. "Didn't I tell you?" She clutches at the woman. "He's keeping me prisoner."

Cutler gives the couple a long-suffering look. "I'm trying to look after her by myself, but sometimes they get to be a handful." He bends and tries to take hold of her to get her to her feet. "Come on, love. Back to the house. We'll watch some nice cartoons on television. You know how you like that."

She pushes him away, fierce, scratching like Moody. "He's trying to make you think I'm crazy," she screeches. "Well, I'm not crazy. You have to help me. He's the one who should be locked up."

"Come on, now, Mother," Cutler says gently, firmly.

"He ran over a poor little boy," she cries, grabbing the woman's hands, desperate to be believed. "And he knows I'll tell on him. And that's why he keeps me locked up." She glares at Cutler. "His own mother."

Over her head, Cutler looks with a regretful smile at the man, and taps his temple with a finger. The man smiles faintly back, gives a wry nod, and puts his sunglasses on again. He is not happy here. "Come on, Anita," he says. "This isn't any of our business."

"Oh, no," Lorraine begs. "Don't leave me. I'm telling you the truth." But the woman pulls free of her twisted grip, and gets to her feet. "You'll be all right now," she croons. She wags a finger. "You try to be a good girl." She puts on her sunglasses. "And don't ever run away again." She takes her man's arm, and they start off, pretending not to hurry.

Lorraine twists in the chair. "Go to the police."

They turn, smile, wave cheerfully. "Bye-bye."

"Your timing was off," Cutler says. "Too bad."

"You devil," she shrieks at him.

He has fallen asleep watching late night film clips of the day's Olympic events. He is naked, half wrapped in a beach towel, already sweating through on the sailcloth cushions of the wicker couch in the living room. Pelletier stands over him, neat and clean, sleek and shiny as if carved out of butter. He wears little gold trunks, very tight. Beyond him, Charles Bronson in bulky furs slogs on snowshoes up a rocky slope among pine trees. Pelletier squats for the control unit that has fallen to the floor, and switches the set off. He straightens, head cocked, mockery in his blue eyes.

"I knew you were weird, Darryl," he says. "But I never knew you went in for crippled old ladies."

Cutler sits up, blinking in the lamplight. He runs a hand down over his face, combs fingers through his hair. "You son of a bitch," he says. "It was you who tipped the immigration service about Eduardo, wasn't it?"

Pelletier shrugs. "I told you I'd figure out a way to make you sorry. When you wouldn't give me the money for Bianchi. Didn't I tell you? Do I ever lie?"

"You never lie." Cutler nods dully. His head aches and his mouth is dry. "You told me." A glass with an inch of warm whiskey in it sits under the lamp. He drinks it off, shudders, lights a cigarette from a pack that lies under the lamp. He peers at Pelletier glumly through the smoke. "We're even, then — is that it?"

"Who's the old broad?" Pelletier says.

"My mother. What do you want, Chick?"

"A drink." Pelletier picks up the empty glass and carries it up the room to the kitchen, where he switches on the lights. "You still keep my light rum?"

"Who else would drink it?" Cutler paws around on the floor for his jeans. "She saw a piece about my movie in the paper." He finds the jeans, puts them on. "I'm rich. I've got a yacht. So she came to live off me."

"And you're letting her? I thought you hated her." Pelletier opens and closes the refrigerator. "This kitchen smells like a Mexican restaurant." He rattles bottles, glasses, ice. "Or is she dying? She looks sick. Arthritis, right? She sleeps like she's full of drugs."

"She's not dying," Cutler says, "worse luck."

"Then why not dump her on a plane and ship her out?"

"It's not that simple." Cutler frowns, turns around, watches Pelletier busy under the white light, hair shining. He is too cheery. He never willingly so much as fetched an ice cube for Cutler before. "What do you want, Chick?"

"Here we go." Pelletier switches off the lights and comes back with the drinks. They jingle. He smiles. His teeth are very white. He puts scotch in Cutler's hand, and drops on the couch beside him. "What's not simple about it?"

Cutler tells him. "And she'll do it, too, the bitch."

"So you're doping her up," Pelletier says, "with those old seconols of Moody's, right? You put it in her food. Mexican stuff, to cover up the taste."

"All it does is make her sleep. Then she stops eating. She doesn't like spicy food. And I have to fix her what she wants. No taste to it. So I can't put in the seconols. And she gets out of control." He swallows some of the scotch, twists out his cigarette, and tells Pelletier about her escape to the beach. "I don't care how crippled she is. Next time she'll crawl up the stairs to the road and stick out her thumb. I know her."

"Not tonight." Pelletier sips his rum.

"Tonight I got her to try spaghetti. I emptied six capsules in the sauce. With about half a ton of basil and oregano. But it's not working, Chick."

"You mean, it's not killing her?"

"You've got some kind of mind," Cutler says.

"Darryl, that stuff isn't lead or arsenic or something. You can't give it in installments. You have to give it all at once. What—about eighty capsules to kill a full size man? She's not very big. Seventy ought to do it."

Cutler stares. "I haven't got seventy. And if I had, how would I get her to take them?"

"Good question." Pelletier yawns, sets his rum aside, and lies across Cutler's legs, stretching an arm for the cigarette pack. Warmth comes off his naked skin, and Cutler feels a surge of lust. Pelletier sets a cigarette going with a cheap little lighter. The lighter rattles on the table top. He sits up again, smoke circling his head, cocks an amused eyebrow, touches Cutler's crotch. "You appear to have a swelling, there."

"Golly," Cutler says, and switches off the lamp. His heart beats fast. He trembles. He says gravely, "Do you think you can reduce it, doctor?"

"Let's see." With a soft laugh in the dark, Pelletier runs down Cutler's zipper. Afterwards, a neat, pale shadow, putting on his swimtrunks again, he says, "Nice," bends, and sets a quick kiss on Cutler's mouth. "You always were the best." He turns on the lamp.

The light makes Cutler flinch. He hates afterwards. Everything that was wrong before comes straight back, afterwards. He looks up at Pelletier. "Help me, Chick. What am I going to do with her? This is supposed to be my god-damn shining hour. Instead, she wants to put me on death row. She always did."

Pelletier drops to his knees for his drink. He sits on his heels like a girl, puts the glass to his mouth, and gazes up at Cutler over it with wide, innocent eyes. "How about a nice cruise on your yacht? Wouldn't she like that?"

Cutler snorts. "I can't sail it. You know that."

"I'll sail it for you." Pelletier jumps up. "My ice is melted." He holds out his hand. "Let me rewire that for you."

But Cutler only stares. "Now? Tonight?"

Pelletier shakes his head, and takes the glass from him. "Not tonight." He walks to the kitchen again, and the lights blink on there again. His voice echoes off the hard surfaces. "Veronica will be home soon. From her therapy group." Ice cubes chink into glasses. "She's trying to kick dope. Free-basing made her sick." Bottles clank, liquid gurgles. "So what does she try to make herself feel better? Shooting up. It damn near killed her. Paramedics, hospital, the works." He sets a bottle down. "So we are very much into straightening out our pretty head, these days."

"What about your pretty head?" Cutler says.

"I quit cold turkey. It was making me paranoid." The kitchen lights go off, and he comes back with the drinks. "You know what I think? She could have quit cold turkey too. But it's the newest thing in chic, right? Taking the cure? Shit, coke isn't chic anymore." He hands Cutler the glass with scotch in it. "It's gotten cheap. Blacks on the streets are doing it." He sits on the floor in front of Cutler again, cross-legged this time, boyish. "But street blacks can't check into the Betty Ford Center, now, can they?"

"When, then?" Cutler wants to know. "Tomorrow night?"

Drinking, Pelletier shakes his head. "Tomorrow, we head up the coast. Monterey. Every rich addict in the west is going. Show business, music business. There's this quack with all the answers. Four day's worth."

Cutler moans. "Oh, no. Tuesday?"

"Yeah, that's when it ends. But it's a long drive, Darryl. Who knows what she'll want to do?" Pelletier takes a deep swallow of his rum. "We better leave it loose. I'll be here when I get here, okay?"

"But Monday night's my movie," Cutler wails. "I already missed the pre-showing at the studio. I'm supposed to watch the telecast at Eddie Axelrod's. With the cast and the director and everybody. Hell, Chick, what am I going to do with her till you show up?"

"Let her watch the picture with you. My son, the screen writer. Togetherness. Touching." Pelletier grins, drains the last of the rum down his beautiful throat. "Got to go." He jumps up, sets the glass under the lamp. Cutler sulks. Pelletier stands over him. "Darryl, I'm doing you a big favor. Who the fuck else can you get? Souza?"

"It has to be you," Cutler says.

"Damn right." Pelletier leaves the circle of lamplight. He turns at the night-black opening to the deck. "You need me, Darryl. You always did. You always will."

25

She peers through smeary dimestore reading glasses at the article in *TV Guide*. Today's entertainment section of the *Times* lies folded on the backgammon table. He has taken away her tray and come back with these things. He doesn't know why. Nor why he gave her a breakfast she liked this morning — eggs scrambled with cream, pink tasteless ham, pale white toast, sugary marmalade. Today he doesn't want her doped, he wants her wide awake. He wants her impressed. What sense does that make? Standing behind her, looking down on her white hair mussed from sleep, a wry smile tugs his mouth and he shakes his head in disgusted wonderment. It's a good thing she will be dead soon. He is turning into a pathetic little boy again, desperate for her approval.

"Mmm," she says drily now, and lays the magazine down. "That's nice." She grunts, reaching for the paper. "And this?" She picks it up with the same bored sigh she used when he gave her his drawings or papers from school. "Oh, I see. They review it ahead of time, do they?"

"They call it the best TV movie in five years." He leans over her shoulder and points. "See? 'The script by newcomer Darryl Cutler is almost flawless, a sure-fire Emmy award contender.' "

" 'His knowledge of the wild elation and desperate heartbreak of amateur athletics runs deep and true.' " She lays the paper down, takes off the glasses, frowns up at him. "I don't understand that. You always hated sports."

"I didn't hate them. You kept saying I'd hurt myself. And I believed you."

"I was only trying to protect you," she says. "You were clumsy. Very poor coordination. Like your father. He killed himself skiing. You know that, don't you?"

"He froze to death in a stalled car," Cutler says. "With that movie actress. They were trying to drive home from skiing. It was in the papers. You kept the clipping. I read it a hundred times."

She has got handy with the chair. She pushes herself to her feet, does a daring, unpropped turn, grips the chair again, and hobbles toward the hallway, leaning on it, shifting it ahead of her at a pretty good clip. "I have to bathe and dress. What time is your movie?"

"Not till tonight," he says. "Eight o'clock."

"I should get my hair done. People will be coming."

"Nobody's coming," he says. "Your hair is all right."

She stops in the hall. "There isn't a single book on sports on those shelves." She jerks her chin at the workroom. "I know what's there. I've been reading them. A person can't watch TV all the time. Trash, most of them. You always did have trashy taste. Comic books." She lurches on down the hallway, the chair creaking. He steps to the bedroom doorway to watch her. She says, "After you ran away, I found where you'd hidden them, and I burned them all."

"You burned up a fortune," he says. "They're collector's items today. Some are worth hundreds."

She gives a derisory hoot, rattles the knob, and the bathroom door swings open. The legs of the chair clack on the tiles. Her swollen feet in their stained, rose-colored slippers shuffle. She gets inside the bathroom, clutches the edge of the door, pulls herself as straight as her crippled joints will let her, and looks at him. "You know what I think, Darryl? I don't think you wrote that movie at all. I think someone else wrote it and you copied it. Like those times in grammar school." She shuts the door.

He runs to it. "I wanted you to praise me." The lock clicks. He shouts, "You never praised me for anything I did. I thought you'd praise me for something some other child did. You always said they were better than me."

"I have to get my hair done. I look a fright."

He draws back his foot to kick the door. He can't. He wants to shout, "I'm going to kill you, old woman," but his throat closes. Just as when he was small, he is terrified that she will hear him — even over the splash of the shower. "I'm going to kill you," he whimpers and, just as when he was small, he bursts into tears.

He keeps away from her. He drinks orange juice and vodka and stares at television. When television has bored him with idiot game shows and soap opera episodes, he goes down for a shower. The heat is no longer breaking records, but it hangs on. He enters the lower level through the workroom, carrying fresh clothes. When she hears him in the hall and calls to him, he does not answer. When he comes back upstairs he dislikes the look of the living room. He takes the sheets, pillows, electric blanket off the couch and stows them in the closet. He vacuums and dusts. Nobody's coming. But he wants the place as neat and shiny as if they were. After this, he feels hungry. He stuffs big avocado halves with fresh crab meat, and opens a bottle of champagne. This he takes out to the deck to eat and drink. He watches the shore birds, the gulls, the tilting sails of wind surfers, red yellow orange blue green. No one much is on the sand. It's Monday. They're working, the fools. He smiles to himself. The sun feels good. He likes the quiet, the steady distant sibilance of the surf. He finishes the champagne. It has made him happy. It has also made him sleepy, and he fetches a beach towel from inside, and sunglasses, and goes to nap on the sand. It is sundown when he wakens. She is shouting his name. Shrilly. He has double-checked to be sure the glass panels from her room and from the workroom are locked. But her voice knifes through the glass and the walls. She is hungry, of course. Taking his time, he gets to his feet, gathers up the towel, wades up the loose sand, and climbs the gritty deck stairs.

"You want your supper?" he calls.

"You forgot my lunch," she cries.

"I didn't forget." He mounts the stairs to the upper deck. His plate and glass and the champagne bottle are still on the table. He takes them indoors. When he has put away the towel, got rid of the bottle, washed plate and glass, he reaches down the amber vial of seconols from the high shelf. Where is that brown bag of chili powder Eduardo brought from some Mexican market in East L.A? He finds it, opens the bag, puts his nose down to it. It is so strong even the smell brings tears to the eyes. He grins, and rummages coarsely chopped beef from the refrigerator, locates onions, a handful of fresh peppers, yellow, red, green. He hauls down a skillet and begins to cook. There is only one person in the country he wants not to see his movie. "The hell with her," he says aloud, pushing the sizzling beef around in the pan. "The hell with her."

On Tuesday night, he tries to telephone Pelletier. In the emptiness of the Quinn house, the phone rings and rings. No one answers. At midnight, he gives up trying. He sleeps fitfully, waking to switch on the lamp and read his watch. Over and over again. At half past six, he stretches an arm to reach the phone, but he doesn't punch the number. If they got home late, Pelletier will be angry to be wakened early. Cutler pulls on warmup pants, goes out, and jogs up the beach. He thinks he is doing this to kill time, but he finds himself twelve minutes later on the new-moon beach of Cormorant Cove, panting, sweating, staring up at the rear deck of the Quinn house. The leaves of the plants in their boxes move in the breeze, but there is no other sign of life. He can't see past the house to the road to learn whether cars stand by the mailbox. He wants to shout to Pelletier to wake up and come help him, that he can't wait any longer, that he can't stand the old hag any longer, not an hour, let alone a day. He doesn't shout. He turns and trudges glumly back home.

*　　*　　*

The boat lies motionless at her moorings in glassy water that wavily reflects her shiny white hull. A blue tarpaulin is tightly stretched across her decks. The naked mast moves very slightly with the motion of the water. The water whispers. It is sunset. Wednesday. Pelletier will surely come tonight. Cutler has tired of reading over the messages that came late Monday, early Tuesday, congratulating him on his script. He has tired of going down to stand in the bedroom doorway and listen to the old woman snore and whimper in sleep. The bedroom is full of the familiar smell of her that haunted his childhood. It is an air he had hoped never to breathe again. He can't wait for her to be gone, gone forever. He will leave the glass panel open for days to rid the place of that smell of hers — some kind of soap, he thinks, though he has sniffed the bars of soap she brought and leaves in the bathroom and they do not smell that way. What is it? Hateful.

"I've got a dozen offers," Eddie Axelrod says on the phone. "Very good money, Darryl. We aren't going to have to wait for the Emmies. Everybody senses you're a winner. Everybody wants you to write their scripts. A dozen projects here. You can take your pick. We can ask the moon."

"Good," Cutler says. "I'll be in in a few days."

"Today," Eddie says. "What's wrong with today?"

"It's personal," Cutler says. "A family thing that has to be cleared up. A crisis."

"We don't want to keep them waiting too long," Eddie says. "They forget in no time. TV is your quintessential evanescence. A picture a week old — who remembers?"

"I'll be there as soon as I can," Cutler says. He

hangs up the phone softly, but he is frantic. He tries Pelletier's number again. No answer. He has to do something. What about the boat? What condition is it in? Have Pelletier and Veronica used it at all? He remembers paying the bills for mooring and security. But shouldn't he check? It would be a hell of a note if they got there in the middle of the night and the boat wasn't usable. What about fuel? He gets a jacket from the closet, picks up his keys from under the lamp by the couch, drops them into a pocket. When he opens the back door to leave, she shouts from below. She wants food. Good. Let her shout. A cloud bank is rolling in. No one will come to the beach. He climbs the stairs.

Now Souza comes slouching along the pier. "I'm surprised," he says. A reek of sweet wine is on his breath. Tobacco. Garlic. "I thought you were never going to sail her again."

"I'm not. I can't. You know that."

Souza glances back toward the carpark. "Chick didn't come with you? Why not?"

"He's out of town," Cutler says. "But he wants to use the boat. Soon. He sent me to see if it's shipshape. Is it shipshape?"

"I'll check it out and fuel it up," Souza says.

"Are you on every night?" Cutler says.

"You going at night?" Souza says. "Only night I get off is Monday. There's this kid on Monday nights. He gets girls down here. They fuck in people's boats." He makes a sour mouth, rubs his beard stubble. "But what can I do? Nobody else wants the job, and if I tell management on him, I won't even get one night off."

The wind has turned cold and damp. It is growing dark. The cloudbank crowding in shuts off the light of the setting sun. Cutler digs out his wallet and lays two twenties in Souza's grimy hand. "Be sure it's ready." He shivers, turns up his collar and, pushing hands into pockets, starts to walk away. "We could want it as soon as tonight."

"You going to deliver another television set?"

Cutler turns back. "What's that supposed to mean?"

"There was a man here today," Souza says, "asking about that time. December eleventh. Wondered could I tell him if you used your boat December eleventh. I says that was when you took out a big television set in a crate."

"Wonderful," Cutler says. "What kind of man?"

"An old guy, white handlebar mustache," Souza says. "Natty dresser. Rich. He drove off in a Rolls-Royce."

"Tony Baron," Cutler says. "Was that his name?"

"He didn't give no name," Souza says. "Just yours."

At first he has a hard time making the car go. His legs are shaking so he can't work the clutch, and the engine stalls. When he is driving the coast road at last, his hands sweat on the wheel, though the evening is chilly. When he reaches home, he has to hold onto the rail of the cliff stairs because the trembling won't stop. He stumbles on the loose sand at the foot of the steps. He drops the keys, trying to unlock the kitchen door. He snatches down the telephone receiver inside, and tries to get Tony Baron's number, but he doesn't know what city to name. He guesses Beverly Hills, Malibu, Newport Beach. They can't find a number. He slams up the receiver, runs heavily down the room, out on the deck, down the deck stairs, and drops the keys again, fumbling with the workroom lock.

He has used the file cabinets to store the business records he thought he'd better keep from the junk Ernie Fargo brought from Moody's that lucky day. He snorts. What the hell is happening to his luck? He paws through the unsorted mess, flinging papers away. He slams one drawer, opens another, rifles through it. Four drawers later, his hand closes on the book he wants. Moody's personal phone directory. He kicks the drawer shut, and whips over the pages. He is still shaking with fright. But he has to know. What does Tony Baron think he is doing? Why is he doing it? Why is he worrying about December eleventh? Why now? Cutler looks around wildly for the telephone. But he unplugged it, didn't he, and took it away? On account of her. Jesus, he's almost forgotten her. Why isn't she yelling for him? She always yells when she hears him come in.

He crosses the hall, opens the bedroom door. It is shadowy inside. The television is a gray rectangle. He peers at the bed. It is open, and she isn't in it. She isn't sitting in either of the chairs. "Lorraine?" He starts to turn, to call to her down the hallway because she must be in the bathroom. And something heavy smashes down on his head. The lamp, he thinks. And has the image of a big, streaky blue ceramic lamp base. And then he doesn't think anymore and sees no more images. When he comes to, he is lying face down on the rug. Something warm and wet is running down the side of his face. He lifts a hand that seems far away and touches the side of his face. He blinks at the hand. His vision is double, blurry. The light is bad. He puts his tongue to his fingertips. Blood. He pushes groggily to his hands and knees. Shards of the lamp lie around him, pale and sharp looking. He shuts his eyes and shakes his head to try to clear his eyesight.

"Filthy old bitch," he mumbles, and tries to get to his feet. Dizziness won't let him. He clutches at the door to keep from collapsing again until the dizziness lets up. "Lorraine!" he shouts, and drags himself to his feet where he stands rocking, suddenly horribly nauseated. He swallows hard. Cold sweat breaks out all over him and the nausea backs off. He breathes deeply a few times, feels better, lets go the door and tries to cross the hall. His legs give and he is down again. She really hit him hard. Where did she get the strength? Plainly she is not half dead—that was wishful thinking, and dangerous.

"Lorraine, come back here."

He totters upright again, and lurches through the office. He left the panel to the deck standing open. That was stupid. He comes to rest, breathing hard, blinking, a shoulder against the metal frame of the panel, and leans there squinting out into the dying daylight. The chair she uses as a walker stands at the foot of the stairs to the upper deck. There is only one chair. That he sees two is the fault of what she has done to his skull. He wobbles onto the deck. It rocks sickeningly and he shuts his eyes for a minute. When he cautiously opens them again, he sees her on the stairs. She is using both hands on one railing to drag herself up, painfully, step by step, right foot, left foot. He must have been unconscious longer than he thought. She has almost reached the top. She is dressed, even to her soiled, rose-colored coat.

He stumbles toward the stairs. "I hope you fall and break your neck."

"The telephone," she gasps, "the telephone."

"No way," he shouts, and tries to run. He falls, banging his knees, scraping his hands. It is hard to get up. He is heavy. It seems to take forever. At last, he manages it, and makes for the stairs again, staggering, deck, house, sea, sky blurring, coming into focus again, blurring again. He half falls toward the steps, groping out to catch hold of the railings. His scraped knees give way, and he is almost down once more. Is he going to have to spend the rest of his life in a wheelchair? Has she done for him before he could do for her? Damn Pelletier. Cutler takes a deep breath, grips the railings tight, sets a foot on the first step, and starts after her. Only when he looks up, she is out of sight. She has made the top. Something scrapes the planks overhead. She has taken one of the chairs of shiny metal tubing and white webbing from beside the table to help her walk.

"Don't do it," he shouts. But looking up has made his head swim again. He shuts his eyes, stands gripping the rails hard, and gasping like a fish. Nausea wells up in him again. He gulps. It slowly wanes, and the cold sweat comes. He opens his eyes and has another go at climbing, arm-pulls doing as much of the work as his numb legs. He shouts, "Lorraine, if you touch that phone, I'll kill you. I mean it. Think about it. They can only hang me once." His head comes above the level of the upper deck. She has not gone indoors. She has waited for this moment. She kicks him in the side of the head. Savagely. He blacks out.

When he comes to, he is back at the foot of the stairs. He can see her through the planks, disappearing into the living room. Where did he leave the phone? On the floor by the couch? He hopes so. Then it is likely covered by newspapers. He struggles to his feet. Shakily. The fall has bunged him up, but there isn't time to check for cuts, abrasions, broken bones. He grips the rails and climbs again. "Keep away from that phone, Lorraine." He sprawls, panting, aching, on the upper deck. The daylight is failing, but he can make her out vaguely, standing in the long room, leaning on the chair whose tubing glints, and gawking frantically around. He was right. The phone squats on the floor beside the couch. But naked. She sees it, shifts the chair, lurches toward it. "No." He groans to his feet, lunges indoors, and grabs her.

26

He is sick and confused. He soaked in a hot tub for a long time to ease the pain out of his bruises. The bathroom has more than its share of mirrors. Pelletier liked that. Now the mirrors help Cutler clean up the ragged, bloody cut in the back of his scalp. It is clumsy work all the same. The hurts he got in the fall downstairs make it agony to lift his arms. He supposes he ought to go someplace for stitches. He has cut the handles off Pelletier's jump-prope, sliced the rope into halves, and tied her hand and foot on the bed, and stuffed a hand towel into her mouth to stop her screaming, but he is afraid to leave the house, all the same. He pours disinfectant on cotton, winds gauze around his head to keep it in place, and tapes the gauze tight.

He dresses in the workroom. Slow going. His head throbs, though he has taken aspirin. He isn't quite over the double vision yet. He puts on four shoes. Maybe a drink will help. His hands shake, putting it together. He sits at the desk, drinking it, and staring at Tony Baron's name, written in Moody's old-maidish script in the address book. He wishes he could think clearly. If Baron wanted to talk to him, he could have come here, and not gone sneaking around to Souza about the boat, about December eleventh. If Cutler phones him, Baron won't tell him what's going on, will he?

Cutler shakes his head, closes the book, stares at

the blank screen of the word processor. Computer. If he fed it the right program, he wouldn't need a clear head. If he put in the information, it would give him the answer. He laughs to himself. What information? He stands up abruptly. A mistake. The white room reels around him. He clutches at the chair. The cold scotch from the glass in his hand runs up his sleeve. He sits down. Hard. He stays very quiet, eyes shut, breathing slowly in and out, waiting to feel better. And hears the cry of the telephone from overhead, muffled by the thickness of the carpet.

"Is anyone watching your house?"

"No. Why should they?" Cutler thought he wasn't going to make it up the stairs, but he did. He sits, heart pounding, head pounding, on the couch in the dark. "Who is this?"

"No names. Your phone could be tapped."

Cutler reaches to turn on the lamp. A stab of pain in his shoulder makes him wince. He knows the voice. Moody's doctor. Medford. So it's no prank. "I don't understand."

"We have to talk. I'm not far off. In a phone booth."

"I can't leave," Cutler says. "Come here."

"Not to the house. It could be bugged. Out on the beach there, all right? In ten minutes. Don't bring a light."

Before Cutler can answer, the line hums. He leans down painfully to drop the receiver in place. Watching the house? Tapping the phone? What for? What the hell is going on? He is scared, and turns off the lamp. He goes out on the dark deck. The breath off the ocean is chilly. He needs a jacket, but he doesn't go back for it. He stands staring into the night. He makes his way shakily down the steps to the lower deck, and from there down to the sand. He walks all around the house, trying to penetrate the night with his eyes, trying to hear. But there's only the wash of the surf, the sound of passing cars and trucks up on the highway.

This is ridiculous. He goes back into the house, switches on lamps, and makes himself another drink. He ought to eat. A bowl of shrimp sits in the refrigerator. He ruined with hot sauce those he cooked for Lorraine, but these are untouched. He pulls off the transparent plastic wrap that covers the bowl, and stands in the light of the open refrigerator, eating the shrimp with his fingers. He licks his fingers, sets the bowl in the sink, throws away the plastic wrap. And hears his name called softly from outside. He shuts the refrigerator, limps down the room, switches off the lamps, and goes out onto the deck. At least, he will meet a living being this time, won't he? It's not like those nightmare times when Quinn called him. All the same, he is afraid. As he crosses the deck, descends the stairs, he trembles, his mouth is dry.

"What is this?" he says, and goes down to the sand again. He can just make out a pale figure in the dark. The sand is soft, and his damaged knees hurt, walking on it. The man is in front of him, trimly muscular, looking if possible even younger than that last morning in Moody's bedroom, with the old man stretched out dead in fresh pajamas on the floor between the bed and the window. "Isn't this kind of melodramatic? Come inside for a drink."

"I mustn't be seen." Medford looks nervously to

his left, to his right. "But I regard you as a friend, and I felt I should warn you. That woman who used to work for Stewart — Fargo? She's stirring up trouble."

"Now? Why? She hates me for selling the business, but that was months ago. What kind of trouble?"

"What happened to your head?" Medford says.

"I missed my footing, fell downstairs, cut my scalp. It's all right. What's this about Fargo?"

"There's a man called Tony Baron. Do you know him?"

"Oh, Christ. Not him, too."

"He came to my office today. He'd already been to Evening Star — the morticians that strewed Stewart's ashes at sea? Fargo had sent him there. For a copy of the death certificate. Striking your head that hard can be serious. Have you seen a doctor? Any dizziness, nausea?"

"It's past now," Cutler says. "Don't worry about it. Death certificate? In God's name, why?"

"Fargo told this Baron man you murdered Stewart for his money, and I conspired with you to falsify the cause of death."

"What? Why? Why would you do that?"

"Because we're both homosexuals."

"Oh, my God. She would. She's crazy. She's got no proof. Of any of it. You know how he died. He had to have oxygen. The tube came loose in his sleep. You saw that."

"What I saw is not the point," Medford says. "This Tony Baron believes her. He's decided there should have been an inquest. He's going to ask for one. I get the impression that he's wealthy and has powerful friends." Medford's hand moves dimly in the dark to touch Cutler's arm. "Of course, I know as well as you do that you're innocent. I know how you cared for Stewart. You did everything for him. I never saw an elderly patient better looked after."

"Thanks," Cutler says bleakly. "An inquest? How can they have an inquest when the body's burned and the ashes were dumped in the ocean?"

"You're thinking of an autopsy," Medford says. "An inquest is a jury hearing with the coroner presiding. To review the facts surrounding the death. To determine if the cause was natural, accidental, or at the hands of another. To decide if somebody has to be tried for murder."

"But there were no witnesses," Cutler says. "What does Fargo claim? That she saw me kill him?"

"It's not like that. It has to do with your young — shall we say 'friend'? The boy with the French name. The one you bought this house for, a new car, a hundred thousand dollar yacht. Fargo told Baron that no sooner had he turned up than Stewart died — that very same night. Baron doesn't believe in coincidences. He believes in cause and effect. He mentioned another coincidence involving you and some man who disappeared. What was the name? Quinn?"

"He doesn't know what he's talking about," Cutler says.

"You ought to have been more discreet about the boy."

"Why? It never entered my head that anyone would think I killed Stewart. He was my whole life."

Medford moves off. "I thought I should warn you."

Cutler reaches out. "Will it make trouble for you?"

"I was his physician of record, saw him regularly,

knew his condition thoroughly. I made a judgment call. That was my right. Not serious trouble, no." The darkness has enfolded him. The sand crunches under his shoes, each step a little farther off. His voice drifts back above the rustling of the surf. "But we'll both get subpoenas."

"You'll tell them how it was, won't you?"

"Of course." The footsteps pause. "But it won't help if they learn I was here tonight."

"I won't tell anyone," Cutler says.

"Goodnight." Medford's footsteps fade into silence.

Pelletier stands in the doorway from the deck and frowns at Cutler in the workroom. "What are you doing?" This night, Thursday night, is colder than last night. He wears his mackinaw, the bulky white turtleneck sweater, blue corduroys, a watch cap. For going to sea. "You never told me you were taking a trip."

Cutler is stuffing grips with his clothes. He has kept his clothes in the workroom closet since Lorraine arrived and took over his room with herself and her smell. Cutler glances at Pelletier, closes a suitcase, zips the lid shut. "You took your time. Where the hell were you?"

"I couldn't tell Veronica I had to rush back so I could help you drown your mother. I had to stop with her to shop and ride horses and sample wines. I told you I'd be here." He comes in, starts lifting clothes from a stack, handing them to Cutler. "Where you going?"

"Rio." Cutler pulls a Pan Am folder from his jacket. "I bought these today. Got my money from the bank. Ordered the gas and water and electricity turned off."

Pelletier slides the ticket flimsies from the folder, reads, looks puzzled. "One way? You're going for good?"

"Tony Baron's after me for killing Moody, for killing Quinn. I don't know why. Don't ask." He flaps down the lid of the second grip and drags the thick-toothed brass zippers shut. "You better believe I'm going for good."

"Tony Baron?" Pelletier slides the flimsies back into the folder and pokes it into Cutler's jacket. "What the fuck does he know? Nothing."

"He suspects. He questioned Fargo. He's asking for an inquest on Moody." Cutler's bruises hurt when he lifts the grips to stand them on the floor. "He also questioned Souza. About that trip we took with the TV crate on board."

"So, what could he say? Darryl, you shouldn't run. What difference does it make if Tony Baron's asking questions? There aren't any answers. But if you run, they'll say that shows you're guilty."

"Souza remembered the date. December eleventh. When Quinn disappeared." Cutler reads his watch. "I should have been gone by now." He carries the grips out to the deck. "Everything took so bloody long. The bank acted like it was their money. Help me with these. My head hurts."

Pelletier comes. "What happened to your head?"

"She ambushed me yesterday." They cross the deck, go down to the sand, carry the grips up the dark slope beside the house. "Hit me from behind with the bedroom lamp. She damn near made it to the phone."

Following him up the cliff steps, Pelletier laughs. "I'd like to have seen that." Cars and trucks roar past on the highway. The Celica waits on the road shoulder. Cutler unlocks the hatchback, they drop in the grips, Cutler slams down the hatchback. Pelletier asks, "What were you going to do about her? What about the house? The boat?"

"I'll figure out a way to sell the house and the boat when I get down there. I've got the papers." Cutler pats the inner pocket of his jacket. "Her?" He takes Pelletier's arm and steers him to the stairs again. "You're going to help me with her." They start down. "You promised."

"Yeah, but what if I hadn't showed up?"

"You had to," Cutler says. "You said it. I need you."

"I said it," Pelletier says.

Because the lamp is broken, Cutler switches on the overhead lights in the bedroom, fluorescents behind milky plastic panels in the ceiling. She lies lumpily on her side, hands tied behind her, ankles tied. She gives a muffled sound and turns her head on the pillow. Strands of white hair cross her face. Her eyes glare through them. She struggles feebly. She has done a lot of struggling, it appears. The spread is rumpled and almost off her.

"You used my jump rope," Pelletier says.

"It's all there was." Cutler lights a cigarette.

Pelletier shakes his head. "It's not enough, Darryl." He takes the cigarette out of Cutler's mouth. "But it gives me an idea." He trots down the room, rolls open the panel, goes out. "I'll be back in a minute." Cutler hears him run lightly up the stairs and across the deck above. When he comes back down again, he doesn't reappear in the bedroom. He stays in the workroom. Cutler looks at the old woman on the bed. She is still glaring at him through tangled hair.

"He's my crew," Cutler tells her. "I've been waiting for him to come back. So we could take a nice little trip on my yacht. You'll like that, won't you?" The rage and resentment in her eyes give way to fear. She shakes her head and struggles again and makes sounds. Smiling at her helplessness, he lights another cigarette, and goes across the hall to see what Pelletier is doing.

"I should have thought of this for Quinn." Pelletier has brought a knife down from the kitchen. Cigarette smoldering in a corner of his lovely mouth, he is kneeling on a Nautilus bench, hacking away with the blade at one of the pulley ropes that holds a weight. The rope is cut. The weight drops with a clatter. "Come help me." Mutely, Cutler goes to him. They lift the weight out of the glittering apparatus. It is heavy. Pelletier drags it across the hallway and into the bright bedroom. He starts to loop the rope around her knees. She kicks and squirms. He slaps her.

"Don't do that," Cutler says.

Pelletier straightens slowly, studies him, head tilted. "What did you say? Darryl, she's nothing but fish food. Four of these weights will take her straight to the bottom. The scavengers."

"I don't want to do it," Cutler says.

"Darryl, we had a deal. A trade-off. I help you get rid of her. You give me title to the boat."

"You never said so," Cutler says.

"What the hell do you think I was so nice to you for?"

"But there's no need to kill her now. I'm leaving. Let her tell the police any lies she wants to. I won't be here to answer for them. It doesn't matter any more."

"Darryl, I need title to that boat." Pelletier twists the rope around her knees again, kneels on the bed, yanks knots into the rope, once, twice. "Those shysters in charge of Phil's estate are delaying and delaying. They're playing investment games with the money instead of turning it over to Veronica like they're supposed to. All she gets is a chickenshit little check every week for expenses." He tugs at the rope to test the knots, nods satisfaction, gets off the bed and heads for the workroom again. "They could keep it up forever. They've always got some new excuse." He picks up the knife from the bench and begins to saw another pulley rope.

"That's your problem," Cutler says.

"I don't have problems that aren't your problems." Pelletier gives him a quick unpleasant sidelong smile and goes on with his rope cutting. "You can't cross me, Darryl. You don't dare. That boat's no good to you. I need the money from that boat."

"For Veronica?" Cutler lays a hand on the jacket pocket that holds the papers. "You know better than that."

The weight crashes down, shaking the floor underfoot. And Pelletier gets off the bench and steps quickly to Cutler and holds the point of the knife to his throat. "Give me the papers, Darryl. Let's get that part out of the way before we sail off and drown her."

Cutler backs against the wall, shaking his head. "I've changed my mind. She's my mother, Chick.

I can't kill my own mother. I don't have to, now. There's no point."

"All right, forget it. Just give me the papers." Pelletier pricks at Cutler's throat above the larynx with the point of the knife. Cutler shifts quickly, like a boxer getting off the ropes. Pelletier starts to attack him and stops, eyes open wide, jaw sagging. Cutler turns.

A man stands in the opening from the deck — dirty rumpled chinos, old tweed jacket with leather elbow patches, straggly gray hair trailing from under a Dodger baseball cap. Irv Liebowitz has been dead for years. But he is not a ghost. He is real, however old and frail. And frail or not, there is nothing to do about him, because he is not alone. Outside stand other figures. One is Tony Baron, not much more vigorous-looking than Liebowitz, though cleaner. Then there are two strangers in flyfront topcoats, who look strong. And beyond them, out in the dark, lurk dimmer beings he can't quite see.

"You stole my script," Liebowitz says.

"Who was in that ditch in the desert?" Cutler says.

"A dead hobo I ran across. Luckiest day of my miserable last years," Liebowitz says. "My height, weight, age. No teeth." He sticks a thumb in his mouth, pulls out dentures, holds them up pink and glistening for Cutler to see and, making a horrible face, puts them back. "I changed my clothes for his, gave him my wallet, checkbook, the works. Drove him twenty miles straight out across the desert to that arroyo and dumped him in. Left my car and walked away. I was drunk. It was an insane thing to do. It should never have worked. But thanks to the buzzards, it did."

"You can't prove you wrote that script," Cutler says. "Your letter to Moody said there was only one copy."

"Darryl, you're talking too much," Pelletier says.

"But Phil Quinn knew all about it, the whole story." Liebowitz takes a pint bottle from a side pocket of the ravelled jacket. "And he told you he knew you didn't write it. He knew I wrote it." Liebowitz unscrews the cap of the bottle, and takes a drink, skinny throat pumping. He wipes his mouth with the back of a grubby hand. "And you killed him, poor bastard."

"He drowned swimming," Cutler says.

"So the news said." Liebowitz recaps the bottle and drops it back into its pocket. "But I didn't believe it. Phil was a powerful swimmer."

"Everybody gets old," Cutler says.

"Don't count on it," Tony Baron says.

"Then, three nights ago," Liebowitz says, "on the little television set tucked up above the bar in the cantina where I pass my dying days, I chanced to see"—he gives a shrug, a silent wry laugh—"well, you know what I saw. And I was a little upset, wasn't I? At the writing credit. Who the hell was Darryl Cutler, for Christ sake? And then I remembered. You worked for Stewart Moody. Where I'd sent the script to be copied."

"So had fifty other writers," Cutler says.

"Not missing, believed dead," Liebowitz says. "And poor old Stewart was dead, too, wasn't he? So he couldn't get in your way. You'd seen to that."

"Don't believe Fargo," Cutler says. "She's just a vindictive bitch. She hates me because Moody left me the business and all his money."

"Another reason for you to kill him." Liebowitz pulls out the whiskey pint again. "You'd met a beautiful boy. This is him, here, right?" He unscrews the tin cap and tilts up the bottle at his mouth again. "Ahh." He smacks his lips. "Not the kind you can keep happy with a Big Mack and Coke." With a soft, dry chuckle, he recaps the bottle and slips it back into his pocket. "It's a basic plot. I worked it out on the plane. Tony very kindly confirmed it for me." He glances over his shoulder. "He knows the ropes. He's written a hundred private eye episodes."

"That's fiction," Cutler says. "In real life, you have to have facts. You haven't got any facts. Fargo's a liar. So is Souza. And a drunk, besides. Will you please clear out, now? This is my house, and you're not invited."

"In a minute." Tony Baron says this, and turns to speak to one of the men in flyfront coats. The man turns and moves off into the darkness of the deck. Baron steps inside to stand next to Liebowitz. "In a minute, we'll all clear out. And so will you. In handcuffs." And the man in the flyfront coat comes in with Veronica Quinn. She is very pale and stares hopelessly at Pelletier, who makes a soft sound in his throat, close behind Cutler. Baron glances at Veronica and looks at Cutler again. "You know this woman?"

"To my sorrow," Cutler says. "Another jealous bitch."

"She was the reason," Liebowitz says, "we were slow in getting here. She was away, and we couldn't locate her." He touches Veronica's arm, who shudders and pulls away. "Don't be frightened, sweetheart. Tell him what you know."

"Don't say anything," Pelletier yelps. "They have to grant you immunity from prosecution first."

"We've already done that," says the man in the flyfront coat. "I'm from the district attorney's office. Go ahead, Mrs. Quinn. Tell Mr. Cutler here what you told us."

"I want immunity too," Pelletier says.

"We'll discuss it," the man says. "Go on, Mrs. Quinn."

"Ph-phil told me about the script," she stammers, "when he read it. He came roaring out of the study in a rage. He told me he was coming here to have it out with you, and he slammed out of the house."

"When he didn't come back," Liebowitz says, "why didn't you go to the police?"

"Because I knew he'd killed Phil," she says. "Just the way he'd killed that old man he worked for. He killed a little boy, too, with his car. I didn't see it. What if I told, and they didn't arrest him? Why wouldn't he kill me?"

"You were afraid of him," Liebowitz says.

She nods, gulps, stares at Cutler as if he were a snake. "We were both terrified. Chick saw the murders, both of them. He made Chick help him get rid of Phil's poor body, take it way out in the ocean and dump it."

The district attorney's man looks at Pelletier. "December eleventh, right? Nailed up in a television crate?"

Pelletier says, "I want a deal. If you won't deal, I want a lawyer. Now."

"We'll deal," the district attorney's man says. "No prosecution for the murders. I can't guarantee more.

You were awfully close, Mr. Pelletier."

"He did it," Pelletier says. "Suffocated Moody with a pillow. Bashed Quinn over the head with a bronze statuette. It's still upstairs. I couldn't stop him."

"And you helped him dump Quinn's body at sea?"

"He'd have killed me if I didn't," Pelletier says. "Look, do you want to know what he's like?" Cutler stands staring at him, dumb, disbelieving. Pelletier goes to the hall door. Out of the corner of his eye, Cutler sees the second man in a flyfront coat draw a gun and point it. Pelletier says, "He's got his mother in the next room. He was going to do to her what he did to Quinn. Only she's still alive. She was witness to that other killing of his — the hit and run in Portland, years ago. He was going to drown her tonight. And he was making me help him."

The man with the gun joins him and they cross the hall. Liebowitz and Baron follow, and the district attorney's man, holding Veronica's arm. Cutler is alone. He runs for the door, but a man in police uniform catches his arm. A very large revolver hangs in a holster at the man's hip. But it isn't the revolver he takes out. He takes handcuffs off his belt, turns Cutler around, and ratchets the handcuffs on Cutler's wrists behind his back.

"You're under arrest," the officer says. "You have the right to remain silent. If you give up that right —" Cutler stops listening. He gazes at the empty beach. The surf thuds and splashes. The night is clear. There are many stars. The officer's voice ceases. He shoulders Cutler back into the glaring room, pushes him along past the exercise equipment, white file cabinets and shelves, white desk with its sleek word processor and glinting bottles. He nudges him across the hallway.

In the bedroom, Liebowitz, Baron, Veronica, Pelletier, and the man from the district attorney's office stand watching the man in the other flyfront coat untie the lumpy body on the bed in its soiled and rumpled rose-colored pants suit. He gently removes the gag from Lorraine Cutler's mouth. She struggles to sit up. He helps her. She pushes with a knuckly swollen hand to try to tidy her scruffy hair. Mockery and triumph are in the look she gives Cutler. Her voice is hoarse from disuse, hardly more than a whisper.

"I heard," she croaks. "You're a murderer. As if I didn't know that. And they've got you, haven't they? Do you know what that means, Darryl? I'm your only living relative. So I get it all—money, house, yacht, everything. They'll put you in the gas chamber. And I'll get it all."